A Roar and A Drumbeat

Tales of Literary Adventures

Anjaly Thomas

GULF BOOK
SERVICES

**GULF BOOK
SERVICES**

Published by **Gulf Book Services Ltd**
20-22 Wenlock Road, London,
NI 7GU, UK
Email: info@gulfbooks.co.uk
Office No: G23,
Sharjah Publishing City Freezone
Sharjah – UAE

First Published by Gulf Book Services Ltd

ISBN: 978-1-917529-06-8
Year: November 2024

Reviews

A magnificent blend of literature and coffee. A great read for lovers of both – **Pankaj Giri**, Author of *The Unforgettable Woman* and *Fragile Threads of Hope*

The author holds the hand of Ernest Hemingway and Lord Byron, connects threads to weave a delightful story, through memoirs, musings, and conversations of a journey through two continents. She possesses an uncanny ability to transport the reader to distant lands, weaving tales of love, loss, and adventure - **Prof. Aloke Kumar**, Author and Cultural Critic

A Roar and A Drumbeat *combines odd bits into a sensible series of ents. Like Byron, she loves Man and Nature and like Hemingway, she loves to write. The book is like a piping hot cuppa. Energizing and uplifting* – **Clement Ilango**, Author of critically acclaimed *She Wore Jasmines* and *The Girl with the Black Mole*

An interesting journey through Africa and Europe, to places where Ernest Hemingway and Lord Byron spent crucial periods of their lives. The author takes us in their footsteps, bringing alive places and letting us imagine the impact they would have had on these writers. Her narration is breezy, but she pays attention to details, be they in architecture, conversations, people, or history. Truly, this is the strongest point of her writing – **Ganesh Vancheeswaran**

Prologue

There are three reasons for this book.

First, travelling in a foreign country, to begin with, is just a collection of odd encounters and likes and dislikes propped against whatever I am accustomed to experiencing. That's why I will not focus on myself or my disjointed experiences; instead, I will start by incorporating odd bits into a sensible stories. That could be the only way to understand it, for it may be so that I never will understand what things mean as one whole.

And secondly, a chance finding of *Childe Harold's Pilgrimage*:

There is a pleasure in the pathless woods,

There is a rapture on the lonely shore,

There is society where none intrudes,

By the deep Sea, and music in its roar:

I love not Man the less, but Nature more…

And thirdly, a visit to Hemingway's home in Chicago, Illinois, where, in his *Memoranda* notebook, as a junior high school student in 1916, he wrote these words that hit me like a cold blow.

"My name is Ernest Miller Hemingway. I want to travel and write."

Through this book, I hope to, even in a small way, practice what he practiced.

Acknowledgements

- Some quotes are, with the permission of the original author, reprinted here.
- The author does not claim to be an expert on literary history.
- A big round of thanks going out to all readers who read with great keenness the initial draft of this book.
- Thank you to every café owner who patiently answered my questions and even to those who did not.

Contents

Lord Byron   *1*

Ernest Hemingway   *3*

Book 1   **5**

Chapter 1   7

Chapter 2   17

Chapter 3   27

Chapter 4   39

Chapter 5   53

Chapter 6   75

Chapter 7   93

Chapter 8   103

Book 2   **125**

Chapter 1   127

Chapter 2   143

Chapter 3   157

Chapter 4   171

Chapter 5   181

Chapter 6   189

Chapter 7   211

Chapter 8   229

Chapter 9   249

About the Author   *259*

Lord Byron

(1788 – 1824)

1. George Gordon Noel, sixth Baron Byron, was born on 22 January 1788 in London. His father died when he was three. He inherited his title from his great-uncle in 1798.

2. Byron was educated at Harrow School and Cambridge University. In 1809, he left for a tour of Mediterranean countries and returned to England in 1811. In 1812, the first two cantos of *Childe Harold's Pilgrimage* were published.

3. In 1814, Byron's half-sister Augusta gave birth to his daughter. The following year, Byron married Annabella Milbanke, with whom he had a daughter. The couple separated in 1816.

4. Mounting pressure after his failed marriage, scandalous affairs, and huge debts forced him to leave England in April 1816, never to return.

5. He spent the summer of 1816 at Lake Geneva with Percy Bysshe Shelley, Mary Shelley, and Mary's half-sister Claire Clairmont, with whom Byron had a daughter.

6. In 1819, while staying in Venice, he had an affair with Teresa Guiccioli, the wife of an Italian nobleman. He wrote some of his most famous works in this period, including *Don Juan*.

7. In July 1823, Byron left Italy to join the Greek insurgents who were fighting a war of independence against the Ottoman Empire.

8. In April 1824, he died from fever at Missolonghi in modern-day Greece. His body was brought back to England and buried at his ancestral home in Nottinghamshire.

Ernest Hemingway
(1899– 1961)

- Ernest Miller Hemingway was born on July 21, 1899 in Oak Park, IL, the second of six children. He graduated from Oak Park High School in 1917, opting not to go to college, instead taking up the role of cub reporter for the Kansas City *Star* newspaper. The *Star's* style guidelines influence his writing style for the rest of his career.
- In 1918, he joined the Red Cross as Ambulance Driver. He was seriously injured by a mortar shell and was discharged from service with a Silver Medal of Military Valour. While recuperating, he falls in love with a nurse, who becomes the inspiration for his book *A Farewell to Arms*.
- In 1921, he married Elizabeth Hadley Richardson, first of his four wives. The couple left for Paris where he worked as foreign correspondent for the Toronto Star and soon falls in with a circle of writers and artists that includes Gertrude Stein and Ezra Pound.
- In 1923, his first book, *Three Stories and Ten Poems*, was published.
- May 1925, Hemingway met Fitzgerald in Paris, and a long friendship was born.
- In 1926, his book *The Sun Also Rises* was published. The novel was critically acclaimed and commercially successful.
- In 1927, Hemingway divorced Hadley and married Pauline Pfeiffer, a fashion writer. The same year his short story collection *Men Without Women* was published.
- In 1928, the couple move back to United States. The following year, his book *A Farewell to Arms* was published.
- In 1932 Hemingway went to Spain to research bullfighting for *Death in the Afternoon*, his critically lauded nonfiction book on

the subject.

- In 1933 Pauline and Ernest travelled to Kenya for a ten-week safari.

- Hemingway fell in love with the continent and his subsequent trips inspired his works, such as the 1935 book *Green Hills of Africa* and short stories including *The Snows of Kilimanjaro* and *The Short Happy Life of Francis Macomber*.

- In 1940, he divorced Pauline Pfeiffer and later married Martha Gellhorn. The same year his book *For Whom the Bell Tolls* was published.

- In 1945 he divorced Martha over professional jealousy and married Mary Welsh a year later.

- On Sep 1, 1952 *The Old Man and the Sea* was published in *Life* magazine. The book brought him commercial and critical success.

- In 1953, Hemingway won the Pulitzer Prize for *The Old Man and the Sea*

- In 1954 he won the Nobel Prize for Literature, becoming the fifth American author to receive the award.

- Hemingway committed suicide on Jul 2, 1961 at his home in Ketchum.

Book 1

Chapter 1

N early every one of my favourite authors has written a book or three on Kenya, thus creating the biggest confusion of my life. I cannot decide *if* they are my favourite because of the books they have written about Kenya or *if* I like Kenya because of the books *they* have written about it.

Therefore, whilst waiting for my coffee in Thorntree Café at Sarova Stanley Hotel, Nairobi, I decide that no matter how trivial, I will not aim to justify my reason for being here. There is no justification to be given.

The simplicity of that open-ended surmise takes me by surprise. At once, my eyes fly open to the accompaniment of a restlessly pounding heart. I believe there is a smile hovering around my lips too, growing wider as the aroma of the coffee grows stronger.

"Asante," I say confidently to the tall, sharply dressed, skinny young waiter, who, believing the smile to be for him, smiles right back, revealing a set of white teeth. He places the cup gently on the table.

"The coffee smells great," I say.

"Yes, Miss. It is our very own beans and our blend. Kenyan coffee is the best in the world. Enjoy, Miss. Good day." He retreats gracefully. He walks with confidence. I notice that particularly.

I pick up the cup and smile at the pitch-black liquid languishing in it. Nothing is more conducive to the moment than a cup of strong black Kenyan coffee, and I am certain that the aroma, the body, and the sensations that will follow will be perfection itself. I sip thoughtfully, awaiting the sensations that follow that first sip.

The hot, bitter brew traces its way down my throat, bringing forth various sensations and a sense of calm that nearly always leads to fantastic desires and sudden decisions. I am gripped with a sudden longing to unravel the secret of the full-bodied flavour of Kenyan coffee alongside Ernest Hemingway's passion for Africa and Lord Byron's dare-devil swim in the Dardanelles, Turkey. These desires are a jumble of loosely gathered thoughts, but with every sip, it all seems possible to achieve. A vague plan of action begins to take shape, but it will take a few cups of coffee to commit to it.

An isolated thought bordering on philosophy pops into my mind.

Is there anything privileged or macabre about the life of travel?

I think not. That perception is best explained by the outcome, but I am sure that in pursuance of my desires, I will reap rich literary rewards besides finding valid reasons to drink as much coffee as I please, and where I please, without fretting over its effect on my blood pressure and my wallet. If that is privilege, so be it.

Before I see the bottom of the cup, the fantastic idea has hit home. I will embark on a coffee-drinking-spree-around-the-world. It is, I believe, just as thrilling as unravelling literary mysteries.

I have found my calling.

*

For the sake of clarity, however, I'll say what I am *not* in Nairobi for.

The wildlife safari. I can do without tracking lions. I've had that pleasure in my earlier trips when I sank small fortunes into those precarious thrills. The smell of lion scat still makes me nauseous, but I don't grudge the past because I see Hemingway's point of view clearly now.

There is no plot to my story. It is, as I concur, going to be a series of sudden decisions and plenty of travel around the continent and beyond.

The very idea is exciting. Someone did say that travel can be undertaken for macabre reasons, but trailing authors and drinking coffee falls short of macabre. At best, I will dare to call it stalking for self-satisfaction or at the very least, adventurous—a trait I believe I have in common with Hemingway.

Well, he did track kudus quite zealously, and no one asked the animal what it felt, right?

*

It is a well-documented fact that Ernest Hemingway, the great lover of Africa, the adventurer, the journalist, and the writer, did after all spend much time at this very hotel during his visits to the city. Of course, the hotel went under a different name then, but it still does not take away its importance in Kenyan history.

It is only serendipitous that I am here right now, connecting the dots to form a logical reason to pursue my fancies. Turns out that Nairobi is Ernest Hemingway and Kenyan coffee in a nutshell, which is just as well because the entire build-up makes it easy for me to retrace Ernest Hemingway in *his* favourite country on the continent of Africa while drinking my way through its finest coffees.

For the time being, this is reason enough to celebrate. In time, things will work itself out.

I am a lover of literature and literary figures; snow-capped mountains, good coffee, and EH tick all the boxes. Sure, he knew how to spin words, but he also knew the right places to travel, the right adventures to have, and of course, the cafes to visit. I have read of his adventures in Paris. It must have been one or all the reasons that he ended up at the erstwhile Stanley Hotel, the present Sarova Stanely, where I am staying for the next few days. Mine is an open-ended plan. It is the only way anything can work.

Hemingway was like that predator that does not always move silently through the bush. He leaves a trail to follow. He makes his presence felt.

I do not know what I will end up with, but I am going to have fun trying.

*

My thoughts briefly wander to another historical figure that I am enamoured with. Lord Byron. He had nothing to do with Kenya or the continent itself, but everything beautiful reminds me of him. From him, I imbibe the knack of finding beauty in everything. Even coffee. It is most unfortunate that Lord Byron never made his way to Africa. For a romantic like him, Africa would have pushed the boundaries of creativity.

Hemingway was luckier to be born in a different era as a journalist and writer, but it was Africa that turned him into a man. And a hunter. Was it the rawness of Africa that propelled him to pick up the gun? Who knows? Who can ever know?

But like everyone else, I do know that some of Hemingway's accounts of Kenya are works of fiction, but one must make allowances for a writer's fancies. Imagination is the key to a good story. Hemingway's adventurous life and his fiction have been so intertwined that I am unsure where to begin. So, I undertake the slow process of elimination, discarding the quest for reconfirming facts and narrowing down my purpose to merely retracing his steps as far as possible.

There is more than one common connection between us.

EH came to the continent twice between 1933-54. Both times it was for game-hunting, and on both occasions, he went through Kenya, Tanganyika (the present Tanzania), and Uganda. I am going that way, too, at least as far as Tanzania. He travelled with a friend named Key West, sought inspiration in the travels of Theodore Roosevelt, and spent the money of his wife Pauline, while I am traveling by myself, seeking inspiration in coffee and rejoicing in the knowledge that, unlike EH, I will not succumb to the stomach bug. I score over him in the number of times I have travelled to Kenya, but I am yet to beat him on the plane crash. Hemingway had that twice, and that took his persona as an adventurer up several notches.

I have had no such luck.

The man did get three books out of his three months spent on the safari collecting trophies that included a lion and a large game roaming the grasslands. *Green Hills of Africa*, the short stories *The Snows of Kilimanjaro*, and *The Short Happy Life of Francis Macomber* were all, I imagine, penned in this very café.

I might, if lucky, get one book out of my latest experiences here.

Have I mentioned that it was also Hemingway who, when recovering from a bout of illness at the former Stanley Hotel, introduced the word *Safari* to the English language and thereby popularized it?

His greatest literary achievement may have been winning the Pulitzer Prize in 1952 and the Nobel Peace Prize in 1954, but his most practical contribution to the world of English literature will be the word, *Safari*.

The word has been in existence and traces its origins to the Arabic world; it was, in turn, adopted into Swahili during the days of trading. *Safari* also finds a mention in Jules Verne's *Five Days in a Balloon* and Rider Haggards *King Solomon's Mines*, but its popularity touched a new high with Ernest Hemingway, and for this, I will remain grateful to him.

*

To understand why and how Sarova Stanley is important to my quest, I undertake a short tour of the hotel on the waiter's suggestions. Yes, there is such a thing. Sarova Stanley is proud of its heritage and is keen to share their past with anyone remotely interested in it.

This morning, I am the only one with any interest.

Captain Trevor, the hotel-appointed guide, looking splendid in his white shirt and a black bowtie, gestures to me to follow him. We march ahead. His opening sentence is uttered in a deep, bass voice, drawing me into the intrigue he is setting me up for. My excitement is building.

The hotel is elegant in a very Victorian way, with dark woodwork and high ceilings. Trevor points at the historic black-and-white photographs of famous guests—Teddy Roosevelt, Queen Elizabeth, Ernest Hemingway, and Lord Baden-Powell of Boy Scout fame.

We pass through the first floor, which now contains a chemist's shop and a few boutique stores.

"Once upon a time," he intones, "in Kenya's colonial days, in the year 1890, a British railroad camp was set up on the Kampala-Mombasa railway. They called it Mile 327. At the time, many Indians came here to build the railway. Some people called the railway 'Lunatic Express' because many people working on the railroad were eaten by lions, and they believed it was utter lunacy to continue building the railway under the circumstances."

He pauses for that information to sink in. I do not react because I am sure the Indians flourished here despite the lion attacks. We are, and by that logic, we sure were, a hardy tribe, not easily deterred by lions.

He continues his narration.

"Mile 327 was the British provincial capital until 1905. It became the centre for the colony's tea and coffee trade and eventually the capital of Independent Kenya in 1963 and was renamed Nairobi.

"When the railroad arrived, there came a lady named Mayence Bent who set up four sparsely furnished rooms over a general store and post office owned by one Mr. Tommy Woods in 1902. She called it the *Victoria Hotel*, probably after the Queen. Bent ran the store and post office for two years quite successfully. One thing led to another, and a few years later, she separated from her husband, remarried, and started the first *Stanley Hotel* with fifteen beds on two floors. There is a strong belief that she named it after Henry Morton Stanley, the Welsh explorer who became famous after locating the missionary and explorer David Livingstone, just so that she could exact revenge on her husband, Bent."

Trevor pauses for breath while I try to recreate the history. Mayence Bent seems like a woman with a motto, and I am impressed by her spirit. I would have liked to meet her kind very much. Trevor breaks into my thoughts with a tragic story.

"A fire destroyed the Stanley Hotel, and Bent relocated it to a new destination, which was soon sold to Nairobi's former postmaster in 1907. Soon after this, Mayence and her new husband Fred Tate, locally famous as 'Nairobi's stationmaster and a pianist at the Railway Institute' and who was fifteen years her junior, built a 60-room hotel on a corner plot at the Junction of Delamere Avenue—today the Kenyatta Avenue—and opened it in 1913. It was called The New Stanley.

"Ten years later, Mayence sold The New Stanley to Abraham

Block, who was once a supplier of her mattress. Abraham is a legend in his own ways."

History, I am beginning to think, is very enlightening. Abraham may be a legend, but I am betting on Mayence.

"That may be so, but I quite like your Mayence," I tell Trevor, who smiles in return. "Spunky, that is what she was."

He nods without a word of appreciation for the good woman, who I believe had an important role to play in the fame of the hotel I am staying at.

Trevor continues his well-rehearsed narration.

"Very soon, people from far and wide began to arrive. Famous authors, journalists, adventurers, people with money… everybody wanted to be here, at this very hotel. Karen Blixen, Elspeth Huxley, and later, Ernest Hemingway made this hotel their base. Very soon, Hollywood actors started visiting Nairobi. When Grace Kelly, Sean Connery, and Michael Caine arrived, Stanley Hotel touched the limits of popularity and became central to the development of the city itself.

"This history is celebrated with pictures that you may see in the indoor portion of the Thorn Tree Cafe."

"Fascinating," I murmur a reply. I know I should have said something more than that, but I am trying to digest these bits of information slowly, and any conversation at this point is unnecessary.

"Yes, miss," Trevor says. "Do you know that today's Nairobi Stock Exchange has its roots in Stanley Hotel, where in 1922 the first stock was floated on 'Gentlemen's Agreement?'"

With that, he opens the door to the Bar, a task he seems to relish. I enter the hallowed halls of the Exchange Bar with its deep brown seats. Here, the fans do not rotate; instead, they wave back and forth slowly, as if propelled by invisible hands.

"I beg you, do not ring the bell," Trevor says. This warning comes as a surprise because I see no reason for it. The Bar is empty, and unless I am stuck inside it—if at all—there is no reason for the bell. I look at him questioningly. Trevor is perhaps expecting this reaction because his eyes dance mischievously.

"If you do, you will buy a round for the house." He waits for my reaction to what he perceives to be a horrifying occurrence, and all I come up with is a "ha."

Not the one to let that dampen his somewhat upbeat spirit, he says rather persuasively. "Might I suggest you come back at night to try our *Dawa?* It is our signature cocktail with vodka, lime, ice, and honey and is very famous."

"I see you have sorted my evening out beautifully, then," I reply. "Thank you kindly."

He then takes me on a brief tour of the suites bearing famous names.

"Today we are the members of Historic Hotels Worldwide," he says, "but we are thankful to these people for bringing us to the world's attention."

I wonder if EH would have ever thought his name would, one day, make it to the door and become the single most powerful name in Stanley's history.

We return to the café, and for the first time, I pay closer attention to it. It is ringed by an extension of the Exchange Bar on the first floor, which is really the second floor, but it is labelled "1" in the elevators—reason enough to confuse anyone.

He points to a tree roofed in glass in the centre—*The Atrium,* he calls it reverently—and continues his narration.

"In 1958, when the hotel was redesigned, a Naivasha thorn tree was planted in its courtyard. When the number of messages pinned on its trunk grew, it turned into Nairobi's unofficial post office."

"When the original acacia tree died, it was replaced with the current one, but the hotel kept the tradition alive by ringing the tree with a message board. This current tree is the third in line, and under it is buried a time capsule that will be opened in 2038 during the replacement of the tree. Did you know that thirty-eight years after the first tree was planted, Tony Wheeler, founder of *Lonely Planet*, who was visiting us, was so inspired by what it stood for that he named his travel forum *Thorn Tree Travel?*

"And now, as we end the tour, allow me to tell you the meaning of Nairobi. In the language of the Maasai, *Nai'robe* means the place of cool waters. To us, Nairobi is an emotion," he concludes with a flourish.

"Wish you a pleasant stay," he says and retreats.

I digest all that he has said in silence. When I can think no more, I simply sit by the window and watch the world go by.

Like Hemingway often did.

Chapter 2

The night is settling in, but I need to stretch my legs and work off the caffeine for a good night's sleep. A short walk from the hotel brings me to the Clock Tower. Nairobi is a familiar city, and I know what to ignore and what to pursue. There is a lot of information to sift through, but it is a task I particularly enjoy.

As Nairobi evenings go, this one is pleasant. Full of life and sounds of a happy place. Like the Nairobi I have known all along. I begin to see traces of another of the most famous literary figures with roots in Nairobi. Karen Blixen. She is everywhere. It is hard to miss her presence.

Blixen is, in fact, the most identifiable name here, even more than EH. While this is slightly disturbing, it does little to usurp EH from my priority list. Blixen, a Danish aristocrat who arrived in the then British East Africa, lived here between 1914 and 1931 through one marriage, bankruptcy, and a tragic love affair. But upon returning to her homeland, she penned her experiences in her book *Out of Africa* and managed to make the most of a situation she would perhaps have loved to avoid in the first place.

I do know of her stint here, particularly her relationship with the Masai Mara, Kenya's top destination safari. And for that reason, a huge part of the Masai Mara is named after her. When not tending to her coffee plantation, Karen's 'restful and limpid' evenings were spent at the Stanley Hotel. The book was adapted into a film by the same name and was set at Muthaiga Country Club, another landmark of Nairobi's colonial past.

It is a pity that Ernest Hemingway arrived in Nairobi in 1933, two years after Karen Blixen left for Denmark, never having

17

the chance to meet her. However, he did eventually become the hunting buddy of Karen's former husband Bror von Blixen.

So much for that. My first night passes peacefully. I have made progress.

*

As a matter of habit, I rise early. Like Hemingway, I want to witness every morning in Kenya and feel happy just witnessing dawn break. I boldly descend into the café in my night dress, not at all surprised to see two other guests dressed the same way. One of them peers at me over his newspaper and the other over a coffee. Both the men smile widely. They are my kind of people. We understand each other.

When it is apparent that the café is going to start filling up, I leave my table and step outside briefly. Breathing the morning air after coffee is the best way to fine-tune the day. I have plenty of time to change and eat breakfast before meeting Tom later in the day.

Tom M is a journalist, a writer, and a father of two who calls himself 'Son of N'ga' which really means nothing, but that is what I am here to find out. His stories on Facebook are hilarious, creative, and original. And that is why we became friends.

Back at Thorntree Café, I ask for the best view of the tree and the street simultaneously. It is brunch time, and against the temptation to order a cold Tusker, I order a coffee. Outside the café, life on the street continues seamlessly.

I wait patiently because I know from experience that time is a fluid concept in Nairobi. But Tom is on time.

Tom is skinnier than his pictures on Facebook, but his smile is the same. Warm and infectious. "So, you are making progress with your good Hemingway? A fine occupation you have there," I say.

"Does it get better from here?" he counters.

"Oh, yes." I match his teasing. "Next on my list is Lord Byron..."

"I'll drink to that," says he. "Are you going to ignore Henry Morton Stanley altogether? He is, you know, the greatest explorer of Africa, and personally, I'd place my bet on him and not Hemingway."

I shudder. I have completely ignored Henry Stanley.

He orders tea nonchalantly while I rearrange my thoughts that are rapidly going askew. The mention of Henry Morton Stanley has opened a new venue of exploration altogether. Maybe... just maybe, I should? I have always associated Stanley's name with Congo and his encounter with David Livingstone, but... maybe there is something to be found in Nairobi, too.

Tom continues the conversation as if I don't exist.

"It is just as well that the good Earth grew tea, and someone clever discovered nicotine in the leaves. And another one—this mischievous other—discovered how to milk bovines, another made safari tea. Oh, and not forgetting the Neanderthal man who discovered fire. Tea is the hallmark of human civilization, only coming second to the good old wine. Stuff of the gods. The Pope should consider the inventor of tea for sainthood."

I nod in affirmation, thinking it should be the founder of coffee and not tea that should get the sainthood.

"May I offer a suggestion?" Tom says. "Considering that you love witch-hunting, I'd strongly advise you to go to Malindi, near Mombasa. Of course, it is not as romantic as stalking Hemingway, but at least you'd get to crack a real mystery. I mean, it is a real ghost town, and you can stuff yourself with pasta if you like that kind of stuff. Me, I like my traditional food…"

"Right ho! Tell me more."

Tom launches into an interesting narration of his train ride to Mombasa not long ago. I can see this is going to be a long and lovely meeting.

"… I sat next to a petite, bodacious babe with nut brown skin, sloping hips, and *na macho kama gololi*—eyes like a ball." He corrected himself. "I kept my eyes closed, smiling to myself, and inhaling her soft perfume. It was getting softly into my brain, but the free therapy session was interrupted when she said *songasonga*. I pulled up my eyelids and looked. I had man spread. I sat properly and grinned. She made a face at me and then smiled.

"She then told me she worked with a local non-profit and was coming from Maasai Mara for some geospatial data gathering assignment. I also learned she was an artist, an upcoming musician, and a writer. We got talking about things and writing in general and winded down the road of Afro history, culture, and heritage. There was laughter and cackling. Her teeth were brilliant white, and the whiff of her breath was warm and minty fresh.

"We were happy with the intellectual vibe we had struck and exchanged numbers so that we could escalate the discourse. Then she showed me a story she had recently written for a competition. It was an Afro-witch story, and it was deeply evocative. I asked this little princess of literature where she got her inspiration, and she promptly said, '*My mother is a witch.*'

"Instantly, there was a shift of feelings. I was shocked but saved my face with a fake smile, gasping, '*How interesting!*' When we alighted, I hugged her ever so lightly. 'I'll see you later,' she called out. I was relieved that she was gone. As I reclined in my car seat, I kept thinking about her witch-mama and what would have happened if I had hit on her daughter. Would Mama have put a curse on me? Would I twitch, fold, curl, and finally transform into a lizard?"

Then we burst out laughing.

"In the meantime, I continue fetching water in weddings, single and very much unavailable. But guess where the babe was going? To Gede. To the ruins."

I stop laughing at once. Tom is such a great storyteller. Just like Hemingway. Is any of it true, though?

The waiter arrives with our drinks.

"There is too much milk in your tea," I say unkindly. "What exactly do you taste then?"

He closes his eyes and leans back slightly, and then opening his eyes wide, he stares at me in mock horror. "Milk, of course. Tea is just an excuse to drink sweet milk."

He looks serious, and I am forced to accept his explanation.

"You are a great storyteller," I say in the end. "Like EH."

"Oh, but your EH had a good imagination too—I mean, he did make up many incidents, including a wife for the love of God. But yes, he was a good storyteller, alright. He was married several times, and yet he invented a fictitious African bride to wean his way into the hearts of Africans, right? Nah. Not charming in the least. You must find yourself that blend of autobiography and fiction about a character named Debba, an 18-year-old girl from the Wakamba tribe who was supposedly his second wife. It is an interesting read."

Tom is no lover of Hemingway, but I will ignore that. How much of his very own stories were his own creations?

"Why don't you leave a note on that board for someone to find?" he cuts in suddenly.

"Maybe I will."

"Did you know that your EH first arrived in Mombasa? People sort of worship him there and even have a hotel in his name. In Watamu."

That is his parting shot. I didn't know that. Tom knows that I don't know. He has the last word.

The best way to find out things, if you come to think of it, is not to ask questions at all. But if you sit still and pretend not to be looking, all the little facts will come and peck around your feet.

These words of author Elspeth Huxley are particularly true of Kenya and the rustic life it offered when she lived here from 1913 to 1925. The author of *The Flame Trees of Thika* frequented the Stanley Hotel and used it as a setting for several of her works. Colonel John Henry Patterson, author of *The Man-eaters of Tsavo* (that inspired the film *Ghost and the Darkness*), also found his inspiration while staying at the Stanley.

History is fascinating, I realize, especially when I am rediscovering it myself.

And Tom had unwittingly opened a new path for me to follow.

*

My trail leads me to the 1904 Tudor-styled Norfolk, what is today Norfolk Fairmont, a few blocks away. It was among the favoured haunts of EH and one I am determined to drink coffee at.

I like the enclosed courtyard. The gardens are blooming with bougainvillea, my favourite tropical flowers. I am welcomed heartily, even though I am not a guest here.

Blixen has left her footprints here, too, and alongside her, author and journalist Alan Moorehead stayed here while researching his book in 1958.

All this is easily gleaned from the serving staff eager to share their association with Nairobi's history.

"We are extremely honoured that Nairobi literally grew around the Norfolk," the staff says. "Nairobians believe that if there wasn't a Norfolk Hotel, there may not have been a Nairobi! And we all know if there was no Nairobi... what would Kenya's history be like?"

I fail to find a fitting reply to this statement, so I smile through the conversation, nodding brightly before finding a gap in the conversation and popping my question.

"Was Hemingway here?"

This starts the second round of gunfire conversation that did not begin with Hemingway. It starts with John Alexander Hunter, a man I'd never heard of.

"I will tell you everything," he begins robustly. "But before your Hemingway, we had many other famous personalities." He raises his left hand and begins counting his fingers. "Scottish-born John Alexander Hunter moved permanently to Nairobi in 1908. He was the number one patron of Norfolk, and all his subsequent books were written here." He touches his second finger; it is for Nairobi's favourite resident, Karen Blixen.

"Karen Blixen had a lover named Denys Finch Hatton, and he loved coming here."

Right now, I am not sure what point he is trying to make—or when he will touch upon Hemingway—but this is turning out to be a great morning.

The second cup of coffee is free.

"For another traveller and author," he says cheerfully. I am moved by this gesture. I hope his words will come true.

"We will add your name on the wall one day," he says meditatively, though not quite meaning it.

"Amen to that."

Nothing more is forthcoming. It seems that Hemingway didn't create much impression on this man. I do my best to introduce EH into the conversation, but the man cleverly sidesteps EH.

Finally, I make my way out feeling quite ignored but somehow satisfied because in my heart, I see Hemingway in his hat and parasol walking alongside me. Hand in hand.

*

Nairobi is thriving. Its urbaneness today may seem to distance it from its wild past, but the connection, however faint, is unbroken. Over the din of the ever-present, highly decorated matatus, I imagine the lions roaring in the world's only national park within the city.

Kenya is an example of the time warp in which Africa is caught. To many visitors, this is simply a nation where you can view wildlife and enjoy the uncluttered coastlines that European explorers encountered a century or more ago. Yet, over the years, Africa has changed. It is no longer the mysterious Dark Continent penetrated by Henry Morton Stanley, and neither is it the playground depicted by the white settlers.

Nairobi itself is two cities: a centre of high-rises and hotels that perpetuates an image of prosperity and comfort shot through with the promise of adventure; and an encircling suburbia of rich folks' villas and poor folks' shanties that belies the image. Nairobi's villas and shanties illuminate the malaise of a continent caught between a lost history and a future of no discernible identity beyond decline.

For the remainder of the day, I retain the services of a boda-boda and strike lucky with the young driver, whose cheerful outlook makes my quest easier. His helmet has a bold picture of an orange lion jumping through fire.

I'd recognize that helmet anywhere.

*

We arrive at the Karen Blixen Museum. It is only fair that I pay homage to Karen, who clearly rules the literary heart of Nairobi. I am surprised to find that Nairobi attracted so many literary greats over the century, making it one of the most culturally and historically rich countries on the continent.

Karen is everywhere, as I mentioned earlier, but her real presence is felt at her former home, and in keeping up with her love of storytelling, the guide at the museum takes me through her life, legacy, and of course, her garden. Her greatest love, Denys Finch Hatton, is buried here.

I round off my quest with tea at Giraffe Manor, a ten-minute ride from the Museum—another evidence of Kenya's colonial past. Its elegant interiors, handsome gardens and courtyards, and not to mention the Rothschild giraffe that joined me for tea, transports me straight into Blixen's Africa. The rooms are named after Denys Finch and Karen and furnished with some of her belongings simply because they are the names everyone in Kenya knows.

*

Footnotes:

*Boda-boda: A motorbike taxi popular in Kenya.

Chapter 3

I am restless. Uneasy. Or maybe it is the lack of caffeine in me, and to fix my predicament, I head to Gibsons Coffee House in the city's central business district to contemplate the success of my visit to Nairobi.

The sun warms up, birds chirp in neem trees, and the sound of cars racing down the road dulls into oblivion. The only sound I hear is my heart beating happily.

To me, Africa has always represented happiness. I wish I could live here forever, especially close to this coffee shop that awakens every cell in my being.

A young man named Johnson appears at my elbow. I call out the request I have learnt from Johnson, the Kenyan barista at Starbucks in Dubai, my favourite haunt.

"*Nataka Kahawa.*"

Johnson beams at me appreciatively. "*Ndiyo Madam.*"

I return the smile.

Just like the Johnson from Dubai. Like homecoming.

It is a pleasant morning. The temperature of my coffee is just right, which instantly puts me in a happy frame of mind.

I have heard it said that getting the desired flavour out of espresso is half in the hands of the barista; the coffee, machine, and other auxiliary details make the other half. Clearly, everything has worked in unison this morning. Ideally, when dealing with a bean as extraordinary as this Kenyan, the person behind the bar must be well-versed in its origin to extract the best flavours from the bean. Here, it seems like they employ only the passionate ones.

As befits the day, I let my mind conjure up a decision while my eyes absently scan the coffee literature hanging on old walls and go over the colourful bags of coffee with pictures of elephants, cheetahs, and rhinos on them. Elephants—a symbol of Gibsons Coffee, a hundred percent Arabica coffee, one of the sweetest and most aromatic beans with a nutty taste and chocolaty aroma and not so acidic but with a bitter aftertaste.

My mind goes over all the time I have spent in Kenya photographing Masai warriors and lions. Being the eager, bright-eyed volunteer keen to make a difference in people's lives away from their country—a task I have wholly immersed myself in. I have helped build roofs over toilets and living spaces in remote villages and held a dying child in my arms once too often.

But now I am ready to experience the real Kenya through its coffee and some of the famous literary figures who made this place their home. Surely there must be a different reason for them to be here, something more than I see.

I summon Johnson with a wave of my hand and ask him why the coffee shop is so empty.

"You see, we produce some of the world's best coffee," he replies, "but coffee-drinking culture is yet to catch on. We people here are very superstitious when it comes to coffee."

I raise a brow and wait for him to continue.

"You have never heard of them?" he asks with a smile. "There are many stories that discourage people from drinking coffee. Sometimes, these stories can make it difficult for you to quietly enjoy your cup of coffee."

Johnson loves to talk.

"Nairobi is very much a society divided by classes, and coffee is mostly a drink for the wealthy. As the average Nairobian is not particularly fond of going to a shop and paying for a premium beverage, he'd rather have a hot drink at home."

When summed up like that, it all begins to make sense.

"Kenya, for all its coffee production and its economic viability, stresses on myths like coffee-induced insomnia, coffee as a cure for hangovers, and coffee as a leading cause of dehydration and a champion of weight loss."

Weight loss, yeah right.

"I agree about the addiction," I say at last. "I am an example of that. But I believe that without coffee, especially Kenyan, the world would find very little to enjoy in life."

Just then, a young couple walks in and calls out their order for Frappuccino. I cringe. How thoughtless, I say to no one in particular. Living in a country that produces the best coffee, all they want is milk and ice in their coffee. I am not sure I can ever forgive the chap Andrew Frank—an erstwhile employee of *Coffee Connection* in Cambridge, Massachusetts—for ruining the coffee-drinking experience of millions of people by putting ice and milk into it.

I am fascinated by the stories of the origin of different types of coffee. Every coffee has a multi-faceted, labyrinthine saga behind how, where, and why it tastes the way it does. For the science-minded or the curiosity-driven, here is something to mull over—the geography, soil make-up, and processing methods influence the flavour of coffee. However, the sociology majors might be more interested in the people responsible for bringing the crop from seed to cup.

I am both.

Johnson returns, muttering inaudibly, almost painfully. I sense his sadness, but he admits the Frappuccino drinkers keep the business running.

"We make friends with the killers of coffee."

*

Despite what Johnson has just said to me, I see a slow upward trend of hanging out in coffee shops in the city.

East Africa has traditionally produced some of the world's finest crops, but few coffees are as highly regarded as Kenyan Coffee. Kenyan farmers re reputed to be highly educated and with strict standards for their crops.

Drinking extraordinary coffee is more than a pleasant way to start the day. It is the human connection in this business that adds to the experience.

Coffee is my world boiled down into one piping hot cup.

*

I am on my way to Kenya's coastal town, Mombasa, aboard the overnight train from Nairobi. This is one of the most epic train journeys in Africa, or, for that matter, anywhere in the world. One can just as easily fly between the two cities, but I am undertaking this unique overland journey for the fun and adventure of it. What a train can do to me, a one-hour flight can never hope to achieve.

The very idea of rattling down the tracks sets my heart aflutter.

I start my journey at the Nairobi Railway Station, an antiquated building from 1899. There are a number of historic displays throughout the waiting areas with photographs and artifacts from Kenya's rail history, including man-eating lions that plagued the workers who laid the tracks more than a century ago, but I engage in people-watching, a singularly enjoyable and educative pastime, while waiting for the train to arrive.

There is a man with a small portable table from which he is selling books about Kenya and its railway history, along with small wood carvings and hand-painted postcards he claims to have made himself featuring various African animals. I chat with him for a while, learn that he is a musician and an artist as well as great storyteller, and end up buying a book on Kenyan birds, a subject I am least interested in. Birds, according to me, are best left in the bush.

Soon, the train, the *Jambo Deluxe*, pulls in. I join a stream of passengers boarding the train. I am travelling second class, which means I am going to share the compartment with three other people. The main difference between the first and second classes is that the first class has a private compartment for two people, while the second class has four bunk beds. So, if you are two people who want to make sure you have a compartment to yourself, first class is the way to go.

Let me put your mind to rest about this train. The *Jambo Deluxe* is one of the oldest trains I have been on, and there is nothing European about it. Not a lot of repairs or renovations have been done to it, and it looks and behaves its age. Many things do not function, such as lights, fans, and other mysterious switches. The toilet has a missing seat, but there is a wash basin inside the compartment. The bedding is clean, and the berths are relatively comfortable. There is really no reason to complain, if you ask me.

I have a couple of bottles of *Tusker* beers tucked away in my luggage, something I had the forethought to buy. My ticket includes dinner and breakfast.

Soon we roll out of the station and out of Nairobi city limits. Darkness slowly envelopes us. I make my way to the dinner car. The unmistakably British formal dining experience gives a faded glimpse into a bygone era of elegance; they still use china, crystal, and silverware, though some of it may be chipped and a little worse for wear. The food tastes great.

I have an enjoyable evening chatting with my table companion who is from Mombasa, having emigrated there from India many years ago. After dinner, I retire to my compartment, and I'm pleased to find that the attendant has made my bed. There are certain privileges to travelling on this train—like the making of the bed.

The beer tastes especially good with a train blanket pulled up to my knees. I have no trouble sleeping.

*

The magic happens in the morning. It's hard to describe what it's like to wake up on a train, the morning sun rising over the African savannah, and to look out the windows glimpsing wildlife, villages, people going about their daily lives, and miles of untouched land.

Waking up to the feel of the train rocking gently beneath me, early dawn seeping in through the windows, and the sight of the savannah as the train makes its way to the coast is nothing short of a miracle. I press my face against the window and watch a herd of gazelles run by. An ostrich dances in the distance, and a flock of birds flies over the train on their way to someplace on the other side. I spend hours just gazing out the windows feasting on the sights around me.

Soon, the train rolls into the city of Mombasa, with its confluence of buildings and the blue ocean coastline beyond. After collecting my belongings and tipping the attendant, I am ready to start my next adventure in Mombasa.

Here and around, according to Tom, I will find a spattering of mystery and history.

*

Mombasa, Kenya's second-largest city, is a melting pot of cultures, combining Kenyan, Arabic, and Portuguese influences with Indian and pan-European aspects. Spend some time here admiring the Arabic and Portuguese architecture and heading to the old town to see the dhows (traditional wooden sailboats) out on the bay before travelling north along the coast to follow in Hemingway's footsteps.

When Hemingway left port in Marseilles for the continent in 1935 with his wife Pauline and his friend Charles Thomson, he disembarked in Mombasa after two weeks at sea. Before heading inland, he explored Mombasa, Malindi, and even Watamu.

I am not about to spend any more time than necessary in Mombasa because I aim to be in Malindi, ninety kilometres away. There is one thing about travel in Kenya that I worry about. It is its inability to set a time; it is either too early or too late. However, I know that in Africa, particularly in Kenya, I should really stop worrying about this and let the local ways carry me along to my destination. It is a place where I often remind myself that time is an illusion, and Kenya always justifies this statement.

The bus journey is not entirely smooth and event-free, but that isn't the thing I am worried about. Kenya, like the rest of Africa, is a developing country with its share of issues. Yes, it is not as safe as Dubai or Singapore. Yes, transport is not often reliable. Yes, I have issues with food, including last night. Yes, I have my share of trouble with thieves and thugs, but that never turned Africa against me. I hope it never will.

After two full hours of jostling about, despite being sandwiched between ample bodies, the journey from Mombasa to Malindi finally ends.

True enough, when I arrive, I feel like I have been transported to Italy. Tom was right. He claimed Malindi had some of the best Italian food outside Italy itself. For him, it was merely hearsay, having never travelled to Italy, but on that front, I can be a judge, having enjoyed Italy's finest in the past. I am pleased with the opportunity to eat Italian food, which will be a welcome break from eating local food.

33

Malindi is everything I thought it would be. This 'little Italy' of Africa is the place Italians sought out thirty years ago and never left. It appears totally dependent on tourism because everywhere I see supermarkets with signboards in Italian. Impulsively, I dash into a supermarket and am not surprised to see huge stocks of olive oil, salami, pasta, and prosciutto, and there are pizza joints everywhere. While this does not make the town entirely 'Italian,' there is a visible influence—in the language, food, and general behaviour.

There is an Italian consulate here, too. Not that I have use for it; it is a mere observation but something that explains a lot.

All this I gather even before I check into my hotel where I am greeted with a *Ciao*. Since I am not expecting to be greeted in Italian, I am at a loss how to respond.

Soon, I am walking the streets, eager to explore this sultry old town. Everything Italian about Malindi is on billboards, and it isn't easy to miss the connection. In fact, I suspect this is what drives tourists here.

I am in love with Malindi and its 15th-century pillar tombs and a thatched 16th-century Portuguese chapel, which is especially pleasing after pursuing Hemingway through his coffee shops and hotels in Nairobi.

My agenda is simple. I intend to forget Hemingway and involve myself in the day-to-day life of Kenyan-Italians whose vocabulary includes *ciao, ciao,* and not *Jambo,* and to relax in this laidback town and eat fresh seafood. I say seafood with not much eagerness because, in the past, I have experienced the not-so-pleasant aftermath of eating seafood in Kenya. Malindi may change that, of course, so I'll take my chances.

The weather is balmy. Pleasantly warm and windy. The kind that encourages long walks on the beach followed by dips in the sea, but I am not particularly attracted to this form of holidaying. I am all for watching the waves, drinking coffee, and letting the sea winds play with my hair.

Malindi's old town is interesting. The Swahili Quarter, dating from 1930 to 1950, has a large and busy market, and on the site where slaves were supposedly auctioned off until 1873 lies the Juma mosque alongside a pair of 15th-century pillar tombs. The said tomb and a few other similar ones are unique to the Swahili Coast. I take myself to the Malindi museum right opposite the main jetty for a peek into the town's historic past. Wooden totems are displayed prominently in the three-storied building, and somewhere beyond this is East Africa's oldest church, a Portuguese Chapel of St Francis Xavier built in 1542 and surrounded by a small but old cemetery. The town's highlight is the Vasco da Gama Pillar, which I can visit because I have a ticket from the museum to visit the headland on which this pillar is built.

When talking to Tom, I had little or no idea what Malindi would turn out to be, and now that I am here, I am pleasantly surprised. Malindi, with its lovely beaches, is rather uncomplicated in the way it is laid out. It has only one main street, Government Road (locally called Baharini Road), which runs parallel to the beach. A shorter street, Sir Ali Road, connects Government Road with the tourist road from Mombasa, officially known as the Mombasa-Malindi Road, and is the site of the market and adjoining bus station, the centre of the community's social and commercial activity.

Another striking feature of this town is the architecture. It is a mix of African clay or wooden rectangular houses with brightly painted doors; however, the seafront is peppered with British seaside villas now serving as vacation homes for wealthy Kenyans. The buildings are set against a background of brilliant-coloured frangipani and bougainvillea.

*

It is when I am cracking a crab shell by the sea in the evening at Umande Restaurant, watching the late beachgoers do their touristy things on the white sands while giggling drunkenly, that I hear, once again, about Gede from the waiter trying to help me with the cracking. Dean Martin's *That's Amore* plays in the background, deepening my impression of being in Italy, except that the words are uttered plainly and simply by blacks. Around me, the aroma of the local specialty, *kuku paka*—chicken cooked in coconut—fills the air.

"These crabs, they are very old. Their shells are like stones," he says as if revealing a secret. "We call them devils. But do you know what is older than crabs? Gede. A defunct ghost town without even a facade to fool visitors."

He scurries away. His words have a dramatic effect on me. A defunct ghost town. Tom was not joking. He did know of it in connection with a ghost.

I can't say if my hands are shivering or the crabs have suddenly come alive because I know they are jumping out of the plate and creeping away…

I await his return impatiently. Did he really say defunct ghost town, or is it my imagination? Lately, I have been imagining things, like walking hand in hand with EH at Norfolk, but here, I need a reconfirmation.

I imagine myself inside an abandoned building flanking the graveyard, with its dark interiors and moss-covered walls. My body erupts in goosebumps when lizards scurry off, leaving an ethereal silence. I like it when an aged door whimpers as if moved by something behind me, only to stop when I look back. My teeth are set on the edge. I am about to call out when the waiter suddenly appears at my side.

"Did you really say a defunct ghost town?" I ask. "Did you? For real? Where is it? You didn't make that up, did you?"

"No, ma'am," he answers with a smile. "And you know what, you can see it for yourself. But before that, I must tell you a story."

We agree to meet at the end of his shift.

*

Chapter 4

The night is quiet and cool. I wait for him to arrive. He arrives suddenly, having changed into his regular clothes. I wouldn't have recognized him without his uniform, but before I can invite him to sit down, he looks over his shoulders furtively and says, "Let me tell you one story so you can understand why I love mystery and why I want to tell you about the ghost town.

"Back in the misty days, when I was growing curious in the shadows of Mt Kenya, I heard a tale of which I cannot reveal much. It is a story without a title and long abandoned secrets."

"One quiet night like this"—he waves his hands expansively and shrugs his shoulders— "a giggling sound was heard in the tombs at the outskirts of town. It went on for days. Silence ate the town. I won't tell you of the whispering winds that would whistle in the silence. Terrible howls that carried strangled screams, faint voices, voices bursting with laughter, receding into far away echoes. A faint glow was always seen in the utter sea of dusk. People spoke about seeing a saw-teeth in the darkness. On the lone narrow street, skinny, mournful cats…"

I wonder where he is going with this. Naturally I don't believe any of this story, and hope he arrives at the point he is trying to make. All this is good, but really, I am not here to speak of myths and legends.

His eyes shine with contained excitement. It appears that he believes all that he is saying.

"A lone dog limped and whimpered down the pitch-dark street…"

"But where is this ghost town?" I ask.

He pauses for a moment and continues as though I don't exist.

"Since the day I heard these stories, I have been looking for mysteries."

I prompt him again, but he ignores me, intent only on recalling tales of hypnotic eyes and flesh-eating grasshoppers. My mind wanders.

Then I hear it. He has finally stopped at a name that sounds to me like Watamu. Yes, that is what he said. Watamu.

There is a faraway look in his eyes. He appears exhausted.

"Watamu," he says again, a little more reverently. "Watamu is the place you must go. Don't be fooled by its handsome beaches, water sports, and of course the food and such like. Watamu hides a big secret, and you must uncover that secret at all costs. Go," he says dramatically, waving his hands at the sea, "go and look through the ruins at Gede. You will find your mystery there. In the ruins of Gede."

He leaves me, muttering to himself, and vanishes into the darkness. The air of mystery clears up as soon as he leaves. "That was rather dramatic," I say to myself, preparing to return to my room. "What yarn! I wonder if any of it is true?"

I didn't even ask for his name. How can I find him again? What would I ask for? The waiter who likes ghosts?

I am left with no option but to return on the restaurant-provided transport back to town and hope the waiter wasn't talking through his hat.

*

On my way to Watamu a day later (in Swahili, Watamu means Sweet People) in the hinterland of the African Coast of the Indian Ocean, I am thrilled at the chance to search for something older than the crab. The Ghosts of Gede.

Watamu is a young town with a history that can be traced to a 1937 shipwreck that washed up an Irish family on the current beach of Turtle Bay.

About four kilometres from this handsome town of Watamu, near the junction of Mombasa-Malindi Main Road, lies a mysterious, ruined city that the local legends say is inhabited by the ghosts widely revered in the area. Gede means 'precious' in Oroma, although its original name was a different one—Kilimani.

Someone materialises from behind the shiny gate and thrusts an identity card at me. Mombo Roberts, the card says. A bonafide guide.

"Good morning, Miss; I think you need a guide?" he announces firmly.

I want to refuse, but I recall the waiter's warning. *The spirits of The Old Ones reside within the sacred environs of Gede.*

"Yes, yes, I think that is a good idea," I reply.

We settle on the price and march forth.

There is never enough time in the world to see all the ruins, but the truth is, ruins are a window into the country's past, I tell myself as I step inside the ruins. It is empty. It is eerie and somewhat magical. Suddenly, I am glad to have Mombo with me.

There is the presence of *someone else* here; I feel as though I am being watched. The place is extraordinary. "Even if you are alone, you are not alone," Mombo says reverently when I mention it. "The Old Ones, the spirits of ancient priests of Gede, are ever present here."

"I hope they are harmless."

"Mostly. You can only come here when you are invited by them," he reveals. "So, it is necessary to show respect, or they can curse you. It has happened. But if you are respectful, you might even have them along for the ride."

Then, he narrates a story.

"In 1948, James Kirkman decided that there were no such things as ghosts and set out to investigate the enchanted walls. However, he had to live outside the ruins because he was visited by the ghosts in the form of wind and storm."

Letting that serve as a warning to me, I stay as close as possible to Mombo.

The Gede Ruins, a National Museum site, is rather well maintained. The buildings are well preserved, nothing like I had imagined. I feel myself walking back in time as we wander through buildings and doorways, passing through the remains of the imposing arched entrance that makes up the palace complex, believed to be the ruler's home. The outlines of several anterooms and courtyards are still visible.

We stroll peacefully past the ruins of mosques, a palace, and merchants' homes, for once glad that there are no other visitors. I am the only one that morning, which means if the ghosts of Gede are real, I am a sitting duck.

The Palace is fascinating. Inside are the men's and women's courtrooms, a bathhouse, and a treasure room. Some rooms are named after household objects, like the *House of Chinese Cash,* the *House of the Iron Lamp,* or *Venetian Bead.*

There are a couple of pillar tombs too, *presumably* belonging to the rich. Presumably, because much is still unknown about Gede.

As I walk around the ruins listening to Mombo, a picture of a very advanced culture emerges. Gede had been a thriving community of about 2,500 people. Here, I see the remains of a flush toilet and bathroom with drains, and Mombo goes over the details of an advanced sanitation system the people adopted back then. Archaeologists have since discovered goods from as far away as China (Ming vase), Spain (scissors), India (lamps), and Italy (beads) at the site, indicating a wealthy settlement. These goods are now displayed in the museum.

Gede was inhabited from as early as the 12th century to as late as the 17th century, but it flourished in the 15th century. Traces of advanced water usage can be seen all over the site—like wells big and small, all over the site. The town architects also collected rainwater and installed lavatories in the stone buildings. Mombo tells me how one of the merchant's houses had a bathtub and swimming pool.

The Great Mosque with three rows of tall pillars and two other smaller mosques built over different periods of time indicate that Islam had been the ruling religion here.

"The town had two walls," Mombo explains. "Within the inner walls, the rich lived in coral houses, while the outer wall surrounded the town and contained farmland, plantations, and houses for the middle or working class. The poor lived beyond the outer walls."

While the site itself feels a little lifeless, in comparison, the baobab and May Flowers, with their roots growing through the walls and foundations, their branches leaning into the ruins, add life to these old ruins. However, the vegetation or the warm winds do little to distract me from the carefully laid out mystery town.

Gede has a fascinating history. It is over 600 years old, yet there is no written reference to the site anywhere. Almost no historical record was ever made, and nor was it marked on maps from that period. The reason for the secrecy is unknown, and the cause of its downfall also remains a historical mystery.

However, in 1927, Gede was given Historical Monument status and later declared a protected monument before finally being declared a National Park in 1948. The original Swahili name for the town had been Kilimani (meaning a hilly place). Mombo tells me that when the Oromo people settled in the area, they renamed it Gede, meaning "precious water and green pastures."

At the edge of the site, partially hidden away, is the Swahili Culture Building—built by the government as a place for dinners and meetings, although it has fallen into disrepair. One of the rooms that serves as a museum houses a small collection of coins, pots, and lamps, and another room exhibits a whale skeleton.

It is rather eerie, especially when you are left alone to admire the whale.

Mombo leads me to the enchanting sacred forest surrounding the ruins. "These are as important as the ruins itself," he says and then explains the traditional rituals and sacrifices done by the surrounding villages. "People came to pray for rain, good harvest, or good health. Not only that, the Sacred Forest is rich in ecological diversity. Look around you." He points to the giant baobab tree, followed by tamarind and fig, and a tree with its smooth bark that even monkeys cannot climb.

Suddenly, I feel very spiritual, as though the *Old Ones* have accepted my presence and are glad for it.

He then puts forward three theories about why the site was abandoned. The first suggests a possible disagreement or war between the sultan of Mombasa, who did not favour Portuguese explorers, and the sultan of Malindi, who did—this or an internal war between the Swahili people and the Oromo people. His second theory proposes a drop in the water level (evidenced by the deepening of the well) that made the residents move away. The third suggests that foreign diseases like the plague killed the residents.

Whether Gede is cursed, haunted, or anonymous, it does not get many tourists, but it holds the key to an important chapter in Kenya's history.

As I walk out, something touches me. Is it the wind? A falling leaf? Or are the spirits of the *Old Ones* telling me something?

I hear a whisper.

"Tell the world about us."

*

Mombo, now relieved of his role as the guide, makes me an offer. "I will tell you more spooky stories and take you to the local witch. Would you like that?"

I do not fear witches. I am Indian, and witches and ghosts live amongst us. We even pray to the spirits, depending on what we seek in life.

We walk briskly for fifteen minutes till my bladder is about to burst. Just as I call for a short break, an old house with a metal sheet roof comes into view.

Mombo shakes a finger at the house.

"You know what comes to mind when I think of this house? Happiness, bliss, and memories of my late great-grandmother."

"Is she the witch?" I ask.

"No, my grandmother is."

We approach silently.

"Grandma loves sitting under that tree. It is the same tree under which my cousins and I played as children. It is the same tree under which I had the last conversation with my grandmother before she lost her mind. But she refuses to go and stay with her sisters in town. That tree still bears leaves and fruit. We call this tree M'bambakofi. The Fever Tree."

The house has a beautiful view of the open fields behind it. To me, it seems other-worldly.

"I spent my early school holidays in this house with my siblings and maternal cousins. It was a house of joy as we lived under the loving care of our grandmother. I don't know how she managed to keep an eye on all of us. She was strict but so, so loving. She cooked for us. We milked her cows, we played, we bathed and washed clothes in nearby streams. We sang songs late into the night, roasted maize over open fire, and told stories passed down from generation to generation, stories of Mbodze and Matsezi, our folklore characters.

"It is the same house where my mother and her siblings grew up. It still stands to date, with its original structure and metal sheet roof. The only change made to this house from my childhood days is the addition of the two front windows, which have now withered too. It previously had no windows, just clay walls with pillars made of stone. Inside, it still retains its earth floor. There is neither electricity nor water supply connected to it. It is a house that has stood still over time.

"The house has stood for decades, watching the souls that come and go into it. We grew up and went away, but one constant is the memory of a beautiful time gone by, a time we wish we could return to but which will never come back. So, I make it a point to visit her as often as I can, though she sometimes doesn't recognise me. My beloved witch in the best place on this earth."

Grandma Witch is a wizened old woman with a sparse tuft of cottony white hair and skin like ancient rolls. Although she appears to be asleep, I know she is looking at me. I feel her gaze. She has dodged death long enough, and I place her age between ninety and a hundred.

I have a feeling she knew every secret in this world worth knowing. She lived alone but had the winds for company. I bet she even speaks to the winds from time to time just to amuse herself.

Suddenly, she grins at us toothlessly.

"Welcome, children," she mumbles hoarsely, spreading a tattered old mat before us. I look at Mombo in alarm. He seems content and peaceful in her presence. My heart is in my throat. But I sit down nonetheless, hoping for the best.

She walks unsteadily into her inky dark kitchen and emerges with a very black pot.

"Eat this all up; it's all yours, tujùjù."

I fervently pray that it is not the soup of white ants or frog eyes. Mombo laughs out loud.

"Eat first, then tell me what tidings you bring." She grins wickedly.

I am not willing to bet on the fact that she knows what I am in Kenya for. None of my authors have ever mentioned a witch in their books, and logically speaking, decades ago, the country should have been full of witches. Or did they just appear recently?

Slowly, I relax. In fact, I am enjoying being spooked. It is a strange kind of feeling, which makes me feel alive.

*

We leave her silently muttering to herself and rush to one of Watamu's well-known Italian café called *Non-Solo Gelato*. The espresso is strong, just what I needed to shake off the spirits.

Hemingway had, at one point in time, spent some time at Watamu. There is a resort named after him, but that is of course a recent addition to the town.

The presence of EH is calming. Somewhat fulfilling, like finding a link to reality. This witch business is all very good but not entirely palatable.

I toy with the idea of snorkelling or diving, which these towns are renowned for and equipped to handle the load of tourists who come here specifically for it. I am eager to see the green and hawksbill turtles here and, in the end, give in to the temptation and add a marine component to my literary and ghostly quest. What a great place to be.

I decide against visiting the snake farm, no matter how hard Mambo tries to convince me. I do not particularly like snakes and refuse to know them, preferring to remain silent on the subject—silent or ignorant, I am not sure. But I do not like snakes in the least. I am tolerant toward them as long as I see them hanging on a tree, a safe distance away, or under a rock I am not standing on.

Ernest Hemingway was nearly thirty-five years old when he saw Kenya for the first time. The hunter of animals and women, as he is known in Kenya, also loved deep-sea fishing. And while coining up the word Safari which was included in the dictionary to mean African Excursion, he went shark fishing near Mombasa, returned dissatisfied, and thereupon came to Malindi and installed himself at the Blue Marlin Hotel. Finally, after two days of deep-sea fishing, he met the marlin, and towards the end of the day, discovered the blue lagoon of Watamu.

Most of EH's life in Africa is closely linked, and some of his award-winning novels, which were later adapted into award-winning films, were undoubtedly inspired by his visits to this part of the world. Unfortunately, his impressions of the place did not get a mention in any of his books, but they changed the outlook of the small sea town forever.

*

I make the return journey to Mombasa on the bus, and from there, I take a short flight to Nairobi. My flight to Kilimanjaro in Tanzania leaves in twenty-three hours, so I decide to stay the night in the city, preferring to spend the evening at Nairobi's Indian Quarter. In no way does it feel like homecoming, except for the occasional Bollywood music over the speakers.

Kenyans adore country music. You hear it on the radio all the time. Elvis or Don Williams—it is all there. Non-stop. Diamond Plaza, an old mall and a jewel in the Indian Quarter, is bursting with restaurants. The area feels like a toy town because everything is two-thirds the scale of the rest of Nairobi, including the streets. In this part of the city, food is served from booths arranged around outdoor tables. I end up eating Anil's chicken tikka on the bone with gooey naan slathered in butter, which I wash down with fresh sugar cane juice laced with ginger.

Back at the hotel, the sky begins to fill with rain-laden clouds. I get ready for bed. It will soon rain, and I want to enjoy a cool night as I float peacefully into slumber.

Kilimanjaro Airport is a short flight from Nairobi, and I board the flight with anticipation and excitement. The last time I was heading to Tanzania, it was on an Ethiopian airline from Addis Ababa in March 2010, but I had been raring to climb Mt Kilimanjaro. It was when Hemingway and Lord Byron were names that I'd known casually, never once having conceived the idea of ever knowing them through their adventures. Sometime in the intervening years, that casual know-how changed into a passion. Or, to be precise, obsession. Hence my presence here.

On the flight is a man who begins a conversation uninvited. Some things haven't changed in the least. I wish they remain so. I am glad he has started the conversation.

How friendly people are. How perfectly normal it feels, too.

He hands me a card. Emmanuel. He is a realtor and runs a chain of modest hotels in Arusha. There is a number on it. He tells me about the family secret of sweet potato soup and the way to raise cows and pigs successfully.

I slip in Ernest Hemingway and Henry Stanley, and just to sound like I knew what I was talking about, I slide the name of

Dr Livingstone into the conversation, and I am glad to find him knowledgeable on the subject. After this conversation, I hope to quiz him on the Tanzanian potato soup.

He doesn't disappoint.

"History is peculiar," he tells me. "Imagine how three simple words Dr *Livingstone, I presume*, catapulted a young journalist into fame? And to think Livingstone did all the hard work? What was so hard about finding him, I ask you?"

I am flabbergasted. All this while I'd known of the young journalist named Henry Stanley of the New York Herald who had in the year 1871, in all earnestness, done a fair bit of exploration in the African bush, looking for updates on the good doctor before happening upon him in a village named Ujiji on the shores of Lake Tanganyika. It did astound me that Stanley's apparent surprise at finding the doctor so suddenly led to this now-famous outburst that catapulted him to fame.

"What, you tell me, was so ground-breaking about an American journalist wandering through the African bush over a century ago? My ancestors grew up in the wild alongside lions, and I can tell you stories of how their lives didn't change when the White Man arrived thundering through the bush to save their souls."

I smile at the thought. There is some truth in what he said. "I see your point, sir," I say candidly. "But I suppose, you know, it is all about timing. Stanley was there at the right time…"

Emmanuel turns to the coffee growing cold on his small pull-out table and takes a small sip. "You must give our local coffee a try, Miss. Promise me you will. Our coffee can look all your commercial coffee in the eye and not back down."

"I will, I promise."

It is time to land. The recipe for the sweet potato soup remains unasked.

He lapses into silence, leaving me to wonder if Stanley was the reason Hemingway came back to the continent years later—and specifically, Tanganyika as it was called then. I know why I am here now, though, and it has everything to do with Hemingway.

He and I belong to different generations, but our mutual love for Africa and its adventures draws us back.

Chapter 5

The road to Moshi has not changed much. During my earlier visit, I had seen potholes large enough to drown a cow, but now I feel they have expanded to fit in a fire truck alongside the cow.

It is the only visible change. Everything else, including its soul, is unchanged. A decade ago, filled with the euphoria of having summitted Mt Kilimanjaro, I'd felt that nothing ever seemed to come close to the feeling of contentment of being here, other than the thought that someday I would scale Mt Everest. Of course, that never happened, and I can grudgingly admit it may never happen, primarily because I have since realized that I might not be cut out to hike vertically over a three-month period and not live to tell the tale.

Tanzania is one of the poorer countries on the African continent, but I can't help but feel the optimism and love of life that the people embrace. Bias and prejudice are hard to find, with diverse ethnic groups and religious traditions living harmoniously side by side. By and large, the local population is kind and generous in spirit, with an undercurrent of respect and politeness.

I check in to Hotel Kindoroko in Moshi, and my impression of it has not changed. Like it did a decade earlier, it seems to rise out of the sidewalk even today. The front street looks a little less chaotic, and the food carts where I had enjoyed *mishkaki* are missing. All the memories come back in a rush. The rains, my first smell of Tanzanian coffee from the hotel kitchen, the wet tables, and the sound of crickets…

There is a spring in my step as I walk towards the hotel reception, smiling widely. The wooden crocodile with its big, open mouth is staring at me. Nothing has changed. Only Jenna, the receptionist with the corn rows, is gone. She'd been the one to introduce me to the local ways of celebration.

"She has two babies now," I am told as a matter of fact. "She moved to Kenya, but whenever she is here, she visits us. Do you want to leave a note for her?"

No one remembers me, but they are happy to hear my stories from a decade ago. I slip into the small garden at the back and ask for my coffee to be served there, eager to reconnect with Moshi and everything in it.

Reliving memories is a wonderful thing, except that it drives home the point that I am now a decade older, and the old bones are not quite what they used to be. It is just as well that I am not attempting to climb Mt Kilimanjaro, despite nursing many random and bold thoughts about it.

*

From the terrace of Hotel Kindoroko, I see the snowy Mt Kilimanjaro. Jenna and I had had some interesting conversations here while sipping milky coffee and discussing the future. Ordinary, simple girl talk. Today, she is married with two kids, and I am following a dead poet and an adventurer. She had expressed a desire to climb the mountain that Hemingway had immortalized in his 1936 book *Snows of Kilimanjaro*, although he had not actually climbed it. Ten years ago, I'd stood on Uhuru Peak, not knowing this truth.

I am overcome with a sudden urge to climb the mountain again, but I console myself that the good Hemingway had never climbed it either.

In hindsight, I can easily associate with every place mentioned in the book. But had I known about the carcass a decade ago, would I have taken the clue from his book and looked for the

Leopard's Point twenty minutes away in the other direction from Gilman's Point at 18,600 feet?

I think not.

If the leopard had been looking for immortality, it found it at the summit of Kilimanjaro, where its frozen carcass lies preserved for all. But for it to gain fame, it must thank Hemingway.

So, did he imagine that carcass of the snow leopard near the summit as he writes in the book?

There is, however, a backstory to this.

In 1926, Richard Reusch, a Lutheran pastor who made multiple climbs up the mountain, discovered a freeze-dried leopard at roughly 18,500 feet along the crater rim of the volcano's loftiest sub-peak, Kibo. A photo exists to this effect. The pastor suspected that the predator had died in pursuit of a goat, the remains of which he also found a few hundred feet away.

He returned the following year and snipped off the leopard's ear as a souvenir. It may be that Hemingway did read this account of Reusch. Eventually, the corpse disappeared, but given the Hemingway shout-out, it was immortalized. The general location of the carcass now holds the unofficial label of 'Leopard Point.'

I contemplate the many myths surrounding it. A decade ago, I'd been consumed with a burning desire to conquer it. And I had. What I didn't know then was how impossibly immense it was. Its base stretches more than fifty miles and spans two countries; the 19,340-foot mountain is so heavy that it depresses the earth's crust.

The Uhuru Peak was known to Ptolemy, the ancient Greek geographer who spoke of a great snow mountain at a latitude of unspeakable heat. But the icy summit that had served as a landmark to Zanzibar traders and slave caravans was dismissed by the Royal Geographical Society in London as a ridiculous rumour until 1849 when Christian missionary Johann Rebmann confirmed the existence of a snow-covered mountain near the equator.

As the story goes, soon after, Queen Victoria redrew the boundary between the British colony of Kenya and the German colony of Tanganyika so she could give Kilimanjaro to her grandson, Kaiser Wilhelm, as a wedding present.

Alas, this is just one more bit of myth swirling around the mountain, and in Moshi, it is okay to go to bed thinking of them.

*

It promises to be a sunny day. I hope it will be too because my former mountain guide Siraji has promised to visit me. I look forward to seeing him again. I hover around the hotel reception, looking at the clock anxiously.

Will he be on time?

He is.

Siraji looks just the same; if it is possible, he looks younger. The decade of separation melts away when he hugs me. In the last ten years, we have remained in touch over social media and if not fully, are aware of each other's lives. He now runs his own trekking company and has a live-in girlfriend and a daughter. I wonder if she knows he is meeting me today.

The young receptionist, unaware of our past, stares at us. Curiosity is writ all over her face.

"You are friends?" It is a question and a statement all at once.

Siraji replies to her, rattling off in Swahili.

"Good, very good," she replies. "Enjoy. I wish you a good day." Then, she vanishes.

"How is your love life?" I ask and playfully jab him in the chest.

"Nothing to celebrate," he counters with a straight face.

"Great. Coffee?"

"Now we have many cafes here. Many good ones. Come, I will take you to one of them now."

Ten years ago, I was not a coffee connoisseur, but the intervening years added some layers of sophistication, and my coffee-drinking habits took on different forms. Now, I am eager to know if Moshi's coffee meets my standards.

*

Siraji leads me to his recently purchased motorbike. *Bajaj,* he calls it. A Bajaj, I recall, is the default name for a *boda-boda,* the local mode of transport. I am unsure if I can handle a bike ride in Moshi right now, but there is no alternative.

They say when in Rome, do as the Romans do, but come to think of it, Romans are expert at being Romans, aren't they? And as a visitor, you have no clue how Roman the Romans are. I say when in Rome, don't do as the Romans do.

He hands me a helmet and says, "You put this on now."

When did helmets become compulsory here?

There is a traffic snarl in Moshi, and I start screaming as soon as we hit one.

"You hold me tight," he shouts through his helmet. It is the best thing I have heard all morning. My screams hit a high when a motor car cuts across oncoming traffic with no care at all. Motorists hoot at him, but the ruthless young man continues nonchalantly, unmoved by the abuses.

I snake my arm around his waist and refuse to let go. Somehow, I feel safer this way. The car driver weaves in and out of traffic, narrowly missing side mirrors, people, car doors, and lamp posts. And, with each scream, I grab him tighter until he almost falls off. Driving in Tanzania is an art. Free-roaming animals are everyday hazards, but so are drivers with their own road rules.

*

We head to the Union Café. This café existed before I set foot here over a decade ago, but as I said earlier, I was not so much of a connoisseur to seek out the best coffee, often contending myself with anything that passed off as coffee and that didn't contain milk, sugar or could be made in a jiffy. Now, I am a different person with a firm opinion on coffee.

There are a few foreign tourists lounging about, looking as if they belonged there. Surprisingly, there are no locals here, and Siraji tells me why. The prices at Café Union are quite high for the average Tanzanian pocket.

"Tourists come here because of their generator and reliable Wi-Fi," he says. "You know Moshi is known to have power cuts quite often."

The waiter arrives with a smile. This is what I have been missing: the smile of a barista that conveys what a good time I am about to have.

Siraji looks through the menu carefully, eventually settling for a honey cappuccino. This surprises me because I know he doesn't like coffee as he prefers soda or cola instead.

"It is good for the throat," he says as though he has known it all along and clears his throat to drive home his point. When it arrives, I take a tiny sip from his cup. He doesn't mind. We go back a long way. It tastes divine, with a sweet aftertaste that is like a balm for the throat.

Siraji doesn't care for the reason I am back in Moshi, much like my "I don't care why you are still single" reason. We have grown together from immaturity to what we are today.

Union Café is like an institution in Moshi, and you can't visit the town without stopping by to have a coffee here. The café belongs to the Kilimanjaro Native Cooperative Union, the major producer of coffee in Tanzania, representing thousands of small coffee farmers. The menu is extensive, including several food options, but in the end, it's all about the coffee. They roast their beans on-site, fresh, and grind them just before making the coffee.

In the middle of our conversation, Siraji suddenly changes tracks. "Do you want to braid your hair, like last time?"

"Oh, err, I think not. But I wouldn't mind one of those, you know, wigs that can be put on with ease."

"My friend can help you then." Something in his voice gives away the fact that she is more than a friend, but I let it pass. The last time I was here, I had braided my hair as a victory celebration of summitting Mt Kilimanjaro, and I had a hard time getting my normal hair back in order once I had unplaited the African-style plaits.

*

The Maasai Market is the same old bustling routine, so we go straight to Siraji's friend's hair store that sells wigs of peculiar designs. I run my hands through these beautiful braids made in the market while enjoying the looks I get as a *mzungu*.

Siraji's lady-friend is warm and friendly and not so pushy. She tells me, "I wish I could have your hair," and I tell her we could trade places.

She tells me how once, when the wind blew off her wig that she lovingly procured in the Kenyatta Market in Nairobi on her first-ever trip there, her son shot past her, exclaiming *Mom mimi sikujui* (I do not know you, Mom).

"That son of Judas," she finishes with mock anger. "I calmly picked up the wig, brushed off the leaves that had collected on it, and sauntered away."

Siraji says nothing, though I can see he wants to laugh. I laugh because it really is a funny story. Her son, it seems, is a miniature Judas.

*

A drive past the Moshi police station revives memories. Stolen money. The suspected porter was proven innocent. Suspicion shifted to another and left there to die a slow death because the charge was never proven. But circumstantial evidence made it all easy to put the puzzle together. And it all pointed to the one person I didn't want to admit. Siraji.

Late in the evening, we return to Hotel Kindoroko, quite drunk on banana wine. I hug Siraji goodbye. He promises to visit me in Arusha soon. I feign happiness, knowing that it is not meant to be. Promising is a very African trait. I know this from experience.

*

In the past, I hadn't paid Arusha much attention, using it as a mere launching pad for my safari trip in the northern circuit. Perhaps Hemingway had done the same? His favourite haunt—where he is said to have hunted kudus—lies in the vicinity of Arusha. I have decided against any wildlife safari, but there is a definite yearning for one.

Looking for surprises is my thing. That is what I excel at. Although those supposed surprises often end up as shockers, I have not lost hope.

Siraji drops me off at the daladala stand at the end of town. It looks the same. Chaos is the trademark of Daladala Park, and without it, the romance of traveling on it would be dead.

I board a particularly well-worn looking daladala with some trepidation. Every kind of emotion flows through me, and I twist my body, enter the contraption, and inch towards the window on the second row behind the driver. In case of any emergency, I will have a remote chance of escaping that way.

Siraji comes to stand by my window, smiling up at me and holding my hand dangling from the window. In some small ways, he is my longest connection with this country and one I am fond of enough to want forever.

We speak of nothing, simply trying to fill the time before we part ways, perhaps forever. I want to promise a lot of things, but I see no point in continuing anything that has no future.

The daladala is nearly full when a good-sized woman enters and sits beside me. I inch closer to the window to accommodate her large bottom, foreseeing an unpleasant journey. Siraji kisses my hand before we pull away, and in my heart, I know I will never see him again.

This daladala is noisy. It is hard to say whether the chaos is from the jarring music or the passengers trying to talk over each other. I rest my head against the window and busy myself with the scenery outside.

It is not a very long journey. From time to time, the fat woman pushes into me, seemingly oblivious to my discomfort. I fight back good-naturedly and lose, but she then makes a half-hearted attempt to shift her weight.

In a little over an hour, we arrive in Arusha. I am not at all surprised by the changes it has undergone. From whatever Siraji had said to me, I was half expecting it.

Arusha, a frontier city located exactly halfway between Cairo and Cape Town, represents a remnant of the British Empire. Marked by a gigantic clock tower, Arusha is the *A-Town* with an energy hard to ignore.

I head to *The Arusha Hotel*, the city's oldest surviving hotel, built in 1894. It is also where I am staying. That means I am sharing space with an erstwhile banker and hunter, Kenyon Painter, and a friend of Teddy Roosevelt, who is believed to have described the hotel as a whitewashed mud brick building with a roof of corrugated iron sheeting. He then purchased the hotel in 1907, naming it The New Arusha Hotel. The hotel then became home to many travellers, including Baron von Blixen (*Out of Africa* fame). During the filming of the 1962 movie *Hatari*, the cast, including its lead actor, John Wayne, frequented the hotel, eventually leading to renaming its bar *Hatari*. Today, it goes by the name 'Four Points by Sheraton.'

The hotel is home to those traveling between the Cape and Cairo. Starting its life as a two-roomed German guesthouse to its current avatar as the city's only five-star hotel, it stands as a testimony of Arusha's formation and prosperity.

In the lobby of our luxury hotel, I see scores of travellers transitioning in and out, many with tremendous amounts of gear, either preparing for or recovering from their trek up the mighty mountain. Arusha is also home to its own mountain, Mt. Meru, which many would-be climbers use as preparation or practice for the more intense climb up Mt. Kilimanjaro. But many more of the travellers are there to embark on safaris, given the proximity Arusha enjoys to many of the country's best national parks.

One thing that annoys me about travel blogs is how so many other writers talk about areas of the world that aren't just little known, practically no one who doesn't travel very often has even heard of them. They assume a level of familiarity with remote, backpacker-centric places without introducing them, explaining where they are, or why the normal, average traveller should even know about them in the first place. I think it is unfair, and I certainly don't want to be that person, that presumptuous, elitist traveller, so while I'm sharing my experiences about a place that most people have never heard of before, I also will explain why it should be on your travel radar.

*

A-Town is a nickname given by the locals, which shortens Arusha to A and adds the word 'town.' The official name remains Arusha and comes from the *waAarusha* ethnic people who lived in the region of northern Tanzania. In the 1830s, Arusha was occupied by the Maasai people, and the town itself had no buildings to speak of, except for a handful of mud and stick homes to suit the semi-nomadic Maasai people's lifestyle. In 1896, following the murder of two missionaries, the area was overtaken by the German military force, which built a German Boma or fortress. At the turn of the 20th century, Galanos, a Greek millionaire, built the Clock Tower, which continues to stand today.

The Clock Tower, an easily recognized landmark, claims to be the mid-point between Cape and Cairo. I spend a few minutes trying to picture it a hundred years ago before walking past the tourist office on Boma Road to the whitewashed buildings built during the German occupation.

Arusha has a fascinating history. During WWI, the Germans were ejected, and the area fell under the control of the British, who boosted trade in the region and set up the railways. The extension of the railroad from Moshi to Arusha in 1928-29 boosted commerce between the two towns, and prosperity came. Three decades later, in 1960, the power returned to the Tanganyika African National Union (TANU), headed by Julius Nyerere. In 1961, Tanganyika became its own state, and three years later, Tanzania was formed as a union of Tanganyika and Zanzibar. It was officially declared a city in 2006.

Today, Arusha is a major trade centre of northern Tanzania, and its proximity to several safari destinations means that tourism is now a major industry in the region, even though mining remains the major contributor to the country's GDP.

*

It is quite warm and nearing lunchtime as I leave the hotel in search of a coffee shop.

Strolling past the Clock Tower towards Boma Road helps me to establish a connection with the city. The sounds reverberate in my being. There is music everywhere. A short walk brings me to *Africafe*, a supposed fixture in the coffee lover's book.

I did not expect to find *Africafe* full, but I find a place easily by the window facing the street, and I am surprised to see the large variety of coffee on the café's menu. People around me are nonchalantly sipping their flat whites, iced lattes, and other European-style cups of coffee. This place has been here for years, a constant staple in Arusha. And for good reason, too, I am led to believe. For starters, the internet is quite reliable.

Another thing I like is that, unlike other Moshi coffee shops, *Africafe* is both an expat and a local place. There are no plastic tables or chairs here. Everything is wood. Brown wood. It has things visitors want: reliable internet, clean bathrooms, coffee, and quick service, but locals come here, too. The other great thing is that they really don't mind if you have a coffee and sit for hours using the internet.

The manager, a lovely young lady with braids close to her scalp and wearing bright violet lipstick, is moving from table to table, speaking with the customers, and from the looks of it, she is familiar to many. For the newcomers, she is making recommendations, asking and answering questions, and helping the waiters bring the correct orders.

Soon, she is at my table, and I invite her to sit down. Her name is Flora.

Her violet lips stretch over her bright white teeth. She rearranges the table out of habit and asks if I have ordered anything yet. I assure her that I have. She slowly relaxes.

"Have you been here before?" she asks. "What brings you to Arusha?"

The best conversation opener, if any. What am I doing in Arusha? If I were to be honest with my answer, we would probably spend all day trying to find an answer. I give her a watered-down version of the real reason and follow it up with a reason she is familiar with.

"The safari, of course," I reply. "But then, I am also looking for the local stories; you know what I mean? Historical scandals and such like."

By the time my coffee arrives, we have become friends.

I take a sip and smile brightly. "Wherever this comes from, it is brilliant."

Flora flashes another of her bright smiles. "I will tell the Barista that he is appreciated."

Flora then tells me the story of a tailor from Goa who put Arusha on the world map and of Mr Khan, the inventor of the chicken-on-the-bonnet.

These stories of Arusha are interesting, particularly the one of Manuel de Souza, a tailor from Goa, India, who is credited with Arusha's international fame.

"Back in the time when Tanzania was called Tanganyika, Manuel qualified as Master Tailor and moved here in the year 1933 after making his way through the remotest places in Africa on foot."

Here, she pauses for effect. I take another sip and nod as a cue for her to continue.

"Perhaps back then, it was the only option available to him anyway," I remark.

She nods in agreement and continues her story.

"In 1939, he began prospecting in the Lupa Goldfields in western Tanganyika, but after World War II, this became unprofitable. So, he moved to Dar er Salaam and returned to tailoring. Soon, his itch for prospecting began, and he left for Shinyanga Diamond fields, but due to political disruptions, he was unable to obtain a license. He travelled again, unarmed, to the area around Lake Victoria, combining tailoring and prospecting to get by."

As the narration progresses, I picture Manuel in the summer of 1967, living in Arusha, where one evening, he collected a group of people, hired a driver, and set off. The driver had apparently refused to go further than the village of Mtakuja, thanks to the bad roads. Instead of returning, he gathered his men and decided to explore the area because, as he later said, he had a good feeling about the place. Three months later, in July 1967, he made the once-in-a-lifetime discovery that changed the gem world. He had discovered Tanzanite (named after Tanzania), the most beautiful and rare gemstones the world had seen.

"Sadly, he died in an accident only two years after this discovery, but his name lives on as the one who brought prosperity to Arusha and as the discoverer of this exquisite gem. You know Tanzanite is the birthstone of December."

Flora has changed the way I perceive Arusha. I will be experiencing Mr Khan's *chicken-on-the-bonnet* on my own later.

*

Much as I'd have liked to spend the evening at Hatari, thinking of John Wayne at the hotel's bar, I decide to give Arusha's favourite chicken place a try.

A brisk walk brings me to the garage-by-day and a chicken-spot-by-night eatery called Khan's BBQ. This eatery is a sign of a culinary shift in Arusha's dining scene. Khan, the owner, is a man of Indian origin whose predecessors moved to Tanzania in the 1920s to work on the railroad. He never left and decided instead to lay out heaps of grilled *Nyama Choma* (or skewered meat) and salad, followed by the famed Indian sweet *jalebi* floating in a sugary syrup, to hungry locals and tourists looking for something to spice up their palate. No matter where you choose to dine in this city, you will end up here sooner or later. Khan is known to *burn it down, smoke it out, and serve it up*.

Dining at Khan's BBQ is not without consequences. My sleep is interrupted by painful visits to the loo.

*

Morning in Arusha comes with its own set of happiness. The sky is clear blue with cottony white clouds peacefully floating about, the sun is warm, and the light wind that blows down Mt Meru is cool. The noise from the streets is stimulating—an indication that Arusha cannot be stopped.

I head to Arusha's central market. Its lively atmosphere is a total assault on the senses. Several languages are being spoken at once. English, Swahili, and Hindi words fly out in all directions. Pushy vendors and hagglers look to lower the price, shilling by shilling. Bins heaped with dried sardines and codfish, meat hanging on the line, abundant locally grown fruits and vegetables, and clothes and bicycle tires indicate that Arusha certainly does not lack prosperity.

I plunge in and haggle hard, and I console myself that even if I get ripped off, which I will, the people on the other side of that 500-shilling note probably need it more than me. The vendors are pushy but friendly and not averse to talking about life as you bargain. Few things have a marked price. That's the fun.

And before long, I am enveloped by the magic of bargaining with the determined and unyielding sellers. I eventually leave, feeling utterly satisfied with a bag of exotic fruits, nuts, and wooden masks.

Arusha is filled with coffee shops, and from the number of cars and motorbikes outside them, they are doing great business, too.

I stroll towards the Blue Plaza on India Street to see and experience Tanzanite, marvelling at the city's transformation. With humble beginnings way back in 1900 as a minor German military garrison, currently, Arusha is not only Tanzania's most active tourism hub, but it is also the headquarters of the wider East African Community (EAC) with a population of nearly 120 million people. In 1961, official documents ceding independence to Tanganyika were signed by the United Kingdom at Arusha, followed by the signing of the Arusha Declaration in 1967. This laid the foundation for a new name, *Geneva of Africa*, a title given by former US President Bill Clinton in 2000 during his visit to the city to witness the Burundi Peace Pact.

Arusha itself is a dusty, charming, mid-sized African city. Its population comprises a vibrant mix of over a hundred nationalities: a melting pot of Swahili, Masai, Hazdabe, and numerous other ethnic and indigenous cultures. Living peacefully, side-by-side, the locals are super friendly and eager to show you their country. To me, it seemed like a city stuck between traditions and modern life. Arusha is not a place most people know, and, I'll be honest, most people will never go. But they should. Arusha is a frontier city, a place of excitement, and a place of opportunity. It's this unlikely place where people from every corner of the planet converge to partake in travel experiences so amazing and unique that they truly live up to the moniker of once-in-a-lifetime. It might not be as sophisticated as some of the larger cities in East Africa, but this dusty town with its colourful markets, vibrant stalls, and hidden oases is a memorable walk down memory lane. It sizzles with excitement and the combined energies of many people embarking on a once-in-a-lifetime adventure. I can't imagine a more exciting sensation or place to be.

I can see why Hemingway was attracted to it.

*

Not wanting to risk a repeat of last night's episode with the chicken, I return to my hotel for lunch when I overhear a conversation about an upcoming three-day safari in Arusha's northern circuit. The three-member group huddled over their beer at the bar are desperately trying to rope in a fourth member to keep the costs down. Without a second thought, I approach them and declare my intention.

Their response is warm, if not tinged with relief. It is settled. Judith, Fred, Mathew, and I will leave early tomorrow morning on the grand safari.

I have lost the challenge with myself.

And despite my original refusal to go on a safari when I was in Nairobi, I am suddenly keen to hear the lion's roar. I blame Karen Blixen for it. She'd said, *"If there were one more thing I could do, it would be to go on safari once again."*

*

At 6 am, we are ready to roll. Our big, sturdy Land Rover waits for us at the door. It is the kind of car that bodes well for things to come and unleashes emotions suited to the moment—a car that is at the heart of my exciting journey ahead. It is the kind of car that hums and roars over dirt tracks and occasionally serves as the resting spot for the fearless cheetah or lion in the wild. It sports a green colour, making it environmentally friendly.

The roof is down, but that is easily fixed by pushing a button. It is built to accommodate four, including baggage, food, tents, and such like.

The driver is young and wiry with a broad smile and charming manners. His name is Joshua. Our agenda is simple. We will drive for six hours to Serengeti National Park and stay the night at Chaka Camp in the northern Serengeti, close to the Mara River. Chaka Camp is a semi-permanent mobile camp located in Serengeti's pristine wilderness. The Camp moves twice a year to ensure its guests are well-placed to witness the Great Wildebeest Migration.

No one seems keen to sit next to Joshua, so I climb in beside him and buckle up. It is a habit and one that Joshua appreciates.

"The roads are bumpy sometimes, you know. So, buckling up is good."

I say I have travelled this way before, and this breaks the ice. We have many things to speak about.

No other member of the safari group talks very much, each keeping to themselves, lost in their dreams. I have forgotten their names, except Judith's. But it turns out that she is not much of a conversationalist either and prefers to bury her nose in a book on African birds. I enjoy the silence, only occasionally speaking with Joshua.

Rural Tanzania is green. And not just any green; it is a lively green, the kind that inspires health freaks or health propagators, and the moment is so wrought with these thoughts that I want to run through the tall green grass, nibble on the tender shoots, and chase butterflies alongside the herd of happy black cows.

Soon, we are driving through an undulating landscape. The car has no trouble negotiating the roads. Red dust clings to the tall bushes by the side of the road despite the recent rain. We are nearly at the park when we have a road surprise—a flat tire. But fate is on our side because not fifty feet from where we stall, there is a small settlement, and as we stand inspecting the tire, ninety-nine percent of the settlers approach us like a swarm of locusts descending on a Russian farm.

Serengeti National Park is an easy park to negotiate, comprising mostly of rolling grasslands and an occasional outburst of trees that the giraffes find interesting. I stick my neck out, trying to bring a giraffe into focus. My eyes travel from somewhere at its feet to the top of its head in admiration. I also spot a particularly old baobab tree, which is interesting because of its shape and that it somewhat resembles Rafiki the Monkey's tree from the film *The Lion King*.

Every part of the baobab tree is valuable, Joshua explains to no one in particular. "You can make ropes and clothes from it, and from its seeds, you can make many types of cosmetics. In summer, elephants eat the skin of the tree because it has water. Our African women use baobab for their beautiful skin."

A low chuckle ensues and dies. The group is back to their windows, and I hear the occasional click of the cameras. Not the frenzied clicks of enthusiasts, just the average clicks of uninterested and tired spectators.

Joshua turns towards me in exasperation. I feel him.

The grass is tall. We drive around, change tracks, and surprise some gazelles out for a graze. It is peaceful. I feel as if I was born for this life. To wake up and greet the spectacular savannah and its inhabitants every morning, gaze at the pale sun through the trees, and watch the slow progress of giant tortoises across the tracks would be a thing I'd enjoy.

Soon, we call it a day. It has been a long day.

After a dinner of warm beans, chapati, and watery chicken, we gather around old benches near the camp and drink warm beer around a campfire. The night promises to be cold. The sounds of the jungles reach us. Somewhere beyond that fence line, the King hunts while we engage in a quiet discussion of the day and listen to the nightly concert of the wilderness.

Someone soon goes over the edge and breaks into a song. Fortunately for us, the camp is quite empty, so there is no one to witness this display of gaiety. Another person launches into stories of encounters with lions, many of them make-believe.

We retire for the night. The camp has fallen silent. Except for the crickets and maybe bats flying about.

I wish, of course, to hear the roar of lions.

I am about to drift into a deep sleep when I am suddenly stirred out of sleep by that evocative African sound: the call of the lion. I will never forget that sound. A roar. I feel it more than I hear it. Is it my imagination? I don't think so. I sit bolt upright in the bed, every hair on my body standing on end and a tense excitement surging through my veins. It doesn't matter how many lions I have heard; I still feel the same nervous excitement. Every. Single. Time.

I stick my neck out of the tent. There it is again. Deeper this time. It is real. Imaginations cannot be that real. I feel the roar. It is a deep sound coming from the depths of ferociousness. From another time. It is fearsome, evoking a primeval, savage-like sensation in me.

I wonder if I am alive or quite possibly, about to die of fulfilment.

I try to establish the direction the lions are calling from, and my subconscious seems to track how close the calls get and where they are headed. The wolf-like wails of the black-backed jackals also throng the African night. I smell the damp soil. It is an unusually dark night.

When the savage voice reaches me the third time, I am sure I am in spiritual heaven.

I wonder if the others have heard it. Quietly, I zip up the tent, lie back, and smile in the darkness.

Some moments are too magnificent for words.

A roar and a drumbeat

Together make Afrika

Like no other place ever be

Born in the savannah

But carried through rivers and valleys

Is a roar and a drumbeat…

*

Our morning drive is undertaken a little before sunrise, which, according to me, is the best time to start. We are a little late because Judith overslept; she had been too scared to sleep after hearing the lions. When she finally arrives, she insists on sitting in the back, away from any possible animal attack.

All of us smile in the darkness and say nothing.

Soon enough, we come across an elephant herd. But more than the peaceful herd, something else catches my attention.

Sunrise. Beyond the horizon, over the dry treetops, is a flaming orange globe: the sun. The elephant pack moves towards the sun, their retreating backs and thin black tails flipping from left to right thoughtlessly. Trumpeting sounds come floating through.

It is a moment of great magic. The magic that made the jungles of Africa so famous in the memoirs of Ernest Hemingway.

The sun comes out from behind the treetops and turns the world into a warmer place. Everything is picture-perfect.

I am happy. Like Hemingway must have been when he wrote:

I never knew of a morning in Africa when I woke up that I was not happy.

The oppressive heat as a thunderstorm builds

The relief when it rains,

The feeling of warmth as the sun rises,

And the joy when it sets

The time everyone takes to ask how you are

And truly listen to the answer

The sounds of camaraderie, of laughter

The smile around every corner of every road

The land, the people, the feeling I have that I'm truly

Home.

This is Africa. My Africa and the Africa that Hemingway left for me.

*

Chapter 6

The traffic builds, slowing our approach to Arusha. Left with nothing to do but curse the traffic, the noise, and the dust, I close my eyes and let my mind wander. It is but a few moments in my ruminations that I am surprised by a question:

Where do I go from here?

I run my grime-coated fingers through my hair, readjust my posture, and make a face. It is a question worth considering, after all. When we finally move again, the answer announces itself.

A conversation I had with Tom at Thorntree Café plays in my subconscious mind, and I delve deeper into that conversation. The name Henry Stanley keeps resurfacing. Before Tom, Captain Trevor had mentioned that name too attributing the name of the hotel to this explorer, but I hadn't been paying close attention. I wish I had. I am sure it is important somehow.

Back at the hotel, I try to redefine my travel plans, subjecting it to a closer look. Until now, I hadn't considered including the lives of two of Africa's great explorers—like Henry Stanley or Joseph Conrad—in my travel itinerary. But I am leaning towards Congo, having read *Heart of Darkness* by Joseph Conrad, a book with many layers and hidden themes.

I know not very much about Henry Stanley. Stanley has been called the greatest explorer of Africa, but a few papers have also called him 'a cruel imperialist who connived with King Leopold II of Belgium in horrific crimes against the people of the Congo.' However, history is full of contradictions.

Should I go for Henry Stanley, someone I have only heard of, or for Joseph Conrad, who I have read? Reading Conrad had taken time and patience, and the only way I remember finishing it was by reading one section at a time. But even then, I felt I had done it some injustice. It is, to say the least, an intellectual book that makes one think and wasn't at all written to entertain the readers. It had forced me to think and question our moral system.

However, I do know that Conrad was disappointed with Stanley, although Stanley's reports on Dr Livingstone could have inspired Conrad to travel to Africa in the first place.

But one thing Stanley, Conrad, and later Hemingway had in common was that all three were journalists.

*

It takes me a while to decide on visiting the Democratic Republic of Congo or simply DRC. While waiting to secure a ticket, I do some reading online, and this is how I come across Michela Wong's *In the footsteps of Mr Kurtz*.

Wong spent six years of her life in Kinshasa, following the political heatmap of a country that eventually went bankrupt. Her account of 'The Leopard,' the president of Zaire for thirty-two years, Mobutu Sese Seko, who showed all the cunning of his namesake—seducing Western powers, buying up the opposition, and dominating his people with a devastating combination of brutality and charm—is quite powerful.

"While the population was pauperized, he plundered the country's copper and diamond resources, downing pink champagne in his jungle palace like some modern-day reincarnation of Joseph Conrad's crazed station manager," she writes in her book.

Michela Wong witnessed Mobutu's last days. She traces the rise and fall of the idealistic young journalist who became the stereotype of an African despot. Engrossing, highly readable, and as funny as it is tragic, *In the Footsteps of Mr. Kurtz* assesses the acts of the villains and the heroes in this fascinating story of the Democratic Republic of Congo.

In the absence of any reason, curiosity takes centre stage. At this point, I step off my literary trail and allow myself to be driven by curiosity to explore what is being called one of the most unsafe countries in Africa. To a little extent, there is that fascination with danger and the desire to see what Joseph Conrad saw and, before him, Henry Morton Stanley.

That said, I am more fascinated by the fictional Mr. Kurtz, the Belgian trader in *Heart of Darkness* by Joseph Conrad, than any river discovered by Henry Stanley.

Mr. Kurtz, a trader of ivory in Africa and commander of a trading post, monopolizes his position as a demigod among native Africans. Kurtz meets the novella's protagonist, Charles Marlow, who returns him to the coast via a steamboat. What an interesting story that is.

*

Africa has remained the stomping ground for journalists and adventurers, both pretty much the same thing, really. Even in the past, you couldn't have been a journalist if you had no sense of adventure. Not much has changed. I say this for a reason.

Henry Stanley was a journalist. Ernest Hemingway was a journalist.

It is a pity Conrad never crossed paths with Henry Stanley. It is peculiar that Hemingway didn't come to this side of Africa, sticking to the East Coast mainly.

I have been both, and in some remote corner of my mind, I nurse a hope that I will get my next big scoop here.

*

I step out into the pleasant morning to find a smiling Jean Paul outside Kigali International Airport.

I am not at all surprised to see a tall, well-built man with a pleasant face and an overflowing tummy, which seems out of sync with the rest of him. He is not nearly as dark as East Africans, being of wheatish complexion. He will take me to Goma, DRC by road on a journey that I hope will revive my love for travel.

He is holding a name card.

I greet him warmly. "I am delighted to be in Rwanda. I hope to be surprised."

Paul is amused. His eyes twinkle as he leads me to an old Toyota sedan with a driver in waiting. I have never seen that make of car before.

"We will go straight to Goma now," Paul says quietly. "To my country."

Paul is Congolese.

It is a beautiful morning here in Rwanda. I feel calm despite the morning rush hour. The streets are spotlessly clean, and the jacaranda trees lining the wide streets are in full bloom. Uniformed municipal workers are bent over long brooms, sweeping up fallen leaves. It is a whole new world.

Rwanda's cleanliness continues beyond the limits of the capital city. We leave the city behind, and an endless parade of soft, terraced hills bursting with bananas, pineapples, and corn and an equally endless parade of people walking in both directions on the road greets me.

Women wrapped in printed, colourful cloths, many with babies tied to their backs, walk effortlessly uphill. One cloth for their lower halves, another for their upper halves, and another small wrapping on their heads—the three rarely coordinated, a riot of contrasting bold colours against one of the lushest and most vibrant arrays of green hues I've ever seen, the blacktop road being the only neutral colour.

The road is flanked on both sides by bougainvillea, cracked mud, or clay brick single-story buildings with tin roofs that go beautifully with all the green on the hills in the valleys behind them.

We stop briefly at Nyaranturama, a small town fuelled by *Akabanga*, Rwanda's famous chili oil. Paul seats himself beside me and picks up the worn menu card disinterestedly. I choose an omelette with chips and meat. It is by far the most familiar-sounding breakfast item on the menu.

The restaurant itself is small, with tables set close to each other haphazardly. But this haphazardness is welcome. This is Africa—the kind of Africa I hope will never change.

There is no coffee on the menu. Paul is quick to recognize my disappointment and hastens to comfort me.

"In my country, we have excellent coffee. In Nyaranturama, you will only find chili oil."

He then laughs at his own little joke. He is no fan of Rwanda.

We stop at a small waterfall where some scraggly children are playing. They abandon their pursuit of happiness and surround me with demands of money. Or a pencil.

Or chocolate.

*

Soon, we arrive at Gisenyi, now renamed Rubavu, the last town before we cross into Paul's homeland and my destination. Rubavu is a plush little town sitting on the shore of Lake Kivu, a lakeside retreat for the rich Rwandese, Paul tells me. I sense a change of tone.

We leave the car and walk towards a swanky building, which is the Rwandan border post. The queue is long, but I am a foreigner, so I am motioned forward.

"Bonjour, miss," greets the immigration officer.

"Good morning," I call out cheerfully. Come to think of it, I am in a cheerful mood, too, despite the lack of caffeine. The Rwandese efficiency is heartwarming. I have now acquired an exit stamp.

"We will see you soon, miss. Have a safe stay in Congo."

Is he trying to tell me something? Did he stress the 'safe stay' a little too much? I cannot be sure, but is it my imagination that he is looking at me curiously? Congo is right there, a few meters away from this building. Do I really need to worry?

"Thank you. Be seeing you soonest," I say and retreat.

Paul has my luggage offloaded and is standing with it proudly. We walk the short distance to the hotchpotch of low, aging buildings that make up the DRC border post. There is every sign of chaos here. There is a sense of latent energy here that was missing on the Rwandan side. People waiting for their visa clearance are lounging about; some are seated on the ground, and some are perched on the car bonnets. It is sunny and warm.

Paul attends to my visa while I wander off towards the lake. But I manage only to peer at it through the tall, mesh fence.

As I am photographing the signboards, Paul walks up to me.

"You must say you are a student, okay?" he says.

"A student? Of what? But, say, do I look like one?"

"Yes, you do."

I am happy to carry on the charade, although I can't help but wonder why this is necessary. Will I succeed in passing off as a student? A senior research student or even a scholar, perhaps? But Paul tells me they must have no suspicions about what I really do.

"To enter Congo as a writer or journalist is tricky. You must have special permission if you are a journalist. Student is the safest way to go."

The immigration officer peers at me when I stand my turn.

"Welcome, Indian," becomes his opening line. "Why do you come to Congo?"

"I am a research student, and I want to see the gorillas, and it is rather expensive in Rwanda. So, I come here. To your country."

I hope I sound sufficiently incoherent and forthcoming. Like a bloody student. He peers over the counter to look at my uncovered legs. It is just as well that I am wearing shorts well above my knee like a student.

My passport is subjected to a closer scrutiny. "You look younger now."

Reverse aging is thus proven at the border crossing of DRC, although another reason is that passport photos are not flattering in the least. I attempt a genuine laugh. "Aw, thank you! You made my day."

I might not look like a student, but I am a woman susceptible to flattery.

My yellow fever documents are quickly approved. He then flips through my passport, glances through all the visas I have on it, and asks me again.

"Research student? You travel very much, I see. You are welcome to Congo."

We leave hurriedly. Paul is quite a popular face here. People wave at him constantly, conveying some secret message in that simple gesture that makes Paul smile. The smile disappears as soon as we enter his old, black Prado. He is like a chameleon, switching on and off with ease. He almost looks human when he smiles. Perhaps I should tell him that?

We endure another passport check before finally entering the Democratic Republic of Congo. The border crossing has been one of the easiest—no bribes, scams, or hassle.

My arrival in Congo isn't what I can call momentous, but I assume it will get better with time. My hopes rest on the coffee I am going to consume.

The contrast between Gisenyi in Rwanda and Goma in the Democratic Republic of Congo is sudden and sharp. Rwanda's cleanliness and orderliness are replaced with chaos, crumbling buildings, garbage, and diabolical roads. Black volcanic rock is everywhere: buildings are built from it, streets are black with it, and massive black boulders line and sometimes block the roads.

A bumpy side road leads us to the lake. Roads, it appears, are not asphalted beyond the main street. Every house we pass has high compound walls crowned with barbed wires and armed security guards. Slowly, I ease into the reality of DRC.

"Say, Paul, how about that coffee you promised? Are there nice coffee shops here? Please say yes!"

"You take coffee now? It is lunchtime; we will eat a Congolese lunch first. Coffee, you can have later."

Paul, in my opinion, does everything by the rules. Noon means no coffee. In my books, there is always time for coffee. Any time is coffee time. I must get Paul to see my view.

"Sounds like a plan, but surely…"

Before he can answer, we arrive at the hotel I am going to stay.

Hotel Caritas is just like the pictures I have googled. It is predictably empty now, thus making my request for a room with a balcony overlooking the lake easy to grant. A bellboy carries my luggage to my room on the second floor. There are no elevators, and I skip upstairs happily. The view from the balcony is gorgeous, and except for the lone pine tree that obstructs the view slightly—just like the pictures—everything is perfect.

Is this the country that people worry about? Is this the land of darkness Joseph Conrad talked about?

Lake Kivu is gorgeous and surprisingly calm. Not a wave or ripple to break the surface. Sun rays dance on the surface, and somewhere far away, there is a watery, sunlit path leading into eternity.

Behind this facade, however, there is a reason to be nervous. Lake Kivu sits on top of 300 cubic kilometres of carbon dioxide and 60 cubic kilometres of methane. The gases are trapped beneath the water, but if something were to happen— like, say, an eruption of the active Mount Nyiragongo—the gas could be disturbed, rise to the surface, and kill millions of people.

Lake Kivu hides this secret well. I launch into a conversation with myself and duly forget that Paul is waiting to show me the city, to be followed by lunch.
The knock on the door snaps me back to reality. It is time to see the real Congo.

The town of Goma is unlike anything I've seen. Cuddling the effervescent Lake Kivu on one side, towered over by a dangerous, active volcano on another, and ruled by wooden load-carrying vehicles called Chikudu, it is a town that has kept the media busy for years. I have heard stories of bullets flying around town, the state of lawlessness, and occasional reportage of kidnapping and extortion, which effectively put an end to tourism in this part of the country. But luck is on our side because we reach the town unhurt.

I feel comfortable about Goma already. A drive through the city proves how much farther from the truth is said about it in the media. This city is far more developed than I thought, with cell phone shops and grocery stores serving the local and expat population. There is a sense of chaos alright, there are far too many *motos* in the town, the sky is a crisscross of electric wires, and the town itself is black, but everything I see opens my eyes to reality a little more.

Congo is primarily a Christian country followed by Muslim minorities and people living out in the bush practicing animistic religions. There are two churches in Goma, and Paul directs his Prado to one of these promptly for some quiet time.

"This Church was almost destroyed in 2002, but God is kind. You will now see for yourself. Here, you can take as many pictures as you want. Here they take no money," kids Paul. "I'll wait here."

The inside of the church is neat and colourful, and even at this time of the day, there are worshippers deep in conversations with their saviour. Light streams in through the stained-glass windows and casts a colourful pattern on the floor. Ten minutes are enough to photograph it all.

We drive back through the town.

Goma was once a popular tourist stop for those adventurous enough to drive from one end of the continent to the other. Not anymore.

"Many hotels today have more cockroaches than guests. There are not many tourists here, and you can see why. It is a little disturbed, this country. Always there is fighting. You be careful when you take photos. Don't take photos of UN people. Even some local people, they will ask for money."

Paul knows his city and its people well. Perhaps he knows something about the two great figures, Morton Stanley and Joseph Conrad?

He doesn't.

The present-day Goma is literally rising from the ashes. Where lava flowed in 2002, houses have been built. The main road in the centre of town is blacktopped, roads have been laid out in the various neighbourhoods, and buses and motorcycle taxis can circulate now. The city is spread out, and the streets are still full of people, a sign of security. Electricity is sporadic, but solar panels have also appeared here and there.

The freshly painted logos of mobile phone networks do not disguise the dilapidated state of most of the buildings. People sit in grime on the streets, trying to sell whatever they can—live chickens, sacks of grain, flimsy towers of eggs, pairs of shoes, and homemade waffles. Children play on a hillock made from hardened clumps of black lava. In the far distance is the silhouette of Nyiragongo volcano—a perpetual menace to this city, looking placid and innocent.

Shiny land cruisers whizz by, but Paul is mum about the presence of numerous UN soldiers. A puzzled expression forms on his face, and while he deliberates upon the subject, I apply myself to taking pictures from the moving car. I tell him I have heard from people who work for the UN and other non-profits throughout the region, including in Goma, that the situation isn't always positive. Along the road to the Goma airport, things are different. Coiled barbed wires run along the high walls of camps with rows of white tents, followed by white military vehicles and white aircraft. This is the base of the UN: the biggest peacekeeping operation the world has ever seen in one of the poorest countries in the world.

We soon ease into a conversation about the UN's ability—or lack of it—to intervene in violent situations, and I repeat my question.

"What are they really doing here?"

"Mineral trafficking—that is what they are doing here," he snaps angrily. "They want our minerals. They say they gave us peace and security. But where is the peace?"

The political and security situation in the Congo, and especially the North Kivu region, remains tense and fragile. What was once a lake-side resort for holidaymakers, Goma is today a mere stopover for those climbing the volcano or going gorilla tracking. So badly was it affected by the 1990s conflict that it destroyed most of its infrastructure. It was never rebuilt to its original glory.

*

So, it comes about that Paul had served with the UN briefly, but when romance led to disillusionment, he left to establish his tour company. That makes me wonder. What do I know about Congo? Nothing. I have heard, of course, of blood diamonds, gorillas, poor roads, and the occasional World Bank offer of assistance in building the roads, but really, that is as far as my knowledge of the country goes.

At lunch in a local restaurant close to the lake, I learn something less gloomy. Congolese people like a good buffet. Paul explains how and why. There is a method to maximizing lunch, he tells me energetically.

"You take what you want and how much you want the first time. If you want a second time, you pay again."

I don't understand it at all. We pile up our small plates with meats, vegetables, fish, steamed tapioca, yams, and fried plantains that get mixed up in the plate that seems too small to hold a large quantity of food. The portions are big and lack visual appeal, but all around me are people piling their plates with this dull-looking food.

The smells, like the food on my plate, are mixed up.

My appetite vanishes the instant I put a piece of pork into my mouth. The pig, succulent though it is, lacks flavour. I put my fork down and stare at the food in dismay. There is no way I can eat that.

"Do you not like the food?" Paul asks. "You want, maybe, some piri-piri?"

"I think, yes, and salt and pepper, perhaps?"

"Piri-piri—we have no pepper here. You try our chili. It is good. Spicy. Indians like it very much."

Miraculously, a waiter appears with a jar of chili paste—a ritual that Paul tells me is akin to welcoming me to a Congolese treat—and places it at my side.

"Thank you," I say. "That, good heavens, even smells hot. I am not so sure about it now."

"You try a little. You will like it."

The said *piri piri* is made of coarsely ground Habanero chili. Suddenly, it seems like everyone is watching, waiting for me to sample their prized offering. Under the force of collective stares, I give in. I am not about to back down. If they want to see a *piri-piri*-eating Indian, then they are going to see one.

Emboldened by my Indian spice-eating heritage, I plunge the spoon into the jar, scoop out a generous portion, and apply it to my little pig.

Nothing happens at first. I am about to let out a gleeful whoop when the fire starts. First on my tongue, then traveling down my throat, burning everything in its path, and ending up in my belly. I feel as though a volcano is about to erupt.

I am sure of a slow, painful death.

*

Watching Lake Kivu break into small ripples as a minor breeze sweeps over the lake is indeed soothing. I am seated at the lakeside restaurant, listening to the offstage sounds of cupboard doors, crockery, and footsteps. It is 4.30 p.m., but darkness is hovering somewhere between the sky and earth. There is every chance of rain tonight.

A waiter walks up to me and slowly sets the table for dinner. I ask for coffee. After a long wait, the coffee appears. It is, without a shadow of a doubt, the most unutterably dreadful cup of coffee ever made.

I try to focus on the lake to avoid finding faults with everything around me. The weather is great. I just wish I could say the same for the coffee.

Someone is approaching me, and that someone is smiling.

He sits on the chair beside me. There is a cup of coffee in his hand, but his expression is not of one who has enjoyed it much.

"Hi there!" I say mournfully. "Lousy coffee, yes?"

"Hello to you," says he. "Of course, the worst."

"Glad you came over. Drinking lousy coffee is worse than drinking lousy coffee all alone."

Constantino is a Spaniard working for an NGO named Fundación CODESPA and is a regular visitor of Goma and, thereby, Hotel Caritas. I tell him that it is brave of him to return to a hotel that makes the worst coffee. He laughs.

"Everywhere it is bad," he says. "But in coffee shops, you can get good coffee."

An ugly shade of grey is forming overhead.

"I hope it does not rain," Constantino says. "You are climbing the volcano, yes? If that bursts, boom—this town will blow up. This lake, too."

"You think so?"

"Yes, they say that everywhere. Goma is ticking."

It is funny—the way he says it. But he is right. Goma is ticking. When you have a lake that can burst into flames the moment magma touches it and a volcano threatening to shoot magma into it, there is nothing more to be said.

It is beautiful here. Quiet.

At 6 p.m., I take his leave after agreeing to meet for dinner at the hotel restaurant.

He promises me a surprise. I want to get into town for a late evening stroll. Constantino is horrified at the thought and is confident enough to voice it.

"You must not go by yourself so late. It is not safe. No, you stay inside. That's better."

But I am curious to know what is so dangerous about night time Goma. Sure, it is not the safest town to be wandering about at night, but Constantino's voice carries concern and fear.

I want to know what everyone is so afraid of. I slip out of the side gate. The security guard runs after me frantically.

"Miss, you don't go out now," he cries. "It is not safe."

"I'll be alright."

My assurance is not convincing, for he shifts uneasily, unsure of the course of action to take to stop me. His unease turns to panic as he requests me to reconsider. In a sudden outpouring of passion, I pat him on his shoulder and depart.

Darkness has enveloped Goma, changing its character from a warm, friendly lakeside town into something shadowy and forlorn. The absence of streetlights is more pronounced as I stumble in the dark before finally turning into a slightly better-lit corner. A moto materializes out of the darkness and comes to stop by me.

"Moto, miss?" he says.

"No, thank you."

The moto doesn't move, and that is somewhat disturbing. I walk briskly past a row of dilapidated shops announcing their business on dimly lit boards. There is no one on the streets or shops. I finally turn past a corner and arrive at the main street, which is no better than the street I have come from. It is eerily empty.

Where are the people?

A sense of unease pervades me, perhaps brought on by the memory of panic on the guard's face or the moto that did not drive away. I abort my plan and return to the hotel the same way I had come.

Suddenly, I am afraid of getting lost.

*

Constantino is in the company of a Congolese man named Frank, and both are well into their third round of Primus.

"This one is the most popular one, yes?" I ask.

The beer arrives in thirty seconds flat.

"You better order dinner now," says Constantino seriously. "They are very slow. Here, only beer comes fast."

The restaurant is filling up with affluent locals. They are not staying at the hotel, or so it appears from their attire. They seem to be just passing the time of the evening with friends in a quiet and safe spot.

"Any suggestions for dinner?" I ask.

"Sambasa."

"Sambasa?"

"It is a small fish from this lake but very good," pipes up Frank, eager to join the conversation. He is clearly fond of sambasa;

his eyes are shining with fond memories of his acquaintance with this fish.

By the time the sambasa arrives, deep fried and topped with onion rings, I am far too drunk to notice its taste.

"You have no idea what is happening in the kitchen here," Constantino says. "Something as simple as beans and rice or fried chicken can take two hours, but beer—it comes very fast."

As a regular guest of the hotel, Constantino is the right person to judge. "Sometimes, I order dinner during lunch, and still it doesn't come on time."

The lake looks ethereal and grey. It is slightly chilly. Soon enough, raindrops begin to fall, and before we know it, the tranquil lake has turned vicious. Furious waves crash underneath us, and the sound drowns out the conversation we are trying to have.

The evening is wearing off, and somewhere to my right, across the fence, a group of musicians tune up their instruments. The music sounds earthy and unpretentious. At the farthest end of the corridor, a makeshift stage is being set up for rumba music to be played later. Goma is readying for the night despite the lashing rain.

I go to bed as lightning flashes over the lake.

I love thunderstorms. They are beautiful—the flashes of lightning, the roaring sounds of thunder, and the pounding rain. How can anything so beautiful be scary?

*

Chapter 7

In the morning, I find Constantino staring sadly into his cup again. I fear the worst.

"This is the land of fucking coffee." Constantino begins, somewhat unhappily. "And yet, no one cares enough to make it drinkable."

"It is consistently bad." I agree, taking a sip. "Not for me—this sub-standard coffee from a plastic tube."

"Thousands of Congolese people may be employed by the coffee industry, and it may be just a few hundred miles from the birthplace of coffee, but it turns out that they don't like coffee that much. Do you need another example of irony?"

"I have half a mind to tell someone what I think," I thunder uncaringly and jab viciously at the sour passion fruit.

"I hear you. There is a coffee shop in town, or so I heard. Perhaps the receptionist can direct you to it."

I am disheartened by Congo's indifference to good coffee.

*

A little after ten, the hotel-arranged Moto-taxi arrives. The number and license of the moto are noted down alongside his telephone number on a piece of paper.

"You don't worry, miss. You are safe," the receptionist assures me. He looks like he means it, too. It appears that I am not in any immediate danger of being attacked or robbed.
I am excited about the prospect of exploring Goma's coffee shops and perhaps finding out a little more about Henry Stanley and Joseph Conrad.

We fetch up at *Au Bon Pain*, located on the second floor of a well-worn building. I am ecstatic. Finally, I am about to walk into a real coffee shop in a coffee-hating town like Goma.

I hope the coffee lives up to its reputation.

Au Bon Pain is a real coffee shop. I mean, it is all about coffee and strictly that. It is tidy and busy, with the smell of coffee oozing from its walls and curtains and chairs. In one deep breath, I smell years of brewing coffee. Why did I think a place like this couldn't exist in a place like Goma? A flaw in my thinking, no doubt.

The barista is smiling from ear to ear, calling out a welcome. This familiarity is appreciated and makes me feel welcome. The café is filled with *Mzungus,* with their heads buried in newspapers and phones.

I run my eyes over the display of mouth-watering pastries, delicious-looking sandwiches, and salads appreciatively before fixing my gaze on an apple pie.

A young girl arrives with a menu.

"What can I get you today," she says, as though I am a regular patron who chooses different things daily.

"A cup of good, strong, black coffee. And apple pie."

The coffee is slow in arriving, and I make two trips to the cash counter to protest their lack of service. An elderly man walks up to me with a smile. He launches into conversation without a preamble.

"You are new around here, aren't you? Things are slow here, like the rest of Africa. Slow. You cannot change it." He sits on the low chair beside me.

"I hope it is worth the wait, though."

"You'll be surprised, I am sure. What are you doing in Goma?"

The conversation is a long one. The coffee is remarkably good.

"But it is brave of you to come to Goma all by yourself, really it is. There are some Indians living here in Goma, and I sometimes eat at their restaurant. Would you like to try something Indian for a change? Local food can be rather limiting in variety, no?"

I tell him of the disaster with *piri-piri,* to which he cackles merrily.

"Those chilies are no good. Trust me, they can easily induce heart attacks. But Congolese, these people are strong; they love their chilies and mayonnaise."

I raise my brows questioningly. He points at the bottles of mayonnaise on the table.

"That, that is what the Belgians left behind. It is on everything these days; for the locals, mayonnaise is manna. Me, I don't understand this fascination."

It is good to be given real-life lessons on local food habits from an expat who clearly loves speaking. His name is Marcus, and he is stationed in Goma to look after the affairs of an NGO headquartered in Switzerland. He is a keen coffee lover. From him, I learn that Congo's coffee export, which, although not significantly high, is on the rise.

"You see, coffee from this country gets sold at Starbucks and some other coffee chain outlets also, I believe, but the locals— they do not like coffee so much. I like the coffee here, at this café, but others, not so much."

"Congo is magnificent," I say, "and it is incredibly beautiful from what I have seen thus far. But it is terrible that my hotel makes the worst coffee. I can't imagine why that is so."

"David Livingstone and Stanley, travellers and adventurers, the good and not-so-good, have all been here over the last few centuries. Pray why?"

I wait for him to continue. It is a treat to lean back on this old sofa, drinking strong and bitter coffee, while Marcus chats on about this and that. He knows a lot about coffee and Joseph Conrad. I had no idea Congo produced any coffee worth mentioning or consuming. But as an industry, coffee has a long way to go here.

There is a place in my heart

For this thing called coffee

The African Long Black, specifically

It is the best there is

And much like its men is this cuppa coffee…

When I open my eyes, Marcus is gone.

*

I arrive at the market filled with everything from coal to clothing, fruits, grains, and car parts. Tiny eateries announce their business on handwritten boards. It is very noisy. There are too many people crammed into a small place. I walk sideways to avoid bumping into passersby, who seem to be in a perpetual hurry to get somewhere.

I do not know if I am being watched or stalked. No one is looking at me, but I am uneasy because my mind is playing games with me. Crime has long been associated with poverty, and my fear is based on that theory alone. Will I be jumped at that corner? I hold my small day pack closer to my chest.

African music blares from almost everywhere, and amidst stark poverty, there is merriment. The girls still want to look pretty, and sardine-tin salons are packed with women who come to perfect their African braids.

So, although I'm painting a grim picture of Goma, it isn't all bad.

*

I rise early and head out to Virunga National Park with Paul and two rangers with AK47s on a three-hour ride over poorly laid dirt roads leading into the heart of DRC. Rains have created havoc everywhere. Gigantic puddles become a constant. Frequently we come to a halt to negotiate cracks in the roads or let oncoming vehicles pass. Heavily loaded trucks swerve dangerously, while one has turned turtle, spilling goods on the roads, adding more chaos to the morning. But not for a moment does my driver appear shaken.

Soon, the landscape changes into a beautiful green one through which the road, now resembling a red-brown vein, winds to its end. This change of scenery is welcome. Our journey is never monotonous due to the difference in height and temperature.

We arrive at the gates of Virunga National Park, and the only signs of life are the armed guards occupying the row of small offices and the large yellow butterflies, and both are warm in their greetings.

Everyone calls out a welcome as they adjust their guns. The rangers, dressed in green, appear friendly but tough, watching every move we make.

"Gorilla conservation is a serious business in Congo. You will learn more in the briefing." Paul assures me.

We troop into the briefing room furnished with old chairs and a long wooden table, and it is a pleasant surprise to find ten other guests waiting. Introductions are made. The chief of rangers arrives, and with him is Paul. The pre-tracking briefing begins in French, and Paul is the translator. The ranger rattles off in French that most of us do not understand, and our attention is riveted on Paul, our saviour.

"Virunga is the jewel of Congo, one of the biggest and most beautiful countries in Africa, and the oldest national park on the continent. This park was established in 1925 by King Albert I of Belgium, and it has everything. You can say it is

diverse, with all kinds of landscapes and wildlife. You will see—it has savannahs, lakes, mountains, rainforests, and two active volcanoes. About eight hundred mountain gorillas are left in the world, but three hundred of them are found in our forests."

We clap at this revelation. The ranger goes into the details of gorilla family names, the naming convention, and the need for maintaining order when watching these primates.

Paul is either a very good translator or years at this job help him carry on the conversation as if it were his own.

"We have eight gorilla families for tourists to see, but of course, on every trip, you will only see one family at close quarters. Each family has one or two silverbacks, several females, and babies. You are forbidden from eating, drinking, or speaking loudly near the gorillas.

"Silverbacks can charge anytime—for two reasons. They want to play with you or kill you. You stay with your guide and follow his orders. They can tell you the gorilla's intention by looking at them.

"If you want to pee or take a dump, you must let the rangers know. They will dig a hole for you. And please cover up when you are done. The gorillas are very curious animals."

We set off in a group of seven flanked by armed rangers to meet with *Rugendo Humba,* a family of nine. There is little to predict when it comes to where the families will be and how long the trek will last.

For the first twenty minutes, we walk steadily uphill. There is a gentle rain shower, and rapidly, the track turns muddy and slippery. The forest is alive with the sounds of insects and birds. Insects fly past us, and vines and branches tear into our skins. We negotiate the narrow, muddy tracks in silence. We are quickly gaining altitude, and that, combined with the heat and humidity, makes for a tiring experience. Faint sounds of collective panting are heard, and the guards allow us a small break.

The forest is filled with butterflies.

After about ninety minutes, we see the first signs of the gorilla—fresh poop. The ranger puts a finger to his lips. We're very close now.

We grab our masks and discard our sticks. Nothing that can be construed as a weapon may be brought into the gorillas' sector because although they are used to rangers, they must not become habituated to aggressors.

"They're moving," is all he says, and we continue silently for ten minutes more.

We are truly in untouched territory here. There are no tracks to follow, no well-trodden path created by tourists. Suddenly, everyone is whispering, and one of the guides is motioning for us to pull on our masks.

"Please do not speak. The gorillas are near us. We must not alarm them. No noise, please! Put your masks on quickly."

For the next few minutes, the only sounds are those of cameras, the shifting of weight on fallen branches, and the grunting of the silverback who promptly takes himself off. We move on softly. I manage to get a picture of his retreating back.

Another silverback soon appears in a small clearing. He seems calm as he stares at us with brooding and bloodshot eyes. I want to smell him. Touch him. Whisper to him. To take off my mask and get a selfie—everything we have been warned not to do.

Here is a big black monkey

Staring as if he is going to eat me

Will he stand up now and, like in the movies,

Dance to an imaginary drumbeat?

The rangers hiss urgently.

"Step back. Stay down. Be quiet. No pictures. Quiet. Quiet."

The giant silverback lumbers slowly towards us, getting closer and closer as we inch backwards into the bushes. He comes closer and closer, and suddenly, there is no place for us to retreat. He can easily reach us with a swipe of his giant black hands. He is so close. I am sure none of us is breathing. The silverback gorilla pulls himself up to his full height, begins thumping his chest rapidly, and lets out a bloodcurdling roar before he drops to all fours and bounds away. It is a shot straight from the pictures! But no matter what you have seen onscreen, to face a silverback in the wild who perhaps doesn't appreciate your presence and shows anger by thumping his chest—a sign he is about to charge—is not reassuring.

We remain on the ground for a few moments, trying to come to terms with the reality of being in the wild with an untamed silverback close at hand.

"Wow! What just happened? Are you guys alright? That was something, wasn't it?"

Someone in my group must have said that, but the rest of us sigh in agreement. "Yes..."

"I didn't even get a picture of that," says someone. "What a fucking waste."

We walk in complete silence till we come upon a happy gorilla family feeding on bamboo shoots. Here, the rangers relax. A family is much more friendly and accommodating.

"Those silverbacks are sometimes dangerous," a ranger says. "But you need not worry. No tourist has ever died of a gorilla attack. You can relax now."

"You have thirty minutes of connection with them," he tells us, pointing at the happy family. "But don't go close. Remember the seven-meter rule."

They are all here, lolling about. A giant silverback lays on the ground, his chin propped up on his fist like a sullen teenager. His wife is sprawled on her back next to him in the dappled sunlight; she gets up and climbs over him for a round of grooming.

A little one tries to get his parents' attention, just like a bored toddler; he also seems keen to interact with us, but the ranger gently herds him back. It is an extraordinary experience. More gorillas spill into the clearing, and now there are six in all. The toddler sneezes and begins to somersault across the jungle floor towards us. To the right of us, a female is pummelling one of her babies in the face with her feet.

In the next clearing, two gorilla children chase each other around a tree trunk in excited circles. It is tough to hold in our squeals when they decide to continue their chase up a nearby tree for a few moments before they both come crashing to the ground.

The rangers chat to the gorillas in what seems to be their own language, warning them off if they get close. This is one of the conservation's great success stories: ten years ago, there were only seventy-five primates in Virunga. Now there are three hundred.

Behind us, an enormous silverback lets out a loud fart.

This is the single best animal encounter of my entire life. The ultimate wildlife experience. As great as traditional safaris are, this really trumps that experience for me.

I wonder if Hemingway ever thought of this.

I wonder if Joseph Conrad, Henry Stanley, or David Livingstone ever had the chance to do this.

Probably not.

*

My being in Rwanda has nothing to do with Hemingway and Byron. This visit is merely a sidetrack meant to rejuvenate my mind and body and to fulfil a long desire to see this country I first heard of in 1994 and later, on reading a book by Lieutenant-General Roméo Dallaire of the Canadian Forces who led the UN Mission at the time of genocide. His book *Shake Hands with The Devil - The Failure of Humanity in Rwanda* was my first real connection with Rwanda. The only other connection was the film *Hotel Rwanda*, which, like every movie, offers a hero.

Chapter 8

The guesthouse I am at was the home of an affluent businessman of Indian origin. Locally made furniture complements the walls and curtains. The coffee is satisfactory, but I wish it were better the next time. The breakfast consists of toast and eggs, passion fruit, pineapple jam, and Rwanda's favourite chili oil, *Akabanga*, a killer oil packed in an eye-dropper-size bottle.

It is a fine morning. The reddish-orange of the unpaved road outside the guesthouse is in sharp contrast to the blueness of the sky, which is bereft of clouds. A gentle breeze carries with it the smells of the soil. Schoolchildren in pretty uniforms are laughing and talking their way to school. Moto-taxis are going up and down the hill, like in Congo, Uganda, or Kenya, but there is one big difference. Moto drivers are wearing orange helmets and a TIGO-branded reflector jacket. There is a sense of uniformity and order here.

A short walk uphill brings me to a street corner where a neat row of motos awaits. Small shops line the street around the moto-bay. There is a large park on the opposite side of the road with its walls painted yellow, a landmark I hope to remember on my way back.

A young man greets me. "Bonjour."

"Errr, hello, bonjour. Do you speak English?"

He nods. "Très peu. Very little."

"My friend," I tell him slowly, deliberately. "I want to see your city. Go anywhere, show me everything. I want to feel Kigali. But first, some coffee."

He nods, hands me a helmet, turns on his moto-meter, and kicks his motor to life.

Oui, bien sûr.

The wide, jacaranda-lined streets of Kigali shine in the morning light. Jacaranda trees are in full bloom; their light-purple flowers add a certain softness to the city that only flowers can. The roads and buildings give the impression of being in a first-world country, an impression cemented by the sight of the Convention Centre in front of us.

Even through the helmet, it looks imposing.

Understanding the geography of Kigali is particularly challenging while sitting astride on a motorbike wearing a helmet, but even through the back of a moto, it is enough to know that third-world is hardly the word suitable to describe the city. The jacaranda trees stay with us through the journey.

Kigali is an ultra-modern, well-maintained city. Traffic is disciplined, and not even a piece of paper or cigarette stub ruins the spotless roads. The streets and buildings are marked clearly with numbered plates and with breathtaking cleanliness and organization.

This is Rwanda, the country which lost nearly a million of its population in the genocide twenty-three years ago. From the depths of memory, I wiggle out these words in French:

Je veux du café.

The driver nods affirmatively, performs a series of deft manoeuvres, and circles back towards the City Centre to arrive at Kigali Heights on KG 7 Avenue in the Kimihurura area.

"Java House is good. I wish you a good day," the driver says.

"*Merci,*" I reply, smiling.

The security guard greets me warmly as I walk through the scanner.

"Good morning, miss, how are you?"

"I am well, thank you. Have a good day."

Shops are only just stirring to life, but Java House is a hive of activity. Smartly dressed waitresses are bustling about. The smell of coffee is in the air. I find a place on the terrace overlooking the Kigali Convention Centre, one of the most expensive buildings on the continent of Africa, built at a whopping $300m.

A smart waitress arrives with a menu card.

"*Bonjour. Comment allez-vous?*" she says politely. Her teeth are very white.

I am embarrassed that my French isn't enough to answer that simple greeting.

"I am fine, thank you. Merci." I manage.

She smiles meaningfully.

"Café Américain," I tell her slowly, deliberately. "You know, just a regular long black."

"I am studying English at the University," she replies pleasantly. "I speak a little English. I will bring your coffee now. Would you like to eat something?"

"*Non, Merci.*"

I am a tourist whose mission here is to understand a little more about Rwanda through its people, food, and post-genocide development. Everything so far has served to please, including the coffee. There is a certain charisma to the city that makes it different from other African countries. I want to understand that difference. I yearn to speak with people, hear their stories, ask questions, and understand their lives. I want to know everything and see if I can get some nuance to my observations.

Learning French has become an absolute necessity, a task I hope can be attended to through Google translate, for Kinyarwanda, the national language of Rwanda, is beyond me. But will I be laughed at my attempt at speaking French? Before my coffee arrives, I learn three French words.

The Java House coffee, the waitress tells me, is locally produced. "Our coffee is delicate with a hint of citrus and a sweet caramelly aroma."

I breathe in the aroma and take a sip appreciatively.

"I can see you like coffee. Like you do, we like our customers to enjoy the coffee through its smell first."

Its delicate flavour grows on me, and I see no reason why Rwandan coffee should not equal Kenyan, Tanzanian, or Ethiopian coffee in demand and taste.

I ask her that.

"One day, we will not be called Alternate Coffee and join the Famous Two—the Kenyan and Ethiopian," she declares. "I hope that day will come soon."

I am loving Rwandan coffee. It is less dramatic than its famous neighbours but is real in taste and suits my mood. I apply myself to learning French and impress the waitress with my skill and speed. The spacious terrace is quickly filling up. Everyone is talking. There is a feeling of contentment in the air. The sun is getting warmer as it climbs higher into the cloudless sky.

Are these the streets where Tutsis were openly maimed and killed just over two decades ago? Rwanda has journeyed through hell and back but continues to prosper, the evidence of which I see around me. Will I fully comprehend what transpired in 1994? Maybe not. What caused the unconscionable, systematic slaughter of 800,000 Rwandans in a hundred days? How did Rwanda survive this catastrophe, and how did it recover from such a harrowing human slaughter? Does the past atrocity influence the interactions between Rwandans today, and what deep, dark holes are left in their hearts?

The answers to these questions are not to be found in the coffee cup where I am looking.

I find the same moto driver waiting outside the mall. I am just as happy as he is. He hands me the helmet and starts his motor.

"Je vais maintenant prendre un autre chemin afin que vous puissiez voir des endroits vraiment sympas," he says.

Google translates it to: "I will now take another route so you can see some nice places."

"Merci," I reply as I take my seat behind him.

He drives me around the presidential palace, the police HQ, and the HQs of several ministries, telling me which one is which. He is excited and cannot stop talking; he narrates how these places have transformed in the last few years. Judged by its setting, Kigali is one of the most beautiful cities on Earth, ringed by mountains, hilly as bubble wrap, and overgrown with trees. I am beginning to see the advantage of riding a moto; it is truly a remarkable way of seeing the city.

By noon, our short tour concludes at UTC Mall. Our goodbye borders on sadness. It has been a good morning. There is something in the air of Rwanda that is doing wonders for my appetite because I am hungry. Eventually, I fetch up at Bourbon Coffee, a delightful spot with fantastic views. The waitress comes over for a chat and suggests coffee, to which I nod in agreement. Her English is good, and she is keen on practicing it on me.

"You come from where? India?" she asks.

"Yes."

"You are visiting Rwanda? I hope you like my country."

"I do. Very much. Say, do you speak French?"

"Yes. But now we are trying to learn English. I am learning English and tourism at the University. All the young people in Rwanda work and study. Our President has a plan for the country with many goals he aims to achieve. We want to reach our country's goals. So, we work hard and study."

Things have come a long way since 1994, and the entire community seems proud of that. They are happy just to be surging ahead. Little does her faith surprise me, for last night at the guesthouse, the receptionist had said something similar when he checked me in.

"Did you visit the genocide memorial centre? There are many in Rwanda you must visit. Our people are buried there," she suggests quite cheerfully.

A shudder passes through me. She says it so easily and without emotion. Her face does not convey any emotion about her ethnicity. Common sense tells me that her people are buried there. One million people had been killed in 1994, roughly one in seven. Considering how crowded the streets are today, it was clearly a large number. A group of older men arrive and seat themselves a table away. What stories do they have?

I want to understand a little more about the country, for I intend to spend some time here. I have to train myself to stop associating everything with genocide and see Rwanda for what it is today. But despite the reasoning, my thoughts go back to genocide. It is hard to imagine that some of the people outside this café at one point were killing their fellow countrymen with crude machetes, and everyone older than twenty-four years of age today has witnessed the massacre, lost family, hands, arms, and feet. One million killed in three months; the thought of all that red blood on the lush green land—what rich, macabre fertilizer.

Briefly, I picture myself in the midst of the bloody civil war with machete-wielding Hutus and child soldiers hacking away at their countrymen. It is an uncomfortable thought.

Two cups of coffee later, I hail a moto outside the mall. The indescribable chaos caused by *boda bodas* in Nairobi and Tanzania is missing here. It is peaceful. Deathly peaceful. I wish for the noise—that would help me drown the sounds of tortured cries rising in my head.

*

In Kigali, evening comes early, and with it comes the desire to drink Primus and Mutzig, Rwanda's famous beer. Refreshed by my afternoon nap, I am ready to see and experience the city at night. This is how I end up at Chez Lando in Remera, a bustling suburb close to my guest house in Kimironko. Every car is checked before being allowed to drive inside the premises.

I am the only one on foot.

The large, airy dining area is full. I am given a table in the centre of this room. The red and white checked tablecloth and dim lights give off a sense of subdued excitement. On the menu are goat brochettes, herb-stuffed tilapia fish, and Chez Lando grilled chicken, not exactly local, everyday food, but Chez Lando is upscale, so the chance of finding local food is bleak. This hotel is one of Kigali's oldest and is considered an important part of their heritage. Its origin is interesting, too— the hotel was built by a Canadian woman and her Rwandan husband in 1980. Like all others, it suffered during the genocide and was rebuilt.

*

I like the noise here. The music is soft, but the patrons are loud and lively. No one is afraid to speak their mind. People are living it up, enjoying tipples and barbequed meats, and discussing life with an air of confidence. Someone instigates a discussion on politics, and the others do not fear to speak their mind. Someone vents and says unemployment is way too high and that the elite own most of the wealth. Most, like the taxi driver, did admit that Rwanda's democracy has challenges but added that due to the country's history, it has to be unique and do things in unconventional ways to get ahead.

Someone who sounds like an NGO worker with an opinion and who is no fan of the government says how appreciated most of the government's high-handed actions are, which have done some public good. The conversation is thought-provoking, the beer is cold, and before I know it, it is 11 p.m. There is a real sense of optimism that pervades Kigali. My urge to remain is strong because, through the course of the evening and many orders of Primus and brochette, I have stopped looking for a reason to be in Rwanda.

Like the Rwandans, I will live a day at a time. I will approach a new adventure or a new place as if I am writing a book. I don't know what the pages will hold, what story will envelope my mind, or if I will fall in love with the experience I recreate or the characters I meet again on those pages. What matters is the sum of everything I see and experience, the good, the bad, and the ugly—the truth of what I see and not what I deem to have seen or understood. Like Rwanda.

*

Today, I hope to find answers to the questions my mind has been asking ever since I arrived. I am not sufficiently prepared for the Kigali Genocide Memorial; afraid it will change what I am beginning to feel about Rwanda.

Visiting genocide sites isn't new to me, but the Rwandan genocide is not just shockingly rapid; it is alarmingly recent.

Kigali Memorial Centre is a neatly kept genocide site, which, to a first-time visitor with no prior knowledge, might appear slightly misleading. It looks peaceful in the morning. Across the site, on another hill, buildings rise into the skies, the streets below it abuzz with traffic.

I am nervous as I approach the gates and walk past an armed security guard, who cheerfully waves me through. A young man of medium height wearing a neat white shirt approaches me no sooner than I am under the arch.

"Welcome to Kigali Genocide Memorial. Do you need a guide?" the young man asks.

"Uh, do I? I am not sure."

"Maybe a guide can explain to you better. Please come with me. You can take an audio guide if you wish." In his kind, gentle voice, he tells me there is no real need for a guide because everything has a French and English explanation.

I ask him one question that I have been yearning to ask. "Do the Hutus and Tutsis hate each other today?"

"No. There is no explicit animosity between us now. But who knows the depth of pain and sense of injustice buried inside?"

There is no bitterness in his voice although if anyone has the right to feel bitter, it is them.

"I was very young then," he says. "My family is buried here."

Briefly, he tells me about the history of the site and shows me the way in. "You can see everything inside."

The inside is very quiet. The walls are covered with photos. As I progress from room to room, the imagery gets disturbing. The visitors are looking in bewilderment at archival documents, photos, video footage, and weapons encased in glass, trying to make sense of it all.

To provide a historical perspective, the indoor exhibit also delves into the sinister ideologies that provoked the world's largest genocidal massacres—from the Namibian genocide to the Holocaust. The Kigali Genocide Memorial is an important reminder that ethnic cleansing of this kind is a global phenomenon.

The indoor exhibit sheds light on the Rwandan genocide as well as its pre-colonial, colonial, and post-colonial roots.

The children's memorial room is particularly disturbing. From the details displayed next to their photos, I learn each child's favourite foods and activities. It is like viewing a family album—except it abruptly ends with how the child's life was violently snuffed out. I sit in a pentagonal room surrounded by thousands of photos of the deceased, trying to look the other visitors in the eye, but everyone avoids eye contact for one reason alone.

Tears.

It seems unjust to try condensing this horrendous event in a nutshell, but I will try. From what I've learned, I mean, from the book I have read and what I have seen just now, the root cause of the genocide was the aftermath of colonial ideology. Death was not the only outcome of the genocide. People were tortured, mutilated, raped, and suffered machete cuts, bullet wounds, infection, and starvation. The country plunged into mayhem, looting, and chaos, with its infrastructure destroyed and its ability to govern ripped to shreds.

I am struggling to put my feelings into words. My faith in humanity is shaken. How the Rwandan genocide could have happened as the international community looked on—just over two decades ago—is unfathomable.

I am yearning for daylight and fresh air. All my energy has been sucked out of me. I try to unsee the pictures of children and perhaps find a place to cry. But I am not the only one. A woman next to me is staring vacantly into space. Another is quietly wiping away a tear.

The experience is core-rattling. I inhale and exhale sharply and slowly walk towards the tombs. Covered by giant plates of concrete, mass graves for over 250,000 victims serve as a place for visitors to honour those lost and for the loved ones of the victims to grieve and remember.

Did the drums beat for 100 days in 1994? When swords wounded and killed, and blood endlessly flowed? Did they fall silent or drown the cries of every man, woman, and child? In Rwanda's darkest days of 1994?

I want to speak to someone, to see a face that has not been affected by this tragedy, perhaps another tourist or someone who comes from a happy place. And yet, I cannot let go. The urge to know more is stronger than before. Perhaps an outsider's perspective will help round off my understanding.

Lt. Gen. Dallaire, the author of *Shake Hands with the Devil*, did not sugarcoat his experience. He witnessed the massacres. He accurately describes the atrocities and the dilemmas to which he was exposed.

In the book, Dallaire explains how, after arriving in Kigali in August 1993, he warned the UN authorities that he lacked sufficient equipment and manpower to carry out his mission. However, a lack of clarity in the UN's intervention procedures coupled with the apparent lack of interest in Rwanda meant that Dallaire's calls for help went unanswered.

His book talks of the day-to-day situation until, eventually, the general's forces are left on their own, without fuel, money, or adequate equipment. In Kigali, corpses of civilians killed by machetes begin piling up, and many of the moderate politicians with whom Dallaire had the mandate to negotiate are also murdered.

*

I walk a little to clear my head before getting a moto to Nyamgenge Market. The sight of crowded markets and the piles of multi-coloured fabric, pots, pans, and plastic toys made in China is comforting.

Life seems normal.

I absently bargain over the price of fabric and discuss designs, all the while thinking about twenty-three years ago.

Were there dead bodies lying when I stand now? Did that forty-something woman see her parents get killed? Is she a Hutu or a Tutsi? I have the urge to hug everyone and offer a word of comfort, a typical reaction every visitor at some point or the other after the visit displays. The reason behind that is a mystery, but that is what I am feeling. Will it do any good? Is it really any of my business to scratch their wound and try healing it with a hug? And then, suddenly, all ill-will has left me, and I smile kindly when pushy women selling fabric in the market try to over-charge me.

For no reason, I take myself to a local bar. There are very few women here, and I am being stared at. This bar is a mass of nationalities—Cameroonian, Burundian, Tanzanian, Belgian, Congolese, and not to mention the Rwandans, who were born or lived much of their lives in Uganda, Zambia, or Malawi. I want to forget what I have seen, but at the same time, I want to hold on to everything I have and try to make sense of it. My mind is thinking of various ways in which I can tell a story differently. Where do I begin? Do I know enough to scratch the surface?

I stare at the faces around me, trying to picture them in their past. Young and old, everyone is talking over Primus or Mutzig beer. Have they seen murder being committed? Did they lose a parent? Friend? Family? How did they get this far? Do they talk about it? To whom? Does anyone care anymore?

A young girl appears at my side.

"Parlez-vous français?" I ask her slowly, deliberately. "Do you speak English?"

"Oui."

I am not linguistically schizophrenic. Rather, I just want to

cover all communication bases. I order Primus. As my order repeats, I get bolder and eventually join a group of young men around the table, simply to be a part of their friendly conversation. I just want to hear them talk. I want to know what they talk about. They are speaking English. It is easy to follow their conversation over the noise.

I soon understand the reasons for this. Until 2008, Rwandan schools and classes were administered in French language. Then, one day, the government declared English the country's official language in schools. Poof. That was it. The reasons for the switch are many: English is more of a universal business language, most of Rwanda's neighbours are English-speaking, and shared business language promotes trade and exchange. The switch further distances the country from Belgium and France and its colonial history with them due to their lack of support during the genocide.

*

I go easy on the guesthouse breakfast because I will spend the day at Des Milles Collins, popular worldwide as Hotel Rwanda. *The Hotel Rwanda.* I debate getting myself a taxi or a moto, unsure if there is a right way of arriving at this hotel at all.

In the end, I get on a moto-taxi. It is the easier and quicker way to get there. I daresay I am dressed rather shabbily, but now, I will not let that worry me. I slept badly last night, imagining all sorts of things about today. What do I hope to find at Hotel Rwanda?

At 10.30 a.m., I arrive at the neatly forested gates of this large, cream-colored building. I walk to the gate and enter feeling beautiful from the inside out. There is a reason for my slight grin: I am in my traveling element. I am finally here—at the place I have long dreamed of visiting. I will take each moment as it comes—no agenda, no expectations.

A tall man at the gate—who looks as if he has been waiting for

me to arrive—greets me warmly, and I have a feeling that he wants to be the first to introduce me to the history of this hotel. His eagerness is writ large on his face, and his eyes shine with an understanding twinkle.

"Good morning," he greets. "Welcome to De Mille Collins. Enjoy your stay."

"Thank you. I am excited to be here. I mean, this is *the* place, after all."

I avoid saying the word genocide as though it will somehow make me unwelcome.

"Yes, miss. This is the place. But it was long ago. Now everything is normal."

Twenty-three years is "long ago" if you were a child in 1994. The security guard looks in his late twenties but has the seriousness of a much older man. I try to picture him as a child in 1994.
Did he see his parents die? Does he have any family left? Does he...

I must stop connecting people to the past or trying to find everything to relate to 1994. I do not know the extent of damage to the present generation, but I must stop being insensitive. I do not know the best way to get them to talk, but what is my need to know?
I am afraid I am turning morbid.

Instead, I ask him the best place to grab a drink, and from the look on his face, I know what he is thinking. It's too early for a drink.

I quickly change it to coffee.

"You go straight into the hotel and beyond the reception area on the terrace; you will get coffee."

I approach the young male receptionist with a smile. His name is Jameson. I do not know how to introduce the subject appropriately, so I plunge straight in, not exactly pleased with myself.

"You might have heard this a hundred times before, but I am wondering if there is anyone around here, who was present here in 1994."

Again, I avoid the word genocide. Should I use a better opening line?

"Sure. Will you please come with me to the terrace?"

I follow Jameson out, hopeful of finding a link to a story developing in my mind. I know when I return home, I will detail my Rwandan experiences, and genocide will be a crucial part of that story. I want to learn the finer points related to the incident.

"Please take a seat," Jameson says. "I will be with you in some time."

Once seated, I take in the beautiful surroundings. The decor is modern and luxurious but not gaudy. If anything, it feels like a peaceful spot in the heart of the city, making it hard to believe it was once the hiding place of hundreds of Tutsis during the genocide. I can't help but reconstruct the incident the way I know it. Paul must have been brave to risk his life for the Tutsis who sought refuge here. What must it be like back then?

I glance over the menu, but I already know what I want. Coffee.

People are splashing about in the pool below.

Jameson is a quarter of an hour in coming, but he does.

"I was looking for the contact of the person who was here in 1994, but he is already old now and doesn't go about much. Maybe I can help you? What do you want to know?"

I tell him.

"I can tell my story," he says confidently. "All of us here, we have stories."

I interpret this as a good omen. I did not come here hoping to strike gold right away, but I think I have. I order coffee for the two of us and settle down, satisfied that my casual curiosity has given way to something real.

"My father was killed when I was six years old. My mother, sister, and I fled to DRC and lived in a refugee camp for a long time. We saw some horrible things happening around us. Months later, we returned to Kigali, and my mother somehow managed to send me to school. I used to wake up at 5 a.m. a few times a week and walk for miles for water. Many times, I would sleep hungry."

Jameson is at university now on a scholarship and does odd jobs to make ends meet, such as working at Hotel Rwanda. He is working hard to connect to the Mzungu culture; he is the sort of person who loves to learn about other cultures. He also knows that learning English and knowing Mzungus is a good way to network and be successful here. He tells me that his Rwandan friends accuse him of trying to be Mzungu.

He asks me several questions about my life, India, Dubai, and my work.

An old man shuffles in and launches into a conversation in French. "*Vous parlez français?*

"*Non,*" I reply.

"*Je ne parle que très peu anglais.* I speak English a little. You speak slow."

"Err, I am sorry. What is this about?"

He launches off in French, and I look at Jameson in bewilderment.

"He wants to tell his story," Jameson explains. "He says he heard you ask about this and offered to help."

So, in a matter of twenty minutes, I have stories of two survivors. Jameson was a little boy, but the old man tells me how he hid in the cave when the attack started, staying hungry for a week. His wife and young sons were slaughtered, and he regrets he could not save them.

"*Je les entends crier*," he concludes and then shuffles away.

I am not sure I want to know anymore. Jameson leaves me, promising to return soon with information on Paul. He is reserved when he mentions the name; there is no sense of pride when speaking of the man whom the Western media made out to be something of a hero. In 2005, US President Bush presented Paul Rusesabagina with the Presidential Medal of Freedom, but Jameson clearly didn't seem moved.

"I will see what I can do," he said as he left.

I remember an article on Paul's real role during the genocide, one which the movie Hotel Rwanda glorified—hinting at Schindler, who rescued 1,100 Jews from the Nazis.

The report ended with 'Rusesabagina was no Schindler.'

*

The pool is full of happy children and mothers chasing them. Tourists randomly engage in conversation, and all are here for a photo and a coffee. But interestingly, it is the youngsters who are keen to take photographs with the hotel as a backdrop.

It will be night soon. The live band has started playing at the pool bar, and I adjourn to the poolside to become a part of this moment. The music is a typical mixture of slow R&B and soul.

The barman tells me that music is one way of bringing people together.

"Has that helped, since you know, the genocide?" I ask.

"Our music heals the heart. I used to listen to the late Kamaliza's song, *Humura Rwanda Nziza* when I was six years

old. The genocide had stopped, but although I can't say that it helped me a lot, it gave me hope for a better tomorrow. In the same way, I want to believe that our songs will still be here long after we are gone. They will educate the future generation, bring them closer, and give them a clear picture of the times their forefathers lived in. I believe this is how music is contributing to the reconciliation process."

It is easy to see what these musical gatherings mean to the locals. I feel myself enveloped in the moment before the noise forces me to grab my drink and return to my earlier spot on the terrace overlooking this lively gathering. Far too many people are jostling for space and talking over the music. The drinks are overpriced, but that hasn't slowed down the trickle of people.

Kigali is slowly turning into a sea of twinkling lights. Beyond the edge of the pool, lights have come up, and the hotel looks warmer by these yellow lights. I head to the rooftop restaurant aptly named Panorama.

There are lights as far as my eyes can see. Lights dancing on hilltops and in the valleys, twinkling like a million stars unmindful of the watchers. It is mesmerizing. Somehow, the night has turned this city of a thousand hills into a fairyland. I have seen no sight like this.

And to crown the moment, rainclouds appear. Lightning flashes, and suddenly, rain pours down. Light catches the falling rain, and as though it was possible, Kigali turns even more beautiful.

I end the night with wine and grilled meats, which don't come cheap. But to be here, watch, breathe, and understand means everything to me.

The music stays with me till I go to bed. In it is hope. Rwanda has done a remarkable job of healing its wounds and has taught me about the power of forgiveness. The day has been an eye-opener, and the night a reminder that morning will come again.

*

Something about Rwanda has touched my heart in a truly unique way, leaving me wanting to know more about what lies beyond Rwanda's beautiful green hillsides and gory past.

Kigali coffee shops, cafés, and restaurants should feature more on the tourism radar. They are independent, open-air jewels in the city's landscape, very different from their overseas counterparts, which can feel generic, dark, and overcrowded. In fact, I believe that a mere visit to all the cafes could easily become its own "must-do" list for coffee lovers or lovers of anything spectacular.

A better insight into the city's backstory comes from an eccentric walking tour offered by a group of local women from Nyamirambo, the Muslim quarter. This sleepless maze is the city's multicultural heart, older than Kigali itself and peopled with migrants from across the continent. Marie, my guide, is vivacious and a keen observer of humanity. She introduces me to her friends as we walk along—milk-sellers, mechanics, drapers, chapati-makers, and musicians.

Everyone is smiling and cheering us on. I am glad it rained earlier in the morning, for all the walking is making me hot. Marie is nostalgic when she explains the history and ethnicity of her district and its stubborn refusal to be redeveloped but perks up quickly when telling me that the latest trend in tailoring in her area comes from Senegal and explains how

Rwandese are "the best tailors and can make your dress in one hour."

Steep paths down the hill pass through villages studded with tiny bars. Children run along and offer little fists. No one is desperate or starving, and although this part of Nyamirambo is considered a slum, it has the feel of a sheltered village, safe and slow.

Nyamirambo, as I see it, is Kigali's most lively neighbourhood and is easily identified by its big green-and-white mosque at the fork in the road. It has a life of its own. Nyamirambo doesn't have gorgeous tree-lined streets like Kigali, but it compensates for its lack of beauty with its food. We have a mini lunch of chapati and some local Rwandese meal that consists of a white elbow of a goat floating in red broth, chips, pilau or flavoured rice, and beans, all for two dollars. Hot chili is a permanent fixture, and it comes free.

I am struck by what a small and strange place it is, but how attached I already feel to its resilience and ambition. Just over a million people are contained within this view—the same number that died in the genocide and its auxiliary massacres. It is incredible, not only for the unfathomable scale of the cruelty, but the extent of the healing since.

Everywhere, in fact, is safe. No other capital city in East Africa can be navigated so widely, at any hour, without harassment, allowing Kigali's nightlife to be greedily explored.

Someday, I will return to Africa, not for any real reason, maybe to the same place I have been before, maybe to a new country, but I promise to be back. Rwanda, in my opinion, has the soul of Africa inside a brand-new country.

I feel exactly what Romeo Dallaire felt when leaving the country.

Still, I did not regret for a moment leaving the bright lights of Manhattan behind in favour of night skies so dark the stars seemed close enough to be streetlights. In the recycled cabin air of the long flight back, I physically longed for Rwanda, its rich red earth, the smell of its wood fires, and its vibrant humanity.

*

Turkish Airlines from Kigali arrived in Istanbul after a brief stop in Entebbe.

Book 2

Chapter 1

On the long flight from Kigali to Istanbul that includes a layover at Entebbe, I begin to understand the importance of travel.

One must credit the travellers for their innovation and their ability to adapt. The longer I am on the flight, the more I am forced to seek answers to an important question: What if EH and LB never left their countries?

*

IIstanbul'a hoş geldiniz hanımefendi.

Teşekkür ederim.

Keyifle kal.

Ataturk Airport is easy to negotiate, made easier by experience. Here in Istanbul, I will reconnect with Lord B, and this thought makes me ecstatic.

The taxi driver is not surprised when I ask to be driven to the Pera Palace Hotel in Beyoğlu. In fact, he is happy for the long ride. We converse through simple words and gestures. To me, conversations that do not require fantastic communication skills and yet make me out to be a sort of linguist are the best kind. In any case, it gets me what I want. In the past, I have explained how learning a new language beyond the basics was impossible, but I am still trying. Like French in Rwanda. Sometimes, I recall what I have learnt, but mostly, I forget everything and start over—and get startled at the familiarity of the words but unable to explain why.

I am in favour of learning new languages, though, even if I fail at it, simply because it makes both parties feel respected and appreciated. The driver is a veteran of ferrying non-Turkish-speaking passengers and excels in the game of broken communication. Turkish is not a language I aim to master. I am off the ground with a few phrases and words I learnt years ago when backpacking and couch-surfing.

*

The elegant, restrained Neo-Classical façade of the seven-storied Pera Palace Hotel does little to prepare you for the opulence of the perfectly preserved interior, which looks very much like it must have done in the 1920s when Agatha Christie stayed here.

I can't properly convey my excitement at securing the Agatha Christie Room No. 411, where, according to the booking site, much of the original and opulent Victorian furniture remains. The valet deposits my belongings in this room and politely withdraws. I utter a joyous glee and break into a little dance as soon as the door shuts behind him.

I swear I see the writer seated at her typewriter, breathing life into Hercule Poirot and endowing him with the faculties to solve the baffling murder on the *Orient Express* train.

"Hello, Ms Christie… we meet at last."

I am aware of the history of this hotel. In every sense, Pera Palace Hotel was born to fascinate. In 1892, Pera Palace, a new hotel as luxurious as the Venice-Simplon Orient Express, was built to serve its important guests like diplomats, actors, journalists, writers, businessmen, and spies who arrived on the train. Pera Palace redefined Istanbul's hospitality by becoming the first building—excluding Ottoman Palaces, of course—with electricity, elevators, and the provision of hot water.

Then, one fine day, the Queen of Crime, Agatha Christie, arrived on the Orient Express and established herself in Room No. 411 to write her bestselling novel *Murder on Orient Express*.

For a moment, as I lapse into history, I forget the reason for my being here, feeling instead absorbed into some event that is about to happen. As though setting myself up for a crime. Or an investigation with Hercule Poirot leading it and I, in my own little ways, stepping in for Captain Hastings or even Miss Lemon.

The room is everything I have imagined it to be. I am easily over the disappointment of knowing Hercule Poirot never stayed here, even if it would have been such an honour to live in the room where my favourite fictional detective stayed. I have a bone to pick with Ms. Christie, though. She was undoubtedly the hotel's most famous guest but had heartlessly lodged Hercule Poirot at Hotel Tokatalian nearby and never once allowed him to enter the Pera Palace Hotel—unlike Fleming's Bond, who appreciated the views of the Golden Horn on the first morning of his arrival... so the story goes.

Something in the room had inspired her. I imagine a stain on the carpet, but I am almost a century too late to know if it is real. I'll admit Pera Palace has a wonderfully sublime feel to it. Soon, I am exploring the hotel. Making my way from Garbo Suites to the Piano Suite to the Hemingway Suite, I fancy shadowy figures, spies, and murderers appearing out of nooks and corners. Years are no barrier between Christie and me— because Pera Palace links us. I draw energy and force from the author's imagination.

Something cold brushes against my spine as I descend the marble stairs. After all, this hotel had been a beehive of activity during the world wars—with an equal number of spies and scribes crawling the corridors, carrying secrets. Surely, there must be some remnants of those days? Something in the air? Isn't it a fact that some secrets are still hidden in Pera Palace? Like Christie's famous key.

Not many hotels come more history-rich or soul-stirring than this. The Pera Palace fits perfectly into an area that, in the 18th,

19th, and 20th centuries, was home to the city's Christian and Jewish minorities and European bankers, diplomats, and traders.

Historical romance drips from every corner of Pera Palace, from its antique furniture to its grand staircases and the red velvet. Everything reflects the splendour of a bygone era. I can practically see Agatha Christie, Ernest Hemingway, Alfred Hitchcock, King Edward VIII, and Greta Garbo lounging about the palace with their scotch.

The original lift, installed in 1892, still works and is a masterpiece of wrought iron and mahogany. French bronze figurines and potted palms on ebony plant stands dot the lobby.

I am not at all surprised when I am told that the hotel is designated as a museum hotel. The bellboy points me towards Room 101, which has been turned into the Ataturk Museum. Mustafa Kemal Ataturk, the president of the newly formed Turkish Republic, is said to have stayed in this room during his visits. The room is painted in the colour of sunrise—dawn pink, Ataturk's favourite colour—and is full of his personal belongings. Room 101 consists of a little entryway, the main sitting room, a bedroom, and a bathroom, and all the rooms have touches of Ataturk—clothes, a tapestry, documents, photos, and mementos.

*

I am brought to the present when the morning sun strikes my face. Shaken out of my imagined world of crime, I set about establishing a literary connection with Istanbul by heading towards the European side, not to see the Blue Mosque or Hagia Sophia again, but for the one place that will kickstart my quest.

The Pudding Shop.

Naturally, I have no intention of eating any pudding. I mean to uncover the romantic origins of the Hippie Trail and what itchy-footed travellers did before flights became cheap and plentiful.

The tram from Karakoy whizzes me across the Golden Horn to the other side. It is, without a doubt, the quickest way to get around the city if one can handle the jostling and warm bodies pressed against each other. There are moments of alarm during the journey when the tram threatens to go off the track at the bends.

At Sultanahmet, the most popular stop on the ride, the tram halts and empties out. My destination in the middle of Sultanahmet Square, in sight of the two most famous buildings in Turkey—Hagia Sophia and the Blue Mosque—is a tiny shop selling overpriced food. I walk briskly towards it. Every step closer takes me back four decades back, when there was less hustle and bustle around the place. I see people in baggy pants, flowering skirts, and mismatched loose clothes; people with unwashed hair and beards—people from Jack Kerouac books and the 1968 Beatles trip to Rishikesh, India.

I am standing here, looking for a passage to Nepal via Afghanistan.

A young man in a white apron comes to stand by my side. He is smiling conspiratorially. He knows what I am thinking. His manner is that of an usher and less like a waiter.

"You are wishing for the good old times, yes?" he says. "I also sometimes wonder what it was like—the good old times. Come in, and I will tell you the story of this place."

"In just a minute," I say. "I want to stare some more, you know, like look into the past somehow. But I suppose much has changed since then, yes?"

"Yes, my father tells me the stories. He was a waiter here at the time. He said one day, he ran away with a German girl on a van but was back two days later, completely broken because she found another boyfriend on the way."

I follow him inside and find myself a table by the door. All around me is the sound of traffic and conversations of people waiting to get inside. Two girls with blonde hair are posing by the noticeboard.

Business is booming at *The Pudding Shop*.

My *sütlac,* a local rice pudding, arrives and is followed by coffee. The waiter urges me to try the chicken pudding next, a dish he says is hugely popular. I decline. I settle for chocolate pudding instead, provided he never brings up chicken and pudding in the same breath again. I couldn't imagine chicken being cooked in milk and sugar, no matter how much I tried.

The Pudding Shop has an interesting backstory. It began as the Lale Restaurant in 1957, a venture by two brothers İdris and Namık Çolpan, before gaining a reputation in the 1960s as a meeting place for hippies and other travellers overlanding between Europe, India, Nepal, and elsewhere in Asia. I had heard of *The Pudding Shop* in a café on Nepal's Freak Street a few years ago. My obsession with historical oddities had led me to Kathmandu's *The Snowman* café—with its psychedelic paintings on the wall—in search of its apple pie and Nepali tea. Then, one thing led to another, and I had become involved with stories of hippies and beatniks.

And on the first page of *Midnight Express* by Billy Hayes, left behind by an unknown traveller, I came across a single sentence written in cursive that changed the course of my life. The line was from *Childe Harold's Pilgrimage.*

There is a pleasure in the pathless woods...

*

The name *The Pudding Shop* replaced its original name because foreign travellers who could not remember the name *Lale*

Restaurant but remembered the excellent selection of puddings sold there called it so.

"In those days, people ate, sang, and played music and did not care how they looked or how the hotel looked. Today, people either come for photos of the place, for the pudding, or the love of travel. They sit with headphones, staring at their mobile phones, smiling at the screens, and sipping coffee without feeling," the waiter laments.

"In its early years, *The Pudding Shop* offered information on transportation to Asia and tourist information on Turkey freely to the customers, who comprised of tourists. Back then, they were simply called hippies. The owners put up a bulletin board inside so that travellers could schedule rides with their fellow travellers and communicate with friends and family members. That is how we became famous."

He beams with pride.

"You must see our famous message from Megan to Malcolm apologizing for the 'business down in Greece.' Today, we hide our messages on WhatsApp. Oh, for the times so simple."

I want to leave a message, too, but one look at the other customers diminishes my enthusiasm. Everyone is engrossed in their phones.

I sip my coffee, trying to live in the moment, and be mesmerized by the Blue Mosque and Hagia Sophia in the distance. Unfortunately, this café didn't exist in the time of Hemingway—or the dictionary would possibly have a new word.

*

I am thinking of Hemingway in Istanbul as a young war reporter for *The Toronto Star* in 1922. After his discharge as an ambulance driver in Italy during World War II, he was sent to Istanbul to cover the end of the Grecco-Turkish War. He arrived at the Sirkeci railway station, the eastern terminus of the world-famous Orient Express.

Something in those three weeks in Istanbul had changed him as a writer. Perhaps I could find an answer at the Pera Palace Hotel, for Hemingway did stay there briefly. As I make plans, a middle-aged British woman sits beside me. It is the only chair available. Her face is friendly, and her smile is infectious.

A conversation ensues, and soon, we are on our way to becoming friends. During our second cup of coffee, she calmly announces, "I moved to Istanbul from London a decade ago and come here as often as I can, for no real reason."

That seals our friendship. I can identify with that, having been party to similar expeditions myself. Julia is a holistic healer. I have no idea what that means, but she is proud of her calling.

Like me, she is a coffee fanatic, though she claims she'd never go around the world drinking in coffee shops frequented by writers. However, she states that she maintains a healthy respect for their work.

"I'll drink to their health and literature and all that, but not the same coffee in the same café, by Jove. That particular form of entertainment is for freaks, I suppose."

There is some sense in what she is saying, but we agree to see things differently. I ignore that she has nearly called me a freak, but I put it down to her being British.

"Come to think of it, you might just be one of those rare species of stalkers in the making—the modern stalker, which, I will admit, is a far sight better than the IG louts."

Such a compliment is hard to ignore. I smile despite myself; Julia has managed to cleanse her aura. I haven't met anyone who could do it better.

Placing me a little above the IG louts was rather decent of her, I guess. Our conversation turns back to *The Pudding Shop*.

"This was somewhat of the start of the trail—or so I have heard people talk about," she tells me. "Speaking of how people journeyed back and forth from here and lived to tell the tale must say a lot about their destiny."

I say quietly, "I wonder what it must have been like to join strangers on an unknown journey to nirvana. Well, the path to greatness was never smooth, was it."

"There's a thing about getting to a place you want to go; I like them all, from flight paths to the hungry trails of backpackers, and there are also meeting points, places to facilitate and catch a ride. This place must have seen pretty much everything— hopes fulfilled, tears shed, relationships made or broken... Every time I come here, I find myself wishing I had lived in those times, you know, to board a bus and simply leave, unworried about returning or making a life or babies.

"They were pilgrims, that's what they were. Eternal pilgrims. Soul-searchers. They had light; they hugged rainbows. But for sure, I would have loved to have seen what went down on the hippie trail all those years ago, what those cities looked like, and all those newspapers saying bad things about the drifters.

"Did you know that Bill Clinton also came here?"

I had. Clinton was amongst the most famous customers of the restaurant, as a hippie in the 1970s and as the U.S. president in 1999.

"Clinton found his calling here. See? Destiny."

That settles the debate about destiny.

*

Finally, Julia and I decide to give some Turkish desserts a try. I am not in the least moved by sweets—but *Asure* is something else. It also goes by the name of Noah's Pudding. It is made in the month following the Sacrifice Feast (Kurban Bayrami) from pulses, dried fruits, and nuts. Legend has it that it was made by Noah, who threw whatever ingredients he had left on the arc into one pot, and *Aşure* was the result of that. Today, it symbolizes diversity and unity, just the sort of thing one needs to seal eternal friendship in Turkey.

"Say, would you like to join me for tea at Pera Palace?" Julia asks.

"Absolutely. Thank you. I had thought of asking you anyway if you hadn't asked me first. Tea sounds so English and all that. I can only hope there will be coffee, too. I can't stand tea for Chrissake."

I really like Julia. She makes me laugh.

*

Today is my day of literary venture. I start with a short walk off Istiklal Avenue, Istanbul's famous shopping area, which Hemingway described as *one narrow, dirty, steep, cobbled, tramcar-filled street*. The walk brings me to Cukurcuma, where a red-coloured building housing a famous literary achievement awaits.

How often did Orhan Pamuk or his protagonists, Füsun and Kemal, walk this way?

But everything is forgotten as I push open the door to the *Museum of Innocence;* in that moment alone, I have catapulted myself into the life of Kemal. *Museum of Innocence* is not just a museum that celebrates history—it lives a story. A real story, perhaps. The author's own.

Each room of the museum's four floors is set up to represent a chapter from Pamuk's Nobel Prize-winning book of the same name. Every article replays Kemal and Füsun's emotions. As a reader who has journeyed through their loves and losses, I establish a connection with thousands of artifacts housed there. Every object, upon minute scrutiny, explodes into a story.

The museum breathes. It is as real as my past, which reveals itself in the form of my letters and diaries. Here are cigarette butts, ashtrays, shawls, letters—everything that Kemal and his lover had touched, felt, seen, experienced, or used. Füsun sighed and laughed within these walls. It was her home.

I spend over four hours in there—drawn into the life of Pamuk, Kemal, and Füsun, walking hand in hand with Füsun, making passionate love to Kemal lying on these silken sheets... unable to snap out of the trance.

Eventually, I pull myself together and hasten to the next hotbed of historical and literary significance—the Nazim Hikmet Cultural Centre in Kadikoy, named after a Turkish-Polish poet. The centre is filled with books and Turkish coffee, and I reach out for both eagerly.

Around me are grave-faced youngsters engrossed in books, but my eyes rest on a particularly animated group of youngsters discussing something, their faces bearing passion and keenness. I am told upon enquiry that they are regular young writers who use the space as a work and meet-up site. I watch them curiously, trying to imagine what goes on in their minds. One of them might just be the next big thing in literature. And maybe—just maybe—someone, decades later, would find it in their hearts to follow their trail across Istanbul.

Today, I hope to achieve much in terms of visiting museums and houses of authors I admire. Shortly, a cable car ride brings me to Pierre Loti Hill, with its spectacular views of the Golden Horn, but I will visit another day to admire the views. For now, I am following the trail of Julien Viaud (Pierre Loti), a French Naval Officer and writer who arrived in Istanbul at age twenty-six in 1876, fell in love with a local woman, and made Istanbul his temporary home. The hill is named after him. Loti was so enchanted by the Ottoman culture that he became a regular to the city and was once welcomed by Sultan Mehmet Reşat himself.

I adjourn to the Pierre Loti Café located on the ridge to admire the view and absorb the magnetic charm of this place over a cup of coffee. This café, the waiter tells me, was nothing like it looks now. Back then, it was a small, humble place with a few stools and a stove for brewing Turkish coffee.

"But the coffee was the best. Today, changes have come," he says.

With every sip, my thoughts sharpen. Somewhere in the distance, traffic roars. The muezzin begins his ritual. I finally understand what makes Istanbul addictive to writers. The morning has been wholly satisfying. I feel the same way the hippies or flower children who set out to seek nirvana felt.

*

As promised, Julia arrives on time for the Afternoon Tea at the Kubbeli Lounge at the Pera Palace Hotel. She looks radiant in her flowing kaftan, which she assures me is perfect for the setting, but in my opinion, it seems like she has come out of a séance.

Julia is charming in the way only a British can be.

Afternoon tea at the hotel's Kubbeli Lounge has been a tradition among the Istanbul elite and tourists. Its high ceilings with domes, crystal chandeliers, Moorish-style arches, walls clad in bands of marble of contrasting colours, and a general feeling of coziness make it the ideal venue for a relaxing afternoon. Julie stares in awe and nearly faints with ecstasy when the live piano begins.

I wait just long enough for the music to take effect before digging into the cakes, puff pastries, mini scones, mini cakes, tarts, and little rectangles of sandwiches while İlham Gencer, the 93-year-old jazz pianist, dazzles the guests. He has played at the Pera Palace since 2012 and is one of Turkey's music legends.

"The tea-time music sounds even more melodious with such a wonderful spread of pastries, mini cupcakes, and donuts," Julia says. "I mean, can you better the white-bread sandwiches with crusts removed, multi-coloured macaroons, and Viennese-style cakes? I envy the grander, more leisured age. I wish I lived in those times."

I say nothing.

*

Julia expresses a keenness to see Agatha Christie's room, so I invite her in. But I'm not at all moved when she exclaims, "What absolute luxury," and unashamedly advances towards the desk. "There, that must be the very place she sat writing. I can only imagine… and all this luxury… what a welcome sight!"

After a momentary silence, she continues. "Good Lord, this must be costing you some money, right? To think I have been here all these years and never thought of visiting her room. It is another thing that I couldn't afford to stay here, but to just look! I should have thought of that. Lucky you and well, lucky me."

Like her, I am drawn into the mystery and gore, not just of this hotel, but of Istanbul itself. Had she thought of that? Istanbul has thrived in the pages of several bestsellers on my bookshelf, but I am eager to see the world the writers created. Bodies in the Bosphorus, a dead cat in the alley, blood stains on the carpets—I wanted to recreate the experiences in the present.

"Why did Agatha Christie choose this particular hotel and city to write *Murder on the Orient Express?*"

Julia's sudden question shocks me. I've had that question on my mind for a while now. What was it about The Pera Palace that attracted her?

"Probably, we'll never know, but we can guess," I say. "That would be so much fun, right?"

"Guessing is a good way to show appreciation to a literary great."

I change the subject.

"Did you know when Ernest Hemingway wrote *The Snows of Kilimanjaro*, he installed his main character, Harry, at The Pera Palace Hotel? Technically, both the writer and his creation have stayed here. Although I suspect he spent more time at the Orient Bar than elsewhere. Over the years, he wrote and dedicated a book to each of his four wives. I think that was rather sweet, albeit slightly twisted."

Each time he got divorced, he married again within the year—but he always left something behind in print. The dedication for *The Sun Also Rises* went to his first wife, Elizabeth Hadley Richardson; *Death in the Afternoon* was dedicated to his second wife, Pauline Pfeiffer; *For Whom the Bell Tolls* was for his third wife, Martha Gellhorn; and *Across the River and Into the Trees* went to Mary."

We discuss another fictional character, Henry Pulling, and his aunt, Augusta Bertram, in Graham Greene's *Travels with My Aunt*, who also stayed at The Pera Palace Hotel. Our conversations inevitably drift back to The Pera Palace. Such a haul of literary greats has walked these hallowed halls that no discussion is enough to cover it all.

Suddenly, she looks at me and says, "I'd love for you to embrace your unique ways of seeing and experiencing the world so you can fulfil your soul purpose by showing up as yourself and being the gift to the world you were created to be."

I am taken aback, but only for a moment. I swear I see a halo around her head as she says this. Julia leaves with a promise to meet me when I return from my journey to Dardanelles, begging forgiveness for her inability to accompany me on this quest, much as she would have liked to, the reason being, 'I have to cleanse the aura of a Turk."

"I'll be damned if I don't," she adds. "Because, you know, I am drawn into this world of your Byron, whether you believe it or not.

"I want to know all about your Byron and his exploits when you return. I'll buy dinner in return for all the stories of the Lord. It's amazing how many weirdos England has produced," she finishes in mock appreciation.

"I hope your Turk is handsome," I say. "That would make it worth skipping this trip to the coast."

I hug her goodbye.

*

Late at night, I stand on the Galata Bridge, looking into the water below. The bridge is lit in neon and purple, and light dances on the water. I stare into the depths, trying to make sense of everything around me.

The waters of Bosphorus indeed run deep and dark.

So much coffee to consume and so many literary trails to follow. I am getting goosebumps just thinking of Lord Byron swimming the Hellespont around here. I can't wait for that moment to come.

I have been waiting for it for so long.

Chapter 2

At the end of the day at the hotel reception, I am informed that the easiest and the best way to explore Canakkale is to book a two-day trip with someone knowledgeable on history, the roads, and the language. Against my better judgement and not to mention the lack of other practical options, I do just that.

*

As a rakishly handsome Turkish guide picks me up from my hotel in a shiny Mercedes van fitted with a small refrigerator and a TV, I relax.

"Everything gets interesting from now on," I tell myself. "This guide must know a lot of the country's past. I suppose I am about to learn the ways of Turks, too. I'm sure Julia would find this turn of events fascinating."

We pick up the other guests, a young Australian couple on their way to pay their respects at the ANZAC Sites. From the way they insist on holding hands all the time, I am sure we aren't going to have any worthwhile conversation.

I turn my attention to the guide.

We ease out of the city's traffic and hit the road along the coastline of the Marmara Sea on the European side. We stop for a breakfast of *burek,* and after a three-hour drive, we arrive at Eceabat and head to Mydos restaurant for a lunch of fish, which is claimed to have been procured from the Dardanelles Strait that we sit looking at.

While the deep blue Dardanelles rises and falls at our feet, we dig into the fishy goodness it produced. The sea breeze is stiff and cool. The lunch is cold no sooner it arrives, but that is the least of my worries.

At the restaurant, I run into a Swedish Professor, Bjorn Ackerman, doing the same thing as I am, only that he is travelling in a different van with a female tour guide. And both of us, having identified the other's needs correctly, are drawn towards the coffee counter. I am glad for the conversation.

*

Lunch over, we embark on the tour of the Gallipoli Peninsula and its fascinating sites, driving from one spot to another and admiring the Brighton Beach, Beach Cemetery, Anzac Cove, Ari Burnu Cemetery, ANZAC Commemoration Site, Lone Pine Australian Memorial, Johnston's Jolly (Turkish & Allied trenches & tunnels), and The Nek among others. Of all the fourteen sites outlined in our itinerary, it is at Johnston's Jolly, the trenches of which were particularly interesting, that I run into Professor Ackerman.

I am glad to share my disinterest in this tour with him, thanks to the overload of war history, and Bjorn agrees with me on the subject quite robustly. To ease our minds off the rather dull turn of events, I tell him about my quest.

In his typical professor way, he says, "It is a strange quest, but good luck."

The Lone Pine Cemetery is somewhat interesting and characterized by a lone pine tree, which perhaps has sad tales to tell. It is the site where most of the Australian soldiers were buried. We stop by the ANZAC Cove on the Gallipoli Peninsular, now a beautiful stretch on the blue Saros Bay. The day is clear, the breeze is cool, and the blue waters are particularly tempting—although swimming is out of the question. This site is of great importance in history; it is said that without this, the Allied forces (France and Britain) during WWI would have been unable to land here. The Allied forces intended to capture Istanbul (then Constantinople) to get to Russia, for the Turks had blocked the route.

History stands witness to the plans of the Allied forces, who aimed to capture the entire Gallipoli Peninsula. The Allied forces included New Zealand, Australian, French, British, and Indian soldiers. Unfortunate circumstances (and history is witness to this) led to the death of thousands from both sides, and the fallen soldiers now lie buried in the many war cemeteries in the area.

A year later, April 25 came to be called ANZAC Day. On that day, scores of tourists from NZ and Australia visit Gallipoli every year to pay respects to their fallen men and take in the beauty of the surrounding areas—as the couple who share my van is doing. Their knowledge of the war is commendable, and when not discussing life on an Australian farm, they engage in profound conversation with the young guide. I have given up on the guide because he does not seem very keen to share information on Lord Byron.

*

Late in the evening, we board the ferry to cross to Canakkale on the Asian side of Dardanelles, our stop for the night.

The captain is a cheery fellow, eager for some conversation, and I soon find myself at the wheel, yanking from right to left under his guidance, all the while talking of the weather and determined to stay on course. The kind man pays no heed to my non-existent navigational skills and watches as I inexpertly guide the passenger ship across the Dardanelles. If there is anyone who would know the history of Dardanelle, it would be him.

"Today, you have boats to go across, but 200 years ago, Lord Byron swam across this strait. It was called Hellespont back then. He was club-footed, but he was bold and proved himself unhindered by his physical lameness by doing so."

That was Byron. The bad, bold Byron. I wish I knew what made him jump into the waters so carelessly. There must have been a reason.

My eyes scan the Dardanelles, which is crawling with passenger and cargo ferries, while I imagine a young Byron throwing himself into the waters.

Today's Dardanelles appears harder to love or swim than in 1810. I have not heard of anyone attempting to do what Byron did. Not in the recent past. I have questions for the captain. I am trying to dust off simple theories and history that miraculously have been recorded, trying to make myself understood, and most difficult of all, to understand what he is telling me.

Without waiting for me to finish, the captain continues.

"His best work was inspired by our legendary Hero and Leander, who died in these waters. You must read it."

His eyes shine at the thought.

*

I walk off the ferry into the bustle of people on the shores of Canakkale, my destination for today. Unimaginatively laid out modern buildings and cafes stare at me apologetically.

I have a couple of hours to myself before my dinner appointment with Bjorn. I walk around town, trying to understand what had brought Byron to this part of the world. Did he ever live here?

The town of Canakkale itself does not have much to hold a visitor's interest even in the present, so what must have been Byron's reason to be here? Well, it does have a traditional Turkish charm not seen in the more touristy cities of Turkey, which perhaps is a good reason to visit unless one is using it as a stopping point before proceeding to the more intriguing ancient city of Troy. The old town's cobbled streets briefly hold my attention; dotted with a handful of Ottoman examples of architecture and houses, it makes for a pretty sight. The Clock Tower is an attraction, and so is the Museum of Archaeology, but since I am not keen to immerse myself in the military history of World War I, I give the Canakkale Naval Museum a miss.

Hands in my pocket, I walk along the pier, feeling a sense of déjà vu. I cannot explain what triggers that feeling, but I get the feeling that I am not walking alone.

A line from Byron's *The Bride of Abydos* comes to mind, and suddenly, *mad, bad Byron* is walking alongside me. I greet him casually, and I swear I hear him respond. And just like that, he is gone, leaving me feeling like I have finally connected with my inner self. I look for evidence of his presence, but there is none to find. History laced with imagination has a peculiar way of finding its way into the present—like it is doing now.

I am in love with Lord Byron.

Instead of finding rapturous joy in this realization, I feel peaceful. I have been looking at my present for my purpose and have found it. It now remains to be seen what will work for me and what not. I am going to follow the threads and see where it takes me.

My eyes scan the waters without focusing on anything in particular. Dardanelles is nearly silent. The few evening walkers are curious about my presence.

I make my way to the more believable version of the legendary Trojan horse dedicated to the local government after wrapping up the shooting of the film *Troy* to meet Bjorn as arranged.

It is time for dinner.

*

In the morning, I continue to the ancient city of Troy (or Truva). Bjorn has decided to return to Istanbul.

Truva or Troy, in my opinion, is not as grand as Ephesus or Hierapolis or other parts of Turkey but is easily more than 2000 years older than any of them and has a lot more to be proud of than just its mythical Trojan horse made famous by Homer's *Iliad*.

But as we walk through the ruins of Troy, I hear a group of visitors snidely remark about the lack of "character" in the ruins and express disappointment over the wooden horse installed at the entrance. Fortunately, I have come with an open mind, which makes even the piles of stones utterly fascinating.

The thick walls that protected the town of Troy centuries ago, the ramps, columns, a small, dilapidated theatre, and earthenware appear in places. Most of the site's information is found at strategic points. According to the information boards, Troy was rebuilt through nine eras. Archaeologists have classified these ears based on the finds, the nature of walls, the built-up areas of the township, the materials used, the shapes of the houses, and other things.

Excavation is still on in the area. If it helps, remember that the ruined walls of Troy clearly indicate why it took the enemies (Achaeans) many years to break into Troy's defences.

Upon returning home, I read more about Troy, and everything slowly starts making sense. The old drawings on the wall that depict Troy during the Trojan War BC make it believable in the present.

*

I return to Istanbul, determined to read everything about Lord Byron. It amuses me that he escaped creditors in England by going on a Grand Tour as any young nobleman in the days, but whose attraction to Islam and Sufi mysticism led him to the shores of Constantinople.

The very idea of being in Byron's footsteps encourages me to revisit a sprinkling of spots in Istanbul, like the Hagia Sophia and the City Walls, which had fascinated him. Byron was deeply influenced by the beauty of Istanbul's natural surroundings, including the serene waters of the Bosporus and the scenic hills overlooking the city. He found inspiration in the interplay between nature and human civilization.

In trying to establish a connection with Byron through these places, I, too, fall in line with his thoughts, and soon, the sight of Turkish burial grounds become 'the loveliest spots on earth.'

Like Byron, there is perhaps a darker side to me, too.

A thorough Google search, at which I am quite adept, takes me to a whole new world. The website I stumble upon disseminates the History of Istanbul from Antiquity to XXI. Century is a work prepared by the cooperation of Türkiye Diyanet Foundation Centre for Islamic Studies (İSAM) and İstanbul Metropolitan Municipality Kültür ve Sanat Ürünleri A.Ş.

Here is what I find:

The list of what Lord Byron read before he came to Istanbul is quite comprehensive. Lord Byron states in his diaries and letters that he read not only about the Ottoman Empire but almost everything to which he had access and was concerned with the Orient. Thomas Moore's biography of Lord Byron (1779 - 1852) reveals that he read the vs of Lady Mary Wortley Montagu and Baron De Tott (d. 1793), as well as all the travelogues he had access to; he also read history books on the Ottomans by Dimitrie Cantemir (Kantemiroğlu) (1673- 1723), Richard Knolles (1545- 1610), Vincent Mignot (dates unknown), and Paul Rycaut (1629- 1700), as well as One Thousand and One Nights.

One of the main reasons for the interest in the Orient is that Greek literature had begun to be taught in schools in Europe. Another reason— also nourished by this interest—is the expansion of the limits of the Grand

Tour taken by the elite European youth; now, this journey also included Istanbul.

One of the main changes in the perception of romanticizing the Orient and Orientalism was that visual representation started to gain importance, not only in architecture and similar branches of art but also in literary genres. Reinhold Schiffer also attributes this change to the fact that the picturesque style was gaining importance. Travelers started to come to Istanbul for a "sublime" experience, particularly at the beginning of the nineteenth century. There is an important correlation between picturesque fashion and the interest of travellers in Istanbul. Above all, this idea is vital, especially for the ethical approach of English travellers to Istanbul, "not only in their depiction of Istanbul but also their description of Istanbul."

This aesthetic ideal, which started in the 1770s in England, gained importance and became increasingly popular. Travellers who came to Istanbul were impressed; the travelogues of Charles Pertusier, Antoine Ignace Melling (d. 1831), and James Stuart are examples of this.

Lord Byron describes picturesque images of Istanbul, and he speaks of how a Turkish warship was anchored in the port of Istanbul, creating a poetic image. (George Gordon Noël Byron, The Works of Lord Byron: Complete in One Volume, Frankfort: Printed by and for H.L. Broenner, 1826, p. 685.)

In addition, he mentions Istanbul in the first canto of Don Juan as "picturesque Constantinople." (Moore, The Life of Lord Byron with His Letters, p. 108).

*

Today's Istanbul is a metropolis, but at the time of Lord Byron's arrival, it was frequented by beggars, disabled people, dervishes, and many graveyards. For reasons I will never know, Lord Byron found graveyards attractive. He called them a place of peace and narrated the beauty of it in detail in his writing. He described picturesque images of Istanbul and spoke of how a Turkish warship was anchored in the port of Istanbul, creating a poetic image.

From his works, I know that historically, coffeehouses were places for men to socialize and watch dancer boys perform. I try to imagine what the coffeehouses were like in the past, but no matter how hard I try, I cannot picture Lord Byron and his friend John Hobhouse visiting such places to simply look at dancer boys dressed as women and share their stories.

But they did.

*

Julia is on time, looking, if that is possible, more radiant than ever. I suspect her cleansing ritual ended well. On the way to Sultanahmet, I fill her in about everything I have learned in the last two days, throwing in a good measure the history of ANZAC.

Her observation shocks me.

"You could have saved the time by reading about that, right?"

"It's not the same, you know. To understand emotion, one must feel it."

I know she is testing me. We wander somewhat aimlessly around Sultanahmet, like any two women, comfortable with the talking of things important or not, and adjoin once again to the *Pudding Shop* for a cup of coffee.

"This place always beckons me," she says and casually orders tea. I will never know what caused that.

The place is crowded; I dislike drinking coffee standing up, so I refuse.

This surprises her, though she doesn't ask me why.

"I have a special place where we're going to have lunch," she says instead. "I remember my promise."

It has taken me a while, but I now realize that when Julie says something like this, she has no idea where we're going but will figure it out as we walk along.

151

We promptly finish the tea, standing up, and suddenly, she exclaims, "Ah, yes. We should eat there. The food is great, and what do you know, it is a famous café in Istanbul."

"There?"

"Yes, there. I don't remember the name just yet, but I know where it is. But first, are you up to exploring the bazaar? I know it like I know my face, but you might get lost in there. But it is fun, I tell you. I know I am in Istanbul when I can hop across the Bosphorus and dash into the Spice Bazaar for nutmeg and pepper. It makes all the difference in the world to my homemade pie."

I tell her I am not fascinated with spices as much as a British woman is, considering my country of birth. We, as Indians, know everything there is to know about spices. We grow them in our backyards and rarely gush over the aroma of cinnamon or sneeze at pepper. To us, pepper spray is not a weapon; it is just the topping on a particularly hot meat dish.

She is quick to decipher my lack of enthusiasm, and, as a peace offering, she agrees to spend time exploring Istanbul's new tourist hotspot, Fener and Balat, in the Greek and Jewish section of the city instead. Hitherto a somewhat diabolical part of Istanbul, it is now climbing the tourists' checklist.

"But a quick dash to the bazaar? Please! You cannot imagine what it is to run out of pepper," she adds sagely. "For all you know, the pepper may have just come from your garden, so why not check it out?"

"Sure."

"The restaurant I mentioned is there," Julia announces. "So it just as well that we are going there."

I finally figure out that we are going to eat 'there', which is 'just there.'

Her aura needs cleaning today.

We plunge into Istanbul's hallowed bazaar, where you can find everything that befits a king, where fragrant saffron and cinnamon share space with dried vegetables, fruits, pistachios, hazelnuts, and a sticky world of honey-drenched sweets. Despite my initial resistance, I enjoy this fascinating world of spices and spend every waking minute admiring the beautiful display of spices or bending over the bags to smell the aroma. Meanwhile, Julia hunts for the perfect nutmeg and pepper to add to her pie.

Occasionally, I catch glimpses of the Bosphorus, which is bursting with boats. Somewhere close at hand are secret underground cisterns, and somewhere beyond it all are the crumbling fort walls, towers, minarets, dark alleys, mysterious hideouts, mosques, churches, and ancient myths.

Every crime story I have read in the past, and every film I have watched comes rushing back. James Bond and Bryan Millis race through the tightly packed narrow lanes within the Bazaar. Barbara Nadel's detective, Çetin Ikmen, and Agatha Christie's Poirot appear in front of my eyes. Scripts and scenes clash in my head.

I am living a story.

"I know what you are thinking." Julia breaks into my thoughts. "This entire setting is just perfect for a crime, right? These spice mountains, these mysterious-looking Turks… Perhaps you should write a book."

I wonder what she would say if I told her I had a few books, and I'd never write another one if I could help it.

*

Julia directs my attention to a new-age coffee shop in Balat, a place, she explains, prepares impeccable coffee. "Coffee can never go wrong there, trust me," she adds quickly, trying to convince me.

Taking her advice, we proceed to the shop named Coffee Department, the very sight of which warms my heart. Momentarily, I forget what I am in Istanbul for. In the neighbourhood filled with coffee shops, this one stands out. It looks a little too hipster for my liking, but she assures me that if I know what I want, I'll never get a cuppa I don't like. I am sold on this idea of drinking coffee in a setting too young and bordering on immature.

But she is soon proved right. The cafe uses freshly roasted beans from their own roastery a few blocks away. My coffee arrives with a small card explaining the bean's flavour profile and origin. It says *Columbia* on mine. Perfect.

Through the gorgeous, tall windows, we watch life go by. On the other side of the street is a quaint little church, and a handful of tourists are staring at it excitedly.

Leaving the coffee shop, we run into an auction on the opposite street.

"Not just any auction," explains Julia. "It is quite charming and pretty useless, but it is where you get to buy broken electronics and gaudy ceramic cat statues."

"But I enjoy watching people inspect these items seriously," I say, slowing down. "The expressions give away far too much of their character."

Julia scowls. "You need to snap out of your Byron-obsession."

Perhaps she is right. We refrain from talking about our serious things and focus on more trivial things.

Like buying a *nazar boncuk*, the eye-shaped blue pendants that keep away the evil eye. On closer inspection, they do look quite pretty and lively.

"There is a belief that one must not buy it if one doesn't have a good heart. One must have pure intentions," she chides.

I cross my heart and bow slightly.

I buy three.

"Just to drive in my rather pure intentions." I smile.

*

Many writers fictionalized their stories, inspired by the city's magical ambience and rich history, making the city their home—if not permanent, at least transient. But then there were the real ones.

Like Hemingway and Lord Byron.

Istanbul has many reasons to celebrate. From my point of view, I have many reasons to celebrate its existence. It is the country common to Lord Byron and Ernest Hemingway.

Chapter 3

Charles De Gulles Airport can cause immense distress not only to a first-time traveller but also to a third-time traveller like me. I have dealt with a fair amount of trouble here earlier, and it simply doesn't get any better.

It gets to me this time, too, but that is not the point I am trying to make. We land a good hour behind schedule. Folks are desperate to get off the plane and run for their connecting flights. This airport is enormous, and the security lines are longer than I have seen anywhere. I doubt some of my fellow passengers will make their flights.

I haven't gotten very far with learning French, an exercise that started and ended in Rwanda. All the blogs on people advising on the shortest way to learn it have yielded little results. Even the apps claiming a quick turnaround have failed. Hard as it is to accept my inability to learn this language, I know that talking to the French might help, but not just yet. I need to find someone with a lot of patience and good humour. I hold myself back from attempting to speak it right now, fearing it will make things worse.

This resolve is broken as I approach the window, lapsing into what I think is French spoken right. I suspect he is humouring me because he has suddenly launched into a full-fledged conversation. I understand only a quarter of what he is saying, but nevertheless, I smile. This lasts until he wants to know the reason for my visit. Then, we both revert to English.

French might be the international language of love, but English remains the international language of reason.

I put off trying to speak French till I succeed in my quest. That way, I stand a better chance of finding the cafes Ernest Hemingway frequented. There is nothing on Lord Byron to be found here except that the hotel where I will stay was named after him. Ironically, the good Byron never set foot in Paris but managed to wean himself into the French literary scene so strongly that at the peak of his influence, the French learnt English just to be able to read him. With this, Byron became one of the biggest influences on French Romanticism, something Goethe or Scott could never be.

*

Lord Byron Hotel, located in a quiet street, is my place of stay simply because it bears the name of Byron and is a short walking distance from Champs-Elysees. On top of that, it combines French elegance with comfort in a way only the French can.

As with most European cities, rains are partial to Paris, making an appearance out of nothing and, for no reason, forcing me to stay indoors.

As a past visitor, I have walked along Champs Elysees, admired the beautiful architecture, sunk money into cafes lining the wide avenues, and thus learnt what Parisian cafes are about. I learnt how the café's serve little more than a snack menu, and sometimes one ends up paying more to sit down and enjoy a coffee than have it standing up. It is here I have met old French gentlemen drinking coffee and enjoying a smoke at midday. I have window-shopped in Sephora without any intention of buying make-up, battled traffic around the Arc de Triomphe, climbed the Eiffel Tower, and visited Sacré-Coeur in Montmartre. I have no reason to stress because not so long ago, I walked through the Louvre to see the Big Three—Mona Lisa, Venus de Milo, and Winged Victory of Samothrace gracing the top of Daru Staircase and enjoyed myself very much.

In other words, I have ticked the boxes and am in no immediate danger of losing the touristic marathon. That is not to say I will not undertake the same journey again because I really love the Louvre, and walking through Champs Elysees makes my heart sing.

Paris is, without a doubt, what Ernest Hemingway said it to be.

If you are lucky enough to have lived in Paris as a young man, then wherever you go for the rest of your life, it stays with you, for Paris is a moveable feast.

As it stands, I am late to the party because in Paris, Ernest Hemingway is somewhat of a legend, and there are many blogs telling the potential tracker how to walk in his footsteps. There are tour companies that make it easier by organizing one for you, which is just as well considering the restraints language puts on one at times. However, I resist the temptation to take a tour. In Paris, there are many stories of adventure attached to Hemingway. I cannot say with certainty whether everything I read about is true, but it is *not* the truth that I am after.

Because the rains do not ease and it is too cold to walk, I spend the evening sipping Bloody Mary in honour of EH. Before long, I start to wonder about the claims he made of Paris.

I am going to figure this out for myself.

If only the rains would stop…

*

Sometime during the night, the rains subside. The morning dawns clear, leaving the city clean and crisp against the backdrop of a deep blue sky.

I have always thought it's a privilege to wake up in Paris— because of the visual perfection it presents. There is beauty everywhere, although here one can never tell what will work or not on a particular day, and this unpredictability is charming because it can mean that one will have an adventurous day. Plus, there is another factor to consider: the Parisian behaviour. That is a random factor because it is hard to predict whether a Frenchman will kick you or kiss you. I have had some experience with the latter.

My list of places to visit in the footsteps of Hemingway is small and incomplete. According to a *New York Times* story, Hemingway arrived in Paris as a reporter for the *Toronto Star* with his wife Hadley in December 1921 and made for the Rive Gauche, the *Hôtel Jacob et d'Angleterre*, which is still operating at 44 rue Jacob.

Another article summed up his life in Paris like this:

When Hemingway arrived, he was 22 years old, and Hadley was eight years his senior. He was penniless, but she had a small inheritance. Ernest would call Paris his home, on and off, for the next six years. When he departed in 1928, he had acquired a new wife, become a successful novelist, and developed a style that redefined modern literature.

That is the gist of his life in Paris, which I learnt after going through various accounts by Hemingway-lovers, newspaper reports, and his books. His posthumous memoir of that era, *A Moveable Feast*, remains one of his best and most accurate account of his life here, with which I aim to trace a part of his life.

Although I have read a fair amount of Hemingway's works, I have still not been able to form an opinion of his character or persona. In fact, I am getting to know him through his love for life, food, and wine. Everything leads back to great food and drinks.

To understand an artist, you must first study his art. In all his works, EH has expressed appreciation for the good life. All evidence points to that. It's there for everyone to see. There are plaques bearing his name in plenty of places he ate and drank at. It is strange how people love historical memories linked to him. It feels like I am retracing the great novels through the recipes and narrations of his most famous dishes, which is fine. I feel ready to host a Hemingway-style dinner for my readers/friends with his favourite dishes.

Seeing that dining and drinking venues figure prominently in Hemingway's Paris experience is a bonus for me, for it is the easiest way to drink at innumerable Parisian cafes without the guilt.

In contrast to Hemingway's voracious appetite, Lord Byron was obsessed with dieting—surviving on thin bread slices and tea without sugar. *One was a poet, and the other a hunter.* The difference was stark and not in the least comparable. There is no question of drawing parallels here. This observation always brings a smile to my face.

I am not at all surprised there is so much media coverage of EH's life here. While I have made piecemeal pilgrimages to various cafes and bars in Africa and Turkey, Paris demands closer scrutiny and an application of journalistic talents.

I am not likely to trace the exact routes made by Hemingway, but I intend to stroll about the city's Left and Right Banks, a randomly enjoyable blend of research and leisure time.

Patience is the key to my quest.

*

The Paris metro is a public transport system I am falling in love with—if such a thing is possible. It is an engineering and planning genius, according to me. It brings me to Lemoine, where Hemingway and his wife Hedley rented a modest two-room flat in the third-floor apartment at 74, rue Cardinal Lemoine. The apartment was tiny and cramped for writing, so Hemingway rented a room around the corner at 39 rue

Descartes. On cold days, he would work in this 4th-floor garret. In good weather, he would work at local cafés where the cost of a cup of coffee was the only rent.

The apartment is not open for public touring, but being able to touch the small board announcing the date and time of Hemingway's stay here is satisfying enough.

I then circle back to Hotel Angleterre in the historic rue Jacob because it is where EH spent much of his time in its iconic cafes, *Les Deux Magots* and *Café de Flore*. Café de Flore is just around the corner from Les Deux Magots and a great introduction to the Parisian café culture of the 1920s. Both these establishments have been drawing artists since the 1880s.

I decide to kick back and enjoy my last cup of coffee for the day at Café de Flore and ruminate on Hemingway and other greats who spent their time here discussing life and literature.

In the 1920s, Paris was an expat paradise. Food was cheap, and after WWI, the exchange rate was the biggest draw for Americans to flock here. Even a starving artist could 'starve in style' back then. Hemingway had acquainted himself with the other expats living in the city, including the famous *Lost Generation* artists like Gertrude Stein, Ezra Pound, Picasso, and James Joyce, who became central to his growth as a writer.

As evening approaches, I realise I have drunk too much coffee and decide to walk to my hotel. The much-needed walk takes me a little over an hour. I am completely captivated by the sights around me. As I walk, I try to place EH somewhere on these streets as a young journalist trying to make it in the world. The caffeine should have pumped out adrenaline, but I feel less enthusiastic than I set out in the morning. Still, I keep moving. That was the trick—to keep moving. No matter what. EH personified that. I keep my ears open to the sounds around me. Through the dull sounds of motor, I hear conversations of people walking past. Some are on the phone, and a few are simply walking home.

I like to listen. I have learned a great deal from listening carefully. Most people never listen.

That is what Hemingway had famously said. How right he was. My literary expedition is turning into a series of life lessons.

*

I head to Rue Delambre, specifically to the *Auberge de Venise*, formerly the *Dingo Bar*, the all-night hangout for American expats in the 1920's. This famous place witnessed the first meeting of Hemingway and Scott Fitzgerald in April 1925, soon after the latter had published *The Great Gatsby*.

That meeting is said to have inspired Hemingway to write a novel besides setting the foundation for a long friendship with Fitzgerald. History is witness that the two men, as different as chalk and cheese, formed a volatile and yet amorous relationship which some call the Jekyll and Hyde equivalent of the literature world—Hemingway, the ultimate man's man, hunter and womanizer, and Fitzgerald, the eternal outsider and hopeless romantic.

But what they famously had in common was a fondness for drinking and good writing.

It is 11 a.m., but *Auberge de Venise* is almost empty. Customers are slow in arriving. The interior is cozy and decently decorated; the distance between tables is roomier than in a typical Parisian restaurant, so there won't be much elbows-rubbing involved.

I find myself a spot by the window and watch Montparnasse's morning foot traffic, imagining a time almost a century ago when the two literary powerhouses clicked their glasses and toasted to success and friendship.

For reasons I cannot recall, I am easily drawn into Hemingway's world of dining and drinking, feeling absolutely no guilt in indulging in the pleasures.

When the hostess puts the menu in front of me, I quickly order the beef carpaccio and a large portion of heirloom tomatoes with fresh mozzarella. While I wait, I casually dig into a dish of salty olives. The restaurant is filling up, but no one is gunning for my seat, so I casually order tiramisu and coffee, much as I'd have liked to enjoy the famous Hemingway cocktail, The Long Island Iced Tea.

That done, I wander around the restaurant, admiring the Hemingway portraits on the walls, small vestiges of a glorious era. The portraits are not that of Hemingway in his struggling days but of the time he became the literary He-Man.

I head to another favourite café of Hemingway and Fitzgerald. What happened there is only limited by one's imagination, but as stated in EH's *A Moveable Feast*—hilariously—it caused a great deal of scandal when it happened. It followed the deepening intimacy between the two and ended with Hemingway checking out Fitzgerald's manhood in the men's room of *Michaud's* for the sake of Fitzgerald's wife, Zelda.

Ultimately, EH convinced Fitzgerald that his physical endowment was of a totally normal size. Hemingway then encouraged his friend to check out some nude statues at the Louvre for confirmation.

Different accounts connecting Hemingway to *Michauds* speak of a time when Hemingway stared through the window at James Joyce and his family eating, all of them talking Italian.

Like thousands of others before me, this account is the reason for a dash to *Michauds*, which now goes by *Le Comptoir des Saints-Pères*. The modern bar-bistro is not particularly charming or suggestive of the atmosphere of the 1920s, except for the ceiling and the bar that has been preserved from that era. It doesn't evoke any idea of the days I seek to recreate, so I am forced to gulp down a coffee standing at the bar before the barista tells me that the bistro is often flooded by requests to see the men's room where said incident happened.

"Would you like to see it too?" he suggests with a smile.

A true chronicler of EH's life story might have ventured in to capture a shot of this legendary lavatory, but I refrain.

"You made the right decision. There is nothing to see," he says and returns to his cups.

*

In the evening, I board the metro from St. Michel de Notre Dame to the Château Rouge Metro Station. Walking through some engaging Parisian neighbourhoods, I stumble upon a little nondescript café where I stuff myself with pastries and coffee.

The pastry is crunchy, delicate, and delicious, and the coffee is intensely black. The café is beautifully designed in a contemporary style with elements of gold and silver. It looks like it has not yet been widely discovered by the public. The baristas are quick, knowledgeable, and on their toes, ready to help with the order.

Walking the hilly streets of Montmartre brings me in contact with charming cafes filled with tourists and local artists sketching out their subjects.

Finally, I make for the Sacré Coeur, the basilica dedicated to the sacred heart of Jesus. The basilica was constructed in 1873, but the grounds weren't consecrated until 1919. It was built with contributions from Parisian Catholics after the Franco-Prussian war between 1870 to 1871. A small crowd is engrossed in a duo of musicians, one playing the guitar and the other a drum.

They put up an interesting show.

I sit on the steps and escape into another world for a moment, a world that is reverberating inside me. Like the roar of a lion. Like the beat of a drum. Steady. Deep. But what I hear now is different. Different from the one that makes my heart sing. Like Africa. The drumbeats that cheer France are not the same as the drumbeats that enliven Africa.

Historically, the African drums were played to communicate, celebrate, mourn, or inspire. They were played during peace, war, planting, harvesting, birth, and death. In Africa, drums have many symbolic meanings. They have been a part of Africans' daily experience for so long that it pulses throughout their collective consciousness. From sending messages to people to healing the sick, they inspire something inside the body as they touch the soul and wake the spirit. Considered the heartbeat of Africa, it unites the people of the continent, binding their pulses together in rhythm with the drumming songs.

In the Western world, drums are mainly for entertainment. Like now. Everyone cheers the drummers, some tapping their feet to its rhythm, and some are making videos on their smartphones. Music has superpowers. It stays with us all our lives. Beginning as a lullaby and unto the grave as goodbye. But in Paris, it is a way of life. Here, it caresses my senses and evokes memories. Listening to it makes places, moments, and sensations appear magically.

I let go of my life's purposes, simply tune in to the moment, and concentrate on feeling alive. I enjoy every moment of the show and leave as the guys begin to play Bob Marley's *This is Love*.

*

Rains are on the horizon this morning as I set out to explore Paris, more specifically, the *Café de la Paix*, near the Paris Opera. As luck would have it, I am stuck without an umbrella, and it has begun to drizzle in that typical Parisian way. Before long, I find myself walking through the Passage Verdeau in the 9th arrondissement, glancing at the fine display of antiques, glad to escape the rain and the following windchill. These covered passages were built to provide a pleasant shopping experience for wealthy people, away from the dirty streets. However, the redesign of Paris—and the building of Grand Boulevard—destroyed most of them.

I alternate between admiring the mosaic-tiled floors, wooden storefronts, and the high glass ceiling when I suddenly recognize a face in the crowd.

Travel serendipity happens all the time, but I'm not sure I am always ready to recognize it. I have a reasonably good memory for faces but fail at remembering names, which often leads to embarrassment and doesn't say much about my efficiency as a journalist. But that is the way it is.

Like now. One such serendipitous moment is about to happen to me because approaching me is a face that is growing brighter at the sight of me. That broad smile is an indication of our acquaintance in the not-so-distant past. That face belongs to a middle-aged man with Arabic features, a tall, slim body, greying hair, and a deep voice.

That voice is booming in a very enthusiastic sort of way. No subtlety there.

"A! Is that really you? Do you remember me? Yes? No? Come on, surely you do."

I hope my eyes don't give away the truth. But when he hugs me, something stirs my memory. Tashkent... yes, that is where I had met him.

We air-kiss thrice, the Arabic way, and that unlocks my brain freeze.

"Yes. Yes. I remember you. Of course! Ghassan. We met in Tashkent. How can I forget that? How lovely it is to see you again."

He looks pleased.

"You came to Paris and did not tell me? Where are you staying? You must stay with us. My wife—she will be glad to see you. I told my son all about you. He is home for the holidays—why don't you come and stay with us? I will show you Paris like a local."

His son. I remember now. A boy they adopted, who is now on his way to becoming a doctor. Ghassan is a Syrian who left his country twenty years ago to make a life in Paris. I tell him where I am staying and outline my agenda for the coming days. He doesn't in the least look shocked. Perhaps he remembers our conversation in Tashkent.

"Still obsessing over Byron, aren't you?" he says. "Or is it the other chap? Hemingway? Clearly, you didn't leave that behind." He gracefully accepts my promise of visiting him when my work is done.

"There is no love like the love dead two centuries ago," he murmurs. I smile to myself.

We watch tourists, businessmen, and ladies with shopping bags waltz, swagger, and rush by. Just like we did in Tashkent station when waiting for the metro. That is how we became acquainted.

"It's not very often that we meet the same people in two different countries, right? Say, Ghassan, why not grab a cup of coffee somewhere to celebrate this serendipity?"

"I agree. Do you have a place in mind?"

"I think I do. *Café de la Paix*, near the Opera. What else!"

"Can't say no to that, can I?"

"No." I smile knowingly.

"Any connection with your man Hemingway?"

"Well... yes... Hemingway and Hadley celebrated their first Christmas lunch there."

"I should have thought so."

We walk briskly to one of Paris's renowned cafés in the 9th Arrondissement—*Café de la Paix* at The Intercontinental Paris, simply because the occasion warrants a celebration. Fortunately, it has stopped raining, although a chill remains. The road is wet, but that doesn't slow us down. I try to match Ghassan's steps but often fall short.

We walk past the outdoor café seating, which is full of people, and enter the restaurant lobby. We have two menu and dining room choices. We choose the bistro.

The florid interior of *Café de la Paix* is welcoming. I will say that no matter where you choose to sit, the choice will be right. From the outdoor patio, you will have a great view of the Paris Opera and get to watch people. If you sit inside, you will be surrounded by beautiful French art and crystal chandeliers.

The café itself is a sight of great cultural significance. When our coffee arrives, it begins to rain again, ever so gently this time, making the whole experience more rewarding.

Nearly nine decades ago, when Hemingway and Hadley supped here, their bill was substantially more than expected, so Hemingway had to run back to the *Hotel d'Angleterre*, a considerable distance on foot, to retrieve more cash while Hadley nervously stalled the waiter.

Or so the story goes.

Ghassan's lack of interest in Hemingway is curious, but I take it in my stride. We drain our coffee cups and smile contentedly at each other. This probably will be our last meeting. I do not tell him so, but I have no immediate plans of visiting Ghassan. Coffee consumed, Ghassan leaves for a prior appointment. He reminds me of my promise to visit him.

"Visit me," he says as he leaves, "when you are done chasing an illusion."

Hemingway and Byron are not illusions. They are as real as the roaring lions in Africa and the music of Paris.

Like a roar and a drumbeat.

I am lost in thought. The rain continues to fall gently, like a lullaby. I order another coffee for no other reason but to linger on. To watch the people. To hear conversations. To enjoy the sensation of being one with Hemingway.

In these few serendipitous moments, I belong to Paris, and Paris belongs to me, among the lively and glamorous. With the shadow of Hemingway over me.

*

I do not intend to present a scholarly or accurate timeline of Hemingway's life in Paris. And unlike the numerous websites presenting Hemingway's Paris, I am only visiting a few cafes, trying to gather an impression of the time when they were frequented by literary greats.

Footnotes:

- *Lord Byron never came to Paris.*
- *The most famous Parisian myth is the supposed invention of Bloody Mary by EH.*

Chapter 4

The TGV Lyria covers the 686 kilometres between Paris and Zurich at a top speed of 320 kilometres an hour on a rather enjoyable ride made more wholesome by the presence of a catering car. The double-decker train is awe-inspiring and has plenty of room to move around, which makes a huge difference to a long train journey.

Soon enough, we pull into the Zurich station on Platform 18 under the historic 1933 steel-and-glass train shed. The Zurich Station is one of the oldest railway stations in Switzerland, with a constant stream of people undertaking their everyday journey here because this also serves as the hub of the city's tram network. Arriving in Zurich is akin to coming home, but despite this familiarity, I am eager to explore this city closely because, in the past, Zurich has hosted many intellectuals and authors of repute.

According to Ian Fleming, this city is the birthplace of *James Bond*. Poet Gottfried Keller was born here. Johanna Spyri died here. John le Carré used a local hotel manager as the model for a character in *The Night Manager,* and James Joyce created his greatest masterpiece, *Ulysses,* right here in this city.

So, it goes without saying that, like a dog in a graveyard, I am tingling with excitement because I am on the hottest literary trial any country can offer. The excitement is two-fold because Lord Byron and Ernest Hemingway have left behind a relatively easy trail for anyone to follow all over Switzerland. My enthusiasm is at its peak because here I can have my pick of authors to trail.

As I edge closer to the tram station, something Hemingway had said echoes in my head: *You can't write about life if you have never lived.*

His sentiment is reflected in my current ambition. It is not as though I am trying to rewrite the man's life around the world, but I am getting closer to literary nirvana; in fact, I am living it up with my journey of knowledge and do not mind going that extra mile or spending that extra euro to experience anything that makes me content.

Zurich has such an intense history, and so many literary giants have spent time in this exact space that it is hard to remain unmoved by their presence. Surely, the city imbibes its character from them. There is satisfaction in knowing that I will unearth something here that will help me tie the loose ends. Arthur Conan Doyle had found something here, too, although that find didn't quite go down well with his publishers or readers. It is funny because he looked for and found a way to kill off his most popular creation, Sherlock Holmes, in Switzerland and zeroed in on a fatal accident at the Reichenbach Falls. I am not the one to judge because I really love Holmes, but Doyle felt that 'Holmes obscured his higher works.' This recollection makes me smile. Doyle turned vengeful against his creation in a place as beautiful as Switzerland, but if were him, I'd forget murder and write poetry here.

Like the good Byron did. However, these thoughts take a backseat when I board the tram for a short ride into Limmatquai because something waits for me there.

Rostii at Café Odeon.

I proceed to this establishment, unmindful of the pretty trams, tourists, and flashy cars. As expected, it is busy, but I am given a table by the large window, which I share with a Chinese couple, tourists, which is evident from their clothes. The frown and concentration with which they look at the map on their phones is another dead giveaway. I peer out the window to my left to see trams doing their runs, a scene that is just as comforting as it is welcome.

Odeon's vintage deco style, with its sparkling chandeliers and rich, earth-tone marbled floor and tabletops, makes it appealing. Particularly fascinating is the red upholstered seating where a conversation is raging. During the wait, I imagine all the past conversations that happened here. What a lot of stories there must have been. Picasso discussing his art, Coco Chanel entertaining her friends and clients, politicians rolling out their ideas and policies, and musicians practicing their charm. Oh, what a load of intellectuals must have passed through its doors since its opening. Einstein frequented the café during his years at the nearby Federal Institute of Technology, and apparently, he did not just take coffee breaks; he gave lectures to his small class right here.

What a charming history Café Odeon has.

It is worth mentioning that in this very café, the Swiss learnt to order champagne by the glass—or, in the local lingo, a glass of Cüpli—with lunch. Before that, champagne was only served by the bottle.

Imagine the consequences had this not been the case.

*

The *rostii* arrives in style, and I am ready to wax lyrical. It is beautifully brown and crisp on the outside and soft and meltingly, well, potato-ey within. It is so good that words can't describe it. This has set the mood for more food, and I promptly order a *Gipfeli*—a freshly baked croissant—like some of history's best literary minds, and a glass of champagne to accompany it. The hostess throws me a look, which I interpret as 'You have ordered far too much, and I hope you don't waste it.'

I smile back knowingly and rub my stomach to show how hungry I am. I am confident of my appetite.

Rostii, a simple, traditional Swiss potato pancake, is top-rated among potato lovers worldwide. At home, I make it once a week and am now close to perfecting it. As a part of my experiments with rostii, I've made it with raw and parboiled potatoes, adding to it at different times bits of bacon, onion, or cheese. But I have finally realized that the rostii made of raw potatoes is the best. However, finding the right recipe has proved elusive.

The Chinese couple leave after a brief argument over which direction to take for the Opera, and I am left to myself to enjoy the rest of my meal. I sip my champagne thoughtfully. It would have been so much fun to have hobnobbed with Hermann Hesse and James Joyce, who wrote good parts of their famous novels *Ulysses* and *Steppenwolf*, in the café.

My hotel room is tiny, the sort that is expected in Europe, but I am far too full and drunk to notice till I hit my head in the shower cubicle.

*

The Zurich morning is expectedly chilly, and I drink a generous amount of hotel coffee before stepping out to brave the chill. My immediate need is breakfast, which I partake in at my old favourite, the Gran Café Motta near Rathaus overlooking Limmat River. Tram No. 4 crawls past, looking warm and welcoming, and looking at it from where I dig into my warm eggs, I want to get on it and head into the morning.

If I were writing a blog, it would perhaps be a listicle of things to do in Zurich in twenty-four hours. At the top of the list would be a suggestion to have breakfast at Gran Café Motta. Because no sooner I have breakfasted, I feel a surge of energy passing through me.

Fascinated that I am with James Joyce's connection with the city, I take myself on the Irish writer's trail, grateful for the crisp morning air because it makes walking easy. Occasionally, I look away from the phone map to enjoy the city's beauty.

James Joyce had arrived in Zurich under peculiar circumstances in 1904. What he thought was an English teaching job waiting for him at the Berlitz School turned out to be non-existent, but he braved on. Eventually, he found a job, lived in Zurich through two World Wars, and sought treatment for his eye problems here, finding not only a cure for his health problems but erotic inspiration too, like in Gertrude, a TB patient who inspired Gerty MacDowell in *Ulysses*.

*

The apartment house on Universitaetsstrasse 38 is quiet. Even the streets are devoid of traffic at this hour. I stare at the house forlornly, trying to make a connection. The only information and image I have of the house is gleaned from the internet, which helps identify it. There are no signs or historic markers to say what I am looking at, even less the historical significance of the building. Without that internet picture to aid me, I certainly would have walked right past and never looked up or discovered anything significant.

The accounts of James Joyce's working module were complex and yet very simple. He, it is said, worked wherever he could find space, be it in the living room, kitchen, and sometimes on his bed. It is fascinating that *Ulysses*, the crown of literary excellence, should have stemmed from such a small apartment block with God-knows-what inside. The apartment house now serves as the James Joyce Foundation and is closed for the day, but that doesn't sadden me in the least because a casual stroll from the memorial plaque and foundation is Buchhanddlung Beer, Zurich's oldest bookstore. In the back of this 17th-century bookstore, I find books centred around Anthroposophy, a philosophy created by Rudolf Steiner. All the authors on display are unfamiliar, but I allow myself a small luxury: purchasing a copy of *Ulysses* and Joyce's poem, *Bahnhofstrasse*.

After this, I stroll down Bahnhofstrasse, hoping to see it through the eyes of the author, reciting the poem in my mind while gazing up at the buildings and streets from time to time. Joyce had famously claimed that *Bahnhofstrasse* was so clean that one could drink minestrone off the pavement. As it stands, it was over a century ago when things were different.

The eyes that mock me sign the way

Whereto I pass at eve of day.

Grey way whose violet signals are

The trysting and the twining star.

Ah star of evil! star of pain!

Highhearted youth comes not again

Nor old heart's wisdom yet to know

The signs that mock me as I go.

A visit to Joyce's grave seems appropriate.

A ten-minute drive from Zurich city centre takes you to the Fluntern Cemetery, Joyce's final resting place. It is not very hard to locate his grave; it lies all the way in the back of the cemetery, surrounded by a green field. A simple slab marks the births and deaths of the writer, his wife, son, and daughter-in-law. There is no sign of anyone having come this way lately. The wind blows through the trees. It is peaceful and calm, a nice place to rest in eternity. There is a statue of Joyce as an old man, reading a book and judging the world with a piqued curiosity only Joyce could have.

*

The James Joyce pub at Pelikanstasse is where I end the day, combining it with a little bit of exploring and an evening of merry-making, chiefly through an excess of wine and beer.

White wine is like electricity. Red wine looks and tastes like liquefied beefsteak, James Joyce once declared. Here, I share his view.

This pub has an interesting backstory.

When the old Jury's Hotel in Dame Street, Dublin, was demolished in the early 70s, it was agreed to spare the old interior of the antique bar and put it up for auction. Then, the Swiss friends of Ireland stepped in, and it was ultimately acquired by the Union Bank of Switzerland and lovingly assembled in Zurich piece by piece.

Dublin's Antique Bar was allegedly one of the author's favourite haunts and featured in many of his novels. The long bar with its counter of thick burnished mahogany, the gleaming brass rail, and the intricately detailed wood, mosaic tiles, and paintings give off a feeling of being in 1940s Dublin. I have not known the Dublin of the 1940s, but like any writer, I am influenced by reading about it and, in equal measure, intrigued by the rich interiors. Stories pop into my mind sooner than I can finish my drink.

I peruse the elegant menu with its informative essay on the history of the building, and I am pleased to find that I can have a choice of three of Ireland's finest whiskeys, Irish coffee, or an exotic concoction of rum, apricot brandy, and orange juice called the Anna Livia Plurabelle. But in the memory of James Joyce, I settle for his favourite white wine, *Fendant de Sion*.

The food is slow in coming, but I am happy just to bite down on the James Joyce burger and the plentiful onion rings in it. Served with a slice of history, the burger helps me tie up the day into a neat little box.

*

For the second day in a row, I am back at Gran Motta café for breakfast, eating the same thing and waving at the same train. The morning is pleasant enough to walk. In some time, however, rain is predicted. But until that happens, I get a move on, seeking inspiration here and there, reminiscing every movie or book set in Zurich. Robert Ludlum's *Jason Bourne* had fled the American Embassy in Zurich, a scene I particularly enjoyed watching. The trams, the people, and the buildings look familiar, mostly from watching the film repeatedly and less from my earlier visits.

Switzerland may not be the world's fashion capital, but strolling along the Bahnhofstrasse, Zurich's shopping street packed with high-end brands might easily convince you otherwise. It is easily one of the world's most expensive and famous shopping streets. If you are up for it, grab designer wear and get boasting rights for shopping here, or of course, you can stick to window shopping.

I have a great fondness for Zurich—although not enough to call it home—but I love walking around, looking for anything I have missed before, especially in the Old Town area. One such discovery was the famous, twin-towered Grossmünster Church. I quickly learnt that the church's fame rests on the Affair of the Sausages, an event that sparked the Protestant Reformation in Switzerland in 1522 on the first Sunday of Lent.

Somehow, the mention of sausages makes me hungry, and I set out to surprise myself by dropping into Haus Hiltl at Sihlstrasse 28 for vegetarian fare. I'd probably not speak of Switzerland and vegetarianism in the same sentence again, but currently, my idea is being challenged. I'm not the one to skip the traditional Swiss meal and go vegetarian, but I am looking forward to the change in diet.

Haus Hiltl is a *Guinness Record* holder for being the world's oldest continuously open vegetarian restaurant. One cannot ignore the fact that places older than Haus Hiltl may exist in Asia, but there is no record of their existence, which puts this Zurich restaurant at the top of the list.

The more popular buffet section is on the ground floor, while a la carte meals are served on the first floor.

When I walk in, I am amazed by the amount of natural light streaming in through the floor-to-ceiling windows that bring the outdoors inside, which, right now, is rain. Through the slanting glass wall of the kitchen, it is possible to peek inside at the chefs absorbed in their curries and pasta. There is a variety of Indian dishes on the menu, too, and I have to resist the temptation to pile my plate too high because here, one pays by weight. I come away extremely satisfied with the beetroot carpaccio and Gnocchi with oven-roasted Pumpkin and a small helping of an eggplant dish, a popular Indian offering.

*

I board the 1.30 p.m. train to Geneva, marvelling at the height and immensity of Swiss double-decker trains standing at the station and involuntarily thanking the Swiss train system. I had begun with a question: How does one follow in the footsteps of Byron in Switzerland? That question is easily answered, considering that you no longer need horses or guides for that purpose. A simple Swiss Pass is the answer because it allows you unlimited travel for four days or longer if you want to linger on and breathe on all railways, boats, and alpine postbuses.

It is, frankly, the only way to travel.

*

Footnotes:

- *Joyce passed away in Switzerland on 13th January 1941, and because Switzerland was his home as much as Dublin was, he was buried here.*
- *Fluntern Cemetery can be reached from the city center by streetcars Nos. 5 or 6 in 20 minutes.*

Chapter 5

M y train to Geneva leaves at noon.

In an article published in the *Chicago Tribune* in 1892, Mark Twain wrote:

There are only two best ways to travel through Switzerland. The first best is afoot. The second best is by open two-horse carriage.

A frequent traveller and not one to shy away from a little grandiloquence, Twain lamented that the construction of ladder railways had destroyed the beauty of the majestic mountains since he had seen them last. *The peasant of the high altitudes will have to carry a lantern when he goes visiting in the night to keep from stumbling over railroads that have been built since his last round,* Twain wrote scathingly.

In the present, I am afraid Twain's observations would be laughed away as presumptuous. Swiss trains are by no means an enemy to the peasants. They are the living and breathing examples of precision and beauty. I laugh lightly as I board the classic red-and-white train heading to Geneva, Switzerland's second most populous city in the French-speaking area of the country.

Situated at the southwest end of Lake Geneva close to the Jura Mountains, Geneva is an important financial centre, and according to author Padraig Rooney, 'has always been a town of worthies.'

Geneva is in a class of its own. It has yielded a significant influence on writers and philosophers. Consider this: Jean-Jacques Rousseau was born in Geneva, and his influence was so powerful that years later, Lord Byron and the Shelleys visited the city because of the influence the Swiss philosopher's bestselling novel *Julie, or the New Heloise,* wielded. Joseph Conrad visited and partly set *Under Western Eyes* in the city. Hitherto, I associated Conrad with Congo, and how little did I know! In more recent times, Robert Ludlum, Stella Rimington, Dan Brown, and Robert Harris set their novels in Geneva.

In 1816, Byron and Shelley had seen no reason to linger here; Byron complained in a letter that he was followed about his hotel garden by 'staring boobies'—or, more politely, English tourists. So, the two groups relocated to the secluded farming village of Cologny near Geneva—Byron to the spectacular Villa Diodati and the Shelleys to the more modest Maison Chapuis by the lakeshore.

Lake Geneva's 167 km shoreline is packed with literary associations. From the 18th-century French philosopher and novelist Jean-Jacques Rousseau to the latter-day poets David Bowie and Freddie Mercury, writers have visited, stayed, and been inspired by the ultra-picturesque combinations of water, mountains, vineyards, and castles that are visible from its shores. For as long as literature has been created here, literary tourism has also been practiced—often by the authors themselves.

But for me, Lake Geneva is the legacy of Byron and the Shelleys. Mary Shelley was inspired by the beauty and terror of its landscape and Byron by its turbulent political history. Henry James took his inspiration from its culture of international luxury travel. In the Lake Geneva region of Switzerland, each of these writers found something that fed their imagination and allowed them to create unique works of literature.

Hoping to get a sense of how Lake Geneva inspired such creativity, I decide to spend a few days tracking down some of the places where the Romantic poets spent their time, a task that will entail visiting one ravishing lakeside village after another.

*

Upon arriving in Geneva, I head straight to Cologny, now a luxurious neighbourhood with a manicured main square. Today, the village is a Geneva suburb and one of Europe's most exclusive residential addresses. But more than its real estate or snob value, it houses today's most famous literary houses in Geneva.

I walk up the steep hill from the bus stop to the imposing Villa Diodati. I experience a sense of pride as I draw closer. I am about to know my muse a little more intimately. The house is privately owned and can't be entered, but a sign in the park next to it welcomes visitors from all over the world to enjoy the superb view of the lake and ponder the origins of one of the world's most famous horror stories.

Its exterior has changed very little from 19th-century engravings, including the expansive balcony where Byron finished the third canto of his epic poem *Childe Harold's Pilgrimage*. However, the vineyards that once tumbled down to the water are now flower-filled gardens, and Maison Chapuis is gone.

This villa was once famous for its scandals; people would stop by to peer at women's underwear on the clothesline, and one British newspaper called it a 'league of incest.'

The gates are open, and I follow a group through it, imagining the bohemians of 1816 in the *Year Without Summer* gathered by candlelight in the upstairs dining room debating, with wine flowing copiously and perhaps laudanum. I picture the surreal atmosphere, the raging storm—within the hearts and outside—and the heated discussions between Lord Byron, John Polidori, and Percy Shelly. I imagine the claustrophobia, the heaviness of words, both said and unsaid, stories churning the minds… and *Frankenstein* being born to Mary Shelly's pen.

Collectively, that summer, they gave the world some of the finest pieces of literature. Byron's poem *The Prisoner of Chillon*, Mary Shelley's *Frankenstein*, and a short story by young physician John Polidori called *The Vampyre*, which went on to become the influence for Bram Stoker's *Dracula*.

Ironically, it was the time everyone believed that the runaway poet Byron was drinking heavily, abusing drugs, and wasting away. Eventually, and thanks to a night in the Year Without Summer, the speculation was finally put to rest.

Here, I quote Patrick Vincent, professor of English and American literature at the University of Neuchâtel.

Everybody was spying on Byron and spreading rumours. The idea he was drinking a lot and taking drugs was a myth. He mainly just wrote when he was here. He was depressed about leaving England and the fact that his wife had left him. He felt guilty and abandoned by his half-sister. There was this tension which was so inspiring and led to great creativity over those five months.

When it is time to leave, I stand on the bench for the last glimpse of the villa beyond its beautifully planted garden, wishing I'd bought a copy of *Frankenstein* and taken a photograph of it at its place of birth.

*

It is not surprising that Geneva has a guided tour of the city's literary heritage, something I am pleasantly surprised to discover. Thus, I end up visiting the House of Rousseau and Literature in the Old Town, which provides an overview of the life and works of this influential Swiss philosopher. Rousseau, the son of a clockmaker, often upset the locals with his radical ideas. He even ran away from the town to avoid being thrashed for stealing apples. His childhood was full of books: "*I read at the worktable, I read on my errands, I read in the wardrobe, and forgot myself for hours together.*"

Voltaire, a fellow philosopher, was not born in Switzerland, but in 1755, he managed to offend royalty. The French King had banned him from Paris, so Voltaire fled to Geneva. His charming home, *Les Délices*, is now the Voltaire Institute and Museum, opened in 1952.

*

In the evening, I stroll around Lake Geneva. People walk their dogs along the lakeshore promenade, and sailboats glide by serenely, and across the lake, the peaks of the French Alps loom. They remind me that here, within the sight of this civilized city, is the majestic and 'terrifically desolate' landscape that inspired Mary Shelley's horror story.

Some old people smile and nod while passing me by. The sky is cloudless and blue, and countless milky swans swim in the lake, oblivious to the pleasure the sight of them brings. Here, life revolves around the big lake in the city's heart. Inside the lake, the Jet d'Eau shoots 140 m above the lake with an impressive five hundred litres of water per second and at 200 km an hour.

*

After the morning coffee is consumed, I allow my thoughts to return to Byron's five months in Switzerland in 1816, which impacted English literature and culture in general and, more specifically, tourism. He had toured the Alps on horseback and by carriage with his companion John Cam Hobhouse, following a guidebook route, and had taken notes. One of his journals contained a letter written for his half-sister Augusta, in which he waxes lyrical about the landscape, the quality of his mattress, and the singing locals:

In the evening, four Swiss peasant girls from Oberhasli came and sang the airs of their country... the airs are so wild and original and at the same time of great sweetness, he wrote.

*

I am not keen on a horseback tour of the Alps, so soon after breakfast, I head to Yvoire on the first class on a passenger ferry. This seems somewhat extravagant, but the idea of sipping coffee out in the open air without jostling with fellow passengers is charming.

Yvoire is a small village nestling on the French side of Lake Geneva, and it is, I am led to understand, straight out of the fairytale. I can do with some fairytales and magic.

My curiosity, if I say so myself, runs ahead of me. Will there be abandoned castles and fancy French wine served in enchanting restaurants?

Every man's life ends the same way. Only the details of how he lived and died distinguish one man from another. I might as well have some magical moments weaved into it.

*

We halt at three different ports before finally arriving at Yvoire. Arriving is an uninspired way of describing the moment—for, I should say, we sail into this beautiful little village springing upwards from the lake, which is overlooked by a castle perched on the headland. It stands there like a sentinel, protecting this village—but that could just be my imagination.

Slowly, I disembark, trying to keep myself from falling over. Like me, the first-time visitors to this magical village are gaping open-mouthed. I don't mind being a tourist this morning.

Yvoire is beautiful, and whoever called it the most beautiful village in France said it right. It is nearing the end of winter, and flowers are springing to life. The village is bathed in the mixed fragrance of spring flowers.

A small brown board announces the highlights, of which I make a mental note and join the stream of tourists up the narrow path. Small restaurants appear within a short distance from the pier, and with that comes the delicious smells of food cooking behind the old wooden doors. Souvenir shops thrive here and are full of precious goods—the kind loved by tourists looking to seal their eternal love with the place in the form of a fridge magnet or a cap.

There is not much time to examine every souvenir on display, for I must make it back to the ferry in three hours. And because I can't trawl the internet for information on Byron or Hemingway's visit here, I put them aside for the moment and immerse myself in the beauty of this 14th-century medieval village, walking rapidly towards The Garden of Five Senses, a spectacular little garden within the castle grounds with enough to please all the senses. Hundreds of fragrant flowers, fruits, and other plants, the labyrinths, and the beautiful architecture provide a unique experience.

The narrow streets of Yvoire are full of old alpine-style buildings with stone walls, steep roofs, wooden balconies, and shutters, and eventually, I arrive at The Saint Pancras Church, a landmark visible from every corner of the village. The Church of Saint Pancras, with its distinct 'onion' dome, is as stunning as it appeared from afar. This church dates back to the 11th century and has undergone many renovations but still retains its antiquity. I dash for the bell tower for a quick overview of the lake and village. It has a quaint charm befitting a fairytale village. There are two gates to enter this little village, which are not too helpful today but were used in the past to keep the enemy away. The gates are classified as Historic Monuments and are protected. I walk around the village, looking up at the old ramparts, and am surprised to see that in the olden days, houses were built into the ramparts!

This quick dash to see the village's highlights has made me hungry, and I see no reason to skip what promises to be a great meal, given the aroma of food wafting through the village.

Every restaurant in sight is packed with customers, and my option is to accept the small chair and a corner of the table to share with a dozen others. I think I am about to eat from my neighbour's plate. Such is the seating arrangement here. No one seems to mind it, though. This is how restaurants function here. People from the cruise boat walk in, eat, and hurry out without lingering aimlessly, scanning the menu, or being anal about their choices. You eat what you get.

I get lamb shanks and coffee.

But under the patch of sun and the noisy crowd, the reality of Yvoire strikes me. The village completely empties out during winter, leaving behind the seventy-five inhabitants and about seven hundred around it. But in the season between June and September, it manages to cater to nearly 1.2 million visitors, a feat not easy to achieve.

I'll give it to the French—they are excellent at stretching their working hours and never drop their smile even with the pressure of thousands of mouths to feed. I think their inspiration comes from the excellent wines.

Slowly, I walk back to the pier with ten minutes to spare, all the while wondering why this village has sunk into anonymity and remained roofless for three centuries.

Chapter 6

A short train journey from Geneva brings me to Lausanne, the Olympic Capital of the World. Lausanne is a city of pretty chalets overlooking Lake Geneva, overshadowed by the snow-capped French Alps. And somewhere in those mountains is a little village named Evian that produces some of the world's most sought-after drinking water.

I am in time to check in to my hotel, which lies within easy walking distance of the train station. Choosing to stay here is the best decision so far because I am not entirely at the mercy of taxis or buses to bring me to the hotel and back to the station. As far as my onward journey to Montreux is concerned, I have little to worry about, considering the number of trains going that way for the short journey. But it is a force of habit.

Lausanne is not a huge city, but from the hotel balcony, I see a small but steep city and recall with some satisfaction what Hemingway had said of Switzerland.

Switzerland is a small, steep country, much more up and down than sideways, and is all stuck over with large brown hotels built on the cuckoo clock style of architecture.

He was, I assume, referring not to all of Switzerland but to Lausanne specifically. The town is laid out on a series of hills, with stunning views across the lake to the French Alps, but it looks rather overbuilt in recent years.

The hotel coffee is passable, but I am counting on finding a café in the Old Town that will do a better job of it. With that thought, I saunter towards Switzerland's first metro built on a steep hill, which is touted as an engineering feat, right outside the train station. The M2 line connects the Old Town to all the tourist attractions.

For over two centuries, artists, poets, and authors have come to Lausanne to find peace, making it somewhat hard to digest the fact that this city was once a military camp for Roman soldiers. But at some point in history, it became a refuge for literary talents.

For example, the French novelist Benjamin Constant was born in Lausanne. The Chinese author of *A Many-Splendoured Thing,* Han Suyin, lived here for years until her death. Georges Simenon, the creator of Inspector Maigret and my favourite mystery writer, died in Lausanne, as did playwright Jean Anouilh. But it could have been the arrival of historian Edward Gibbon in Lausanne—to finish writing *The Decline and Fall of the Roman Empire*—that changed the city's reputation, which led to the famous visit by Byron and Shelly.

Ernest Hemingway's connection with Lausanne is well documented. He first breezed into Switzerland from Paris in 1922 to cover the International Peace Conference in Lausanne for the *Toronto Star.* Later, he put his protagonists, a nurse, and a recovering, war-wounded soldier in his famous *A Farewell to Arms*, in neutral Switzerland. In the book, the nurse gets pregnant, but it ends in a stillbirth in a Lausanne hospital.

Hemingway's initial days in Lausanne may not have been very joyous, considering that his wife Hadley was robbed at Gare de Lyon, Paris, on her way to join him in Lausanne, thereby losing all of his manuscripts and notes.

It contained everything I had written. She was bringing the manuscripts down to me to Lausanne as a surprise. She had put in the originals, the typescripts and the carbons, all in manila folders, he later wrote.

Despite this setback, the couple spent four months in the hinterland above Montreux. But the marriage didn't last. Five years later, in 1927, Hemingway returned to Switzerland with his second wife, the Vogue correspondent Pauline Pfeiffer. She shared her husband's journalistic views.

*

The M2 is a fully automated subway system connecting Ouchy to the northern suburb via the central station, Flon, with several stops in Old Town. The metro system is a little surprising, with some very steep stations, particularly the Gare, which is tilted about 30 degrees. The Bessieres station near the cathedral, for which I need to take the elevator from the station up to the bridge, also gives me a chance to see the city directly below through the windows, a kind of experience I have never had before.

Lausanne's Old Town is cobbled and steep, and I am grateful for my shoes, but once too often, I am forced to stop for breath, inviting smiles and disapproving stares alternatively. The one thing that strikes me is Lausanne's coziness. It is there in the buildings, the streets, the people jostling about, and the aroma of food, which is a particularly welcome change. Lausanne feels festive. I am sure the locals are very proud of it, too. The city's skyline is pleasantly devoid of skyscrapers or tower blocks. In their place are delightfully crooked rooftops and ornate spires, but that's not to say Lausanne is stuck in the past. Remember what I mentioned about it being the world's Olympic Capital? Being here makes me feel connected with the heart of Lausanne and its fabulous Renaissance buildings. The combination of old and new is present in everything, from the culinary scene to the architecture, and is reflected in the very core of its existence.

Soon, I find myself in the middle of Lausanne's main shopping area, and a series of wrong turns later, I reach Place de la Palud, where the splendid Town Hall lies. I say this because of the massive, animated clock, which has a band of Vaudois gentlemen marching across it at noon. This place is packed. It takes some effort to recreate the scene in 1787 when Edward

Gibbon penned the last line of *The History of the Decline and Fall of the Roman Empire.*

"The silver orb of the moon was reflected from the waters, and all nature was silent," Gibbon had written of Lausanne. Here, I must confess I haven't read Gibbon's big book. It's on my bucket list.

At present, Lausanne is at its noisy best, and it takes a huge amount of historical imagination to picture this city as a quiet, pastoral village. However, the success of the book, especially among Romantic writers, put Lausanne on the literary map. That leads me to wonder why

Lausanne never created the buzz of Paris in the 1920s, even though a steady stream of writers like Shelley, Victor Hugo, Charles Dickens, and Thomas Hardy followed Gibbon to Lausanne.

Gibbon, the hero of the Romantic movement, and his house, *La Grotte*, became a literary magnet. Less than three decades after Gibbon's death, Byron undertook a literary pilgrimage to his residence on June 27, the anniversary of the date when Gibbon penned the last line of *The Decline and Fall.* Later, the house was knocked down to make way for the Lausanne Post Office in 1896.

Lausanne has the attractions of a metropolis but without the size.

And this is just what makes strolling around such a pleasure. The pedestrian area, like the Place de la Palud and the Rue de Bourg, has some particularly charming boutiques if one likes to shop.

I don't.

*

Perhaps Lausanne's best-kept secret is the Escaliers du Marché, a series of covered wooden stairs leading up to the

Gothic Cathedral from Place de la Palud. What is interesting is that these steps are over 400 years old. It is well preserved, with no dangerous or ugly cracks in the wood. After briefly exploring the shops, galleries, and restaurants to the left of the stairways, I begin my slow climb up the stairs. The bookshop owner tells me the stairs are the most direct way to the Rue Pierre-Viret, which lies below the cathedral.

It is, without a doubt, steep, but from a few vantage points, it offers breathtaking views of Lausanne. I discover this because I am forced to stop once too often to catch my breath, which is embarrassing, for more than once, locals of advanced age easily climb past me without pausing for breath.

Google says: *The upper part of the stairway was interrupted in 1911 with the construction of Rue Pierre-Viret, the continuation of the Pont Bessières bridge. Until the 14th century, the city market was held on a square built to the right of the staircase, hence the name. Traces of it can still be seen in the shade of the trees at the bottom of Rue Pierre-Viret.*

For those who get short of breath, there are other, less strenuous ways up to the cathedral, but these creaky old covered wooden stairs are the most picturesque. Some of the wooden pillars and beams are ancient, and partway up is a shaded courtyard with a fountain and benches.

The houses alongside the stairs are pretty to look at, too; you can easily find a chocolatier, a store of arms (on every picture of Lausanne taken from the cathedral, you can't miss the ARMES written on top of a building), or boutiques. The ARMES, of course, is a dead giveaway as to the nature of its business!

At the top of the stairs on the left is Le Barbare, a historical café known for its thick hot chocolate; one version says the chocolate is so thick you can stand the spoon up in it. I am taking it at face value because, at any given time, I am all for coffee to restore my mettle.

This establishment has been awarded the label of *Café historique de Lausanne*.

When I finally reach the cathedral, I am breathless but in total awe of the city. The cathedral is surrounded by lovely old buildings, mostly from the 17th and 18th centuries. Near the cathedral is the 15th century Château St-Maire, where the Vaudois government sits.

The cathedral was originally the residence of the Bishops of Lausanne, but when the Canton de Vaud was part of Bern, it became the residence of the Bernese bailiffs.

The cathedral was built in the 12th and 13th centuries and continues to woo people looking for Gothic architecture. The façade, however, looks like it has had a facelift recently, but it does not take away the romance associated with it. Feeling particularly bucked up after the coffee, I climb to the top of the tower, marvelling at the view of the lake, the French Alps, and the city of Lausanne itself.

Interestingly, this cathedral is one of the last few cathedrals in Europe to have a night watchman who cries the hours between 10 p.m. and 2 a.m.

I walk back to my hotel. The distance as the crow flies is short, but I make a few stops in between to nourish my mind and spirit, spending a good hour in Flon, the city's nightspot.

Stumbling into my hotel, I am greeted by the stern-looking doorman.

From his manner, I figure he is used to guests arriving in a similar state. He politely wishes me a good night and directs me to the lift. I have some difficulty remembering my floor at first, but after tugging at my hair sharply, I suddenly remember.

From my hotel balcony, the city appears like a twinkling—a somewhat miniature version of Kigali, Rwanda.

I go to bed thinking of the night watchman bellowing out the time. It doesn't feel at all unusual.

*

Following a light breakfast of eggs and coffee, I head out to Ouchy for my Lausanne connection with Lord Byron, retracing my steps to the M2 slowly, unworried about the onward journey to Montreux.

Hotel Angleterre.

Byron had arrived at this hotel—that went by the name of Hôtel de l'Ancre—on a replica of a Napoleon coach with his monkey and a peacock. He wrote *The Prisoner of Chillon* while staying here.

From the outside, it looks like a classic Swiss resort, with manicured gardens and stone façades, set at the edge of Lake Geneva. I stroll around the gardens blooming with flowers like I assume lord Byron would have done, with my hands in my pockets and my head tilted at an angle to suggest deep thought. Unsurprisingly, a handful of people are doing the same, watching ferries cruising the lake in the distance and imagining the hotel's original appeal. Hotel Angleterre is sufficiently high-functioning and appears to be the local top choice for conferences. One such conference is taking place now, going by the number of parked cars and suited men dashing in and out.

I go in for a beer and look at the insides. The hotel does not lack history or atmosphere. Hotel Angleterre counts Lord Byron as a one-time resident. I imagine the hotel has significantly changed since 1816, so that's still impressive.

I find a table for two at L'Accademia easily. A smiling waiter in black and white appears out of nowhere and pulls out the chair for me. He then arranges the menu and waits politely by my side. I look up at his face and smile. He is tall, with white hair parted at the side. His narrow face and smile lines put him at around fifty years of age. His eyes are grey, like the reflection of the lake outside the glass windows.

My order is simple. Beer.

"I'll look at the lunch menu later," I say.

The waiter bows slightly and marches away with a grace only a waiter of a long-standing service can.

To my far left is a group of women huddled over the table, murmuring passionately while their small white dogs nap under the tables, looking just as aristocratic as one imagines the guests in Byron's day. The tables to my right are unoccupied, and apart from five other guests enjoying lunch or beer, there is little else to distract the water.

My beer arrives cold. I am eager to talk.

"May I have a word?" I ask.

"Yes, Madam. I am happy to help."

On his cue, I order lunch because it will be at least twenty minutes in the making. My lunch is a mix of pasta from Napoli and seasonal fish stew, an excellent choice, according to him.

He goes away with my order. When he returns, he seems more relaxed and even begins the conversation with a smile.

"Now, we can talk. How can I help you? You are looking for information, yes? The hotel's history?"

I don't ask him how he figured that out and instead pick his brains as best as I can. Perhaps he is not expecting a Q&A about a poet who died two centuries ago, but he gives his best shot at handing information to me he is privy to.

"You can still feel the presence of greatness in these walls. Lord Byron had been our honoured guest."

He exudes the pride of a time his forefathers must have witnessed.

*

To follow the footsteps of Byron in Switzerland, a train journey to Montreux and Castle Chillon is de rigueur.

An early evening train takes me to Montreux, a lovely town on the northeast shore of Lake Geneva, in the Swiss Riviera—the gateway to Chillon Castle. I know very little about Montreux, but I intend to make my first trip to this ritzy town memorable. All I know of this city is through the song *Smoke on the Water* by Deep Purple, which, in turn, was inspired by a fire that broke out during a Frank Zappa performance long before I was born. The fire ate up the venue and sent smoke across Lake Geneva, thus inspiring that song. That association is not entirely pleasant.

The train conductors are rather grumpy, and the cars are stuffy and unclean. There is nobody in my car except for an old gentleman who appears quite drunk and a young mother and her daughter wrapped up in wool. The young mother smiles at me and attempts a conversation in French. The conversation develops thanks to Google Translate, and she tells me quite excitedly, "*Vladimir Nabokov. Vous devez visiter la tombe de Nabokov.*"

I understand what that means, but until now, I had not given that activity a deeper thought.

I nod affirmative and follow that up with a smile and a thumbs up. As I look outside the train's window, I see the Swiss landscape passing by like a dream. Old farmhouses sail by one after another in an endless show of beauty.

"How very beautiful," I say to no one in particular. "A place suited for the gods."

"Oui, beautiful." Her accent is odd, but it manages to convey her thoughts on the subject. Language is no impediment when trying to express an emotion. The train stops. We have arrived.

For historians, this chocolate-box town on Lac Léman represents the signing of the Montreux Convention of 1936, through which Soviet Russia, Turkey, Bulgaria, and other nations sought to regulate the status of the Black Sea straits. To its visitors, Montreux is, above all, a place of music and musicians—be it jazz, blues, or classic rock. A monumental Freddie Mercury stands on the lakefront, posing as a tap dancer and greeting the tourists.

But for me, Montreux is the most important stop on my Byronic trail.

The station is pretty, and the very sight of it puts me in a better mood. I picture myself bumping into Hemingway and being invited for coffee at The Buffet de la Gare, standing at the station platform. The smile doesn't leave my face as I take myself to this café, which became the setting for Hemingway's short story, *A Homage to Switzerland*, a quiet, understated story unlike the usual Hemingway-style. In the story, a young waitress who speaks German and French becomes the target of the lust of three American men. One of them offers his money to spend the night with him. She refuses.

The story of Hemingway goes like this: he arrived in Montreux on the Simplon-Montreux train and waited awhile for another train to take him up to Les Avants, where he rented a house. At the time of his arrival, he was writing *A Farewell to Arms*. So moved was he by the beauty of Montreux that he turned it into a haven for his characters—nurse Catherine Barkley and her lover Lieutenant Henry.

The city did not leave Hemingway because, forty years later, Hemingway remembered Montreux in *A Moveable Feast*.

*

Hemingway was the one for gossip, as history has me believe. And he loved trains so much that he knew all the train timetables of the world by heart. A man after my own heart, as I have always maintained. Like Lord Byron, he was among the few celebrities and artists who eventually found fame and left their mark on this city. Lovers of Hemingway following him to Montreux to this day continue what he did decades earlier while waiting for the train—have a coffee and a croissant while waiting for their train or going about their destination.

Not the one to break tradition, I quietly order the same, although, in my heart, I believe that he'd have preferred a Bloody Mary over coffee any day. That was more his style. No one is surprised at this. Around me, everyone is enjoying the same order. Papa lives on in Montreux's coffeehouse, ever present like that steam in a coffee cup.

The café's simple appearance belies the treasures of this old restaurant. Its tranquillity and the stunning view of the lake are unmatched. Coffee partaken I make my way to Hotel Suisse Majestic. I am looking forward to a long walk along the lake.

*

In the early evening, the view from the quay is jaw-dropping, with its vista of the lake and the impressive Dents du Midi mountains that change colours from blue to pink and white to gold. Montreux is magnificent. The countless silhouettes of the hills and mountains stand out picturesquely against the pink sky. A full moon shines as the icing on the cake of the scenery.

It is the sort of setting that allows my mind to wander and ruminate. My being here is the result of my wanderings in Kathmandu, Nepal. It was there I'd heard of the *Pudding Shop* in Istanbul. It was there I learned about Lord Byron through my desperate urge for apple pie from the famed *Snowman café* on Freak Street. Had it not been for that chilly evening in Kathmandu, the lights going out, my bag rolling off the table and scattering everything on the floor, me rummaging in the pale light from the paraffin lamps, I'd have never found that book—*Midnight Express* by Billy Hayes. When the lights had flickered back on, I realized I had picked up someone else's book from under the table. Drawn to the title, I opened the book to find these lines written in cursive, like someone justifying their travel choice to a loved one.

There is a pleasure in the pathless woods...

Under that line was a name I couldn't read, but that one sentence stuck. It kept playing back to me. When I eventually found where it came from, I was already sold on the idea of finding pleasure in pathless woods and Byron.

From the dusty, fading interiors of *The Snowman* café in Nepal to the mystic Istanbul café named *The Pudding Shop* to the glitzy Montreux, I have come a long way in the steps of Byron, but it is in this city that those words ring true.

Montreux has not seen marijuana-smoking hippies since the 1960s. Instead, it has seen advancements in science and literature, starting with the pharmacist Henri Nestlé, who developed the first milk formula for infants; Igor Stravinsky, who composed part of Rite of Spring; and Tchaikovsky, who wrote Violin Concerto after fleeing from his wife. Tchaikovsky stayed in a villa on the quay nearby, previously occupied by William the Third, the eccentric King of the Netherlands.

Is it just possible that I hear Tchaikovsky's music in the lake? Or do I see tendrils of smoke rising from the lake?
Not far away, the Montreux Palace Hotel towers grandly above the quay. I stare at it thoughtfully. It was Vladimir Nabokov's home following the success of his novel *Lolita*. Montreux invites great appreciation, and nothing pleases me more than a closer inspection of it.

French-speaking Montreux has always enjoyed a star status among the world's rich and famous. The famous American actor Charlie Chaplin was smitten by the city and spent 25 years at Manoir de Ban during his self-imposed exile in Switzerland. Nearby, Villeneuve welcomed Mahatma Gandhi and Victor Hugo in the past.

To get a feel of Old Town, I amble around its narrow cobblestone alleys. The streets flaunt ornate Belle Epoque buildings. Trams and cars purr about the 17th and 18th-century mansions, and I enjoy the breathtaking Alpine views, inhaling what I assume to be the scent of pines. I can't be sure, though. I continue strolling until I reach the Town Centre, where I spend time in an elegant, covered market brimming with fresh produce.

*

Today is my day to reconnect with Lord Byron. My arrival in Montreux yesterday was not so momentous, but today is the most important in my journey. It is a journey I am looking forward to. Today, I will venture into the heart of my quest. I finally understand what Ghassan had said to me in Paris.

There is no love like the love for someone who died two centuries ago.

Yes. That kind of love. Unrequited, soulful, and imaginary. That is what I am feeling right now. I hope my visit to Chillon Castle will prove to be a double pilgrimage, complimenting the multilayered nature of my literary question.

Byron's visit in 1816 produced *The Prisoner of Chillon,* and sixty years after him came American author Henry James, who found inspiration in the simple act of literary tourism. That led him to Chillon castle, and like Byron, he set a vital part of his book *Daisy Miller* there. The only irony is that Bonivard, the protagonist of Byron's poem, was a 15th-century patriot chained for four years in the castle's dungeons, while Daisy of James's story was a free spirit imprisoned by social convention.

I am going to see the castle that inspired both versions.

*

The way I proceed to my destination does not differ vastly from that of Byron—both of us choosing the way of the water on a side-wheeled paddle steamer (although mine is electricity-powered) operated by the Lake Geneva Navigation Company.

The scenery is spectacular, but it gets better as we approach the château, the home of the former Counts of Savoy. The château's turrets, swans, clouds, and mountains are reflected in the blue lake, giving an incredible allure in contrast to the power struggles and conflicts that mark Chillon's history. As we draw closer, my first thought is that I have travelled through time to become a part of a vintage painting.

The oval-shaped castle is set on a rocky outcrop and looks forlorn and cold. Byron wasn't as fascinated with the pretty exterior as he was with what lay within its stone walls, and he'd later declared that *Chillon was a great place to visit, but I couldn't imagine living there.* His impressions were created by the story of Francois Bonivard, and mine is the result of Byron's observation.

I am about to discover why Byron has that effect on me.

*

I discover that a self-guided tour of the castle is just as enlightening as a guided tour. The audio commentary is excellent. I listen intently to every bit of information pouring into my ears. It turns out that this castle was not just a summer residence for the Savoy's but a profitable toll station and housed a prison in its depths. It is not a big castle. Stairs lead you through endless chambers—many with traces of the original medieval frescoes—into the highest keep, where every arrow slit offers a stunning lake view.

I proceed to the prison chambers, the site where, once upon a time, witches were tortured before being burnt alive in the castle's courtyard. The waters of Lake Geneva crash into the prison walls, and the soft sound carries inside the dungeons, making me shudder slightly.

Byron had once descended into one of these subterranean chambers, pictured Bonivard shackled to the pillar, and devised the heart-rending poem. He had then etched his name on the column, although this fact is subject to discussion. He took away a sense of the place, which echoed in his work.

Lake Leman lies by Chillon's walls:

A thousand feet in depth below

Its massy waters meet and flow;

Thus much the fathom-line was sent

From Chillon's snow-white battlement,

Which round about the wave inthralls:

A double dungeon wall and wave

Have made—and like a living grave

Below the surface of the lake

The dark vault lies wherein we lay:

We heard it ripple night and day;

Sounding o'er our heads it knock'd;

And I have felt the winter's spray

Wash through the bars when winds were high

And wanton in the happy sky;

And then the very rock hath rock'd,

And I have felt it shake, unshock'd,

Because I could have smiled to see

The death that would have set me free…

In these lines, François Bonivard comes alive. The romantic narrative Byron weaved, imagining the impact of the death of his brothers before his eyes and his own torment and wish for death, makes for a powerful reflection of the dark times. That poem alone is why Château de Chillon has remained one of Switzerland's most popular tourist attractions for the past two hundred years.

*

For as long as I've known of Byron, I have considered him a great lover, poet, romantic, mischievous, self-centred, blasphemous, and even gay. There was some joy in knowing someone so similar in nature to myself that I rarely thought of him as a man. But momentarily, when I run my fingers over his name on the pillar in the dungeon, he comes alive. It is as though I am caressing him, then kissing his lips gently before sliding my hands down his back and pulling him close. I bend down to kiss his name with my eyes closed, and I picture us together, here in the dungeon with the cold seeping out of the walls, and his…

In this moment of thoughtfulness, he belongs to me.

*

After this, there is nothing left to see. I have had my moment with Lord Byron. I don't think I will ever come so close to feeling him within me again. I sit by the lake and watch the people weaving in and out of the chateau, some with dismay on their faces and some with a smile. The few children accompanying their parents on this tour appear glad to be out in the open. The sky is turning grey, and suddenly, the water changes colour. The sudden change is unsettling.

Strange as it may seem, Byron, while struck by the beauty of the Swiss countryside, his attitude towards the Swiss people was far from friendly. He didn't think highly about living here.

In this regard, I defer from Byron because I believe the beauty of Switzerland is unmatched, and to live in these environs would be a definite advantage. Byron had been bold about expressing his opinions to Thomas Moore in 1821— *Switzerland is a curst selfish, swinish country of brutes, placed in the most romantic region of the world. I never could bear the inhabitants, and still less their English visitors.*

The Swiss are no brutes, but clearly, Byron thought otherwise. Fortunately, Byron-mania peaked in Europe, ensuring Switzerland witnessed a steady stream of tourists and gained popularity as a top destination. Book publishers cashed in on their travel books, some going up to about fifty releases a year between 1845 and 1850.

Byron fans, including French writer Victor Hugo, made pilgrimages to Lake Geneva, the Château de Chillon, and the Alps to follow in his footsteps. They were assisted in their quest by books like Murray's *Handbook for Travellers in Switzerland*, published in 1836 by the son of Byron's English publisher. Packed with Byron quotations, tourists could relive his emotions in front of the Jungfrau and at other spots.

Slowly, I pull myself up to begin the short walk back to the hotel. The lakeshore path is tree-lined, but a pale sun pushes through the overhanging branches. I feel as though Chillon has cast a spell on me because the tingling sensation in my body doesn't cease.

Few things are as good for the spirit as walking. It is not a long, arduous walk, but I soon feel breathless. Perhaps in a few months or years, I will forget the effort I am putting into this cause because by then, I would have moved on to admiring or following other agendas. Maybe I will find my nirvana in watching the flight of an eagle, dodging a snake, or simply looking at the horizon while thinking I will get there someday. Maybe I will meet other people interested in climbing mountains, follow their path, and share their stories and lives, but right now, I am concerned about my breathlessness. It is somewhat worrying.

While walking down the path, I notice that Byron's influence has not waned. Local entrepreneurs are also quick to exploit the literary rockstar's appeal. *'Byron stayed here'* plaques appear on buildings, and English tourists pack new establishments like the luxury Hotel Byron near the Château de Chillon. Today, literary places are no longer exclusively for literary lovers researching about a writer. Instead, these places now attract many tourists. Literature today seems to have become a form of alternative tourism, a transition welcomed by many who see it as a source of income.

Before I arrive at the hotel, I am running a fever, which forces me to stay in for the afternoon till it passes. I turn to my trusted Vicks VapoRub, my cure for every ailment, particularly cold and fever. A little dab behind my ears, a touch across my forehead, and applying some on my chest always works wonders.

I have exhausted every possible emotion in my visit to the Chateau. I have no explanation for it.

The otherwise perfect end to the day comes on the terrace of my hotel, watching dusk descend over the lake and drinking rum as recommended by the hotel staff.

But rum is a good alternative, and soon, I am stumbling to bed, ready to sleep off the fever.

*

My fever is gone, and I have just one thing left to do this morning before I check out and head to the train station for my onward journey. I head out to the cemetery of Clarens, a twenty-five-minute walk from Montreux station and into one of the most beautiful parks in the area. That is where Nabokov is buried. When I arrive, I am surprised to see a recent edition of *Lolita* and a candle on Nabokov's grave. Clearly, the man has some passionate followers in Montreux. I kick myself for not having thought about bringing flowers to the grave.

*

The 4.53 p.m. train to Interlaken Ost winds up the hillside above the lake, leaving Montreux behind. The scenery is spectacular. The bustle of the so-called Swiss Riviera gives way to the tranquil farming countryside. I know exactly where I am heading. Two hours and two train changes later, I will arrive in Interlaken, my last point in Switzerland, chasing Byron.

Two centuries ago, this was possible only on horseback, but even the tormented Byron seemed to enjoy himself in this celestial mountain scenery. On one occasion, crossing a high pass, he apparently lightened up so much that he 'made a snowball and threw it at Hobhouse' according to a report by British journalist Elma Dangerfield. She served as Secretary and then director of the Byron Society for three decades.

*

Interlaken itself isn't huge, and its main street runs between the two train stations and is lined with shops, luxurious hotels of Belle Epoque, and modernistic buildings serving the seekers of winter snows or summer meadows. Moreover, it is surrounded by towering mountains and lakes, which, I imagine, sparkle when the sun shines.

A leisurely twenty-minute walk brings me to Hotel Interlaken, a favourite of Lord Byron, who had parked himself there awhile in 1816. This low-rent hotel isn't at all wearing well; the decor has been unchanged since the 1970s, but the restaurant is unexpectedly good, enriched in so many ways by just being here.

*

The morning weather is conducive for walking, for it is dark, cold, and clear. Maintaining a slow pace, I walk to the end of the street and am surprised to see people up and about so early. I am pleasantly surprised to see that most of those people are Asians and, to break it down further, Indians. An elderly couple stops me to ask directions for any Indian restaurant serving vegetarian breakfast. I throw up my hands in the air and beg forgiveness. The woman looks at me as though I have sinned by not sharing her dislike of 'European food' and ambles away grimly, husband in tow. If I weren't hungry, I would have found that funny, but I make haste to the hotel for breakfast and to get a move on.

I leave on a blue-and-yellow narrow-gauge train of the Berner Oberland Bahn (BOB) from Interlaken OST to the picturesque Grindelwald, where I switch to a 26-seater Eiger Express for the fifteen-minute ride to Eigergletscher, which is followed by a ride in the cogwheel train to Jungfraujoch through a tunnel.

Jungfraujoch is a little like heaven and has the most captivating viewing point in the Bernese Alps. Jungfraujoch is worth all the hype. As the icy wind brushes my face, I draw my waterproof jacket closer to my body, the cold coming in the way of admiring the beauty unhindered. The glacier-lined mountains and the majestic cliffs render me speechless, and soon, I repair to the nearest feeding station to warm myself with a cup of hot chocolate.

The weather changes quickly in the mountains, so when I return, Grindelwald, which had inspired Byron's creation of *Manfred*, is covered in mist. Unfortunately, it is a day that doesn't show Grindelwald at its best, which leaves me wondering if Western romanticism would have existed had Grindelwald been as obscured in mist when Lord Byron went through it.

Probably not. And I'd probably be only imagining it.

Byron only spent six months in Switzerland, but much of his work and legend is connected to that land of mountains and lakes, especially the area surrounding Lake Geneva, and a large part of Switzerland's success as a tourist destination is owed to Lord Byron's short stint here. Despite his lack of fondness for the Swiss people, he did manage, after all, to catapult this tiny mountainous country into the limelight.

Come to think of it, Byron was somewhat of a blogger in his time. He had travelled a lot, spinning his journeys to exotic locations into two volumes of his long narrative poem *Childe Harold's Pilgrimage*—essentially a travelogue of Byron's own journeys.

Or what we call today—a blog.

*

Footnotes:

- *Frankenstein Summer of 1816 was the interlude of happiness in lives marked by tragedy. In 1822, Percy Shelley drowned in Italy at age 29; Dr Polidori committed suicide in 1821, aged 25. Claire's daughter with Byron died at age 5. Byron died in Greece in 1824, aged 36.*
- *Byron left Switzerland in October 1816, heading to Italy and then Greece.*
- *American-British poet T.S. Eliot wrote much of The Waste Land while under the care of a Lausanne psychiatrist. His landmark modernist poem was published in 1922.*

Chapter 7

Tracking Hemingway in Italy is fraught with difficulties because I seem not to find a hot trail to pursue. I have read many accounts of Hemingway in Italy that throw light on his association with Italy during WWI when he served as an ambulance driver for the Red Cross on the Italian Front. Besides moving wounded soldiers, he transported supplies.

Somehow, it seems like a cut-and-dry version of a life otherwise lived with so much gaiety.

But the most vivid account I have read is written by Steve Paul, a Kansas-based author and journalist, in his book *Hemingway at Eighteen*. The other, *A Farewell to Arms*, written by Hemingway himself, gives an exaggerated account of his role in the war and a love affair with a nurse in Italy. Given his propensity for fictionalizing facts, I console myself with the knowledge that at least one version of his life is true. It is of some comfort to know that, and I quote Steve Paul:

In the winter and spring of 1918, Ernest Hemingway churned out several feature stories for The Kansas City Star about military recruiting campaigns. The Navy, the Tank Corps, and even the British had set up local offices to seek troops after the United States joined its allies in Europe.

Hemingway at the time was a recent high school graduate who had landed a reporting job in Kansas City in lieu of going to college or enlisting. At 18, he was too young to join without parental permission, but he talked a lot about getting into the war, a desire he expressed in several letters to his sister Marcelline. After arriving in Kansas City in mid-October 1917, he joined the Missouri Guard and even trained at Swope Park. Further military service was not in the cards, but a Kansas City friendship led him down another path toward serving in the war. In February 1918, the

American Red Cross announced it was seeking volunteers to join the ambulance service in Italy. Hemingway most likely heard about this directly from Dell D. Dutton, who ran the Red Cross office in Kansas City.

Hemingway had learned much about the wartime ambulance corps from Theodore Brumback. The son of a prominent judge, Brumback had spent five months as an ambulance driver in the war-ravaged countryside of northern France. Hemingway met Brumback on the latter's return to Kansas City in November 1917 and interviewed him in The Star's newsroom. Brumback eventually wrote a lengthy, action-filled account of his dangerous posting in France, which appeared in the newspaper in February 1918, about the time the young men volunteered. Hemingway finished his reporting job at the end of April, returned home to Oak Park briefly and corresponded with Brumback about their forthcoming mission to Italy.

Hemingway, Brumback and their fellow volunteers spent two weeks training and sightseeing in New York. After an Atlantic crossing aboard a grimy French steamship and fleeting stops in Bordeaux and Paris, Hemingway arrived in Milan in early June 1918. An unexpected assignment turned up immediately. Hemingway and others were sent to the gruesome site of a munitions plant explosion a dozen miles outside Milan. Bodies and body parts were strewn everywhere. "We carried them in like at the General Hospital, Kansas City," the young man reported on a postcard he sent back to his former colleagues at The Star. Despite the horrific detail of his "baptism of fire," which Hemingway detailed years later ("A Natural History of the Dead"), he couldn't hide his enthusiasm over arriving in Italy: "Having a wonderful time!!!"

The next day Hemingway and Brumback were split up and sent to different sections of the Red Cross service. Hemingway landed in Schio, 150 miles northeast of Milan in a valley below the Dolomite Mountains. There is little evidence to suggest that Hemingway actually drove an ambulance during his stint there. Hemingway, in fact, expressed a sense of boredom, because there wasn't enough to do. In mid-June, hostilities resumed as Austro-German forces began an offensive along a wide stretch of the Piave River. Italian defences stiffened and casualties mounted throughout the rain-drenched countryside. When an opportunity to get closer to the action arose later in June, Hemingway eagerly signed on. He left the relative quiet of his ambulance unit and took over a rolling canteen operation near the villages of Fornaci and Fossalta. As he reported to his mother in a letter that year, the change gave him yet more wartime experience: "I have glimpsed the making of large gobs of history during the Great Battle of the Piave and have been all along the Front From the mountains to the Sea."

Hemingway's daily routine at Fossalta involved handing out coffee, chocolate, cigarettes and postcards to Italian soldiers in the trench, about 20 yards off the Piave. Rather than a motorized vehicle, Hemingway travelled by bicycle. Hemingway observed snipers in action. He saw and felt artillery blasts in the night. Then, on the night of July 8, 1918, an Austrian Minenwerfer mortar shell screamed through the darkness and exploded just feet away from Hemingway. It killed an Italian soldier, wounded others and blasted Hemingway unconscious. Two hundred twenty-seven shards of metal pierced his flesh, and Hemingway ended up spending most of the rest of the war in the American Red Cross hospital in Milan.

Hemingway's hospital experience is a thing of legend. There was booze and there was an epic love affair that lasted weeks beyond the Armistice. Hemingway immortalized his relationship with the Red Cross nurse Agnes von Kurowsky years later in A Farewell to Arms. About 10 years his senior, she wrote it off as innocent puppy love, and when she finally broke it off, after Hemingway returned to the states, he was devastated.

By the end of 1918 Hemingway received an Italian medal of valour for having served in his supporting role with honour. He also earned an Italian war cross, apparently in recognition that Hemingway served during an Italian campaign in the mountains in late October. That appearance ended quickly when Hemingway came down with a case of jaundice and returned to the hospital.

Hemingway's experiences in Italy, including the physical therapy that continued into December 1918, contributed to at least two of his future novels and several pieces of short fiction. Most notable are the novel A Farewell to Arms and three short stories set in Italy and featuring Nick Adams, who is often read as Hemingway's alter-ego – "Now I Lay Me," "In Another Country" and "A Way You'll Never Be."

Debates continue among scholars about the aura of heroism that accrued around Hemingway following his wounding. Did the teen-ager, still only eighteen years old, really carry a wounded Italian on his shoulders to safety through a hail of machine-gun bullets? Very unlikely. But as with much of the Hemingway legend, in Italy and beyond, it makes for a compelling tale.

*

The above account fairly covers all aspects of his life in Italy and how he made it thus far. I suppose there is nothing left for me to find.

"There is nothing else than now. There is neither yesterday, certainly, nor is there any tomorrow. How old must you be before you know that? There is only now, and if now is only two days, then two days is your life and everything in it will be in proportion. This is how you live a life in two days. And if you stop complaining and asking for what you never will get, you will have a good life. A good life is not measured by any biblical span."

---Ernest Hemingway

The lucky devil that he was, EH was awarded the *Italian Silver Metal of Bravery*.

I suspect that Italy attracted more romantics than journalists, and thanks to young English poets such as Keats, Shelley, and Lord Byron, it came to be known as 'Paradise of the Exiles.' Sunnier, cheaper, and full of art and culture than their homeland, it was the perfect destination for these bohemians.

Unfortunately, Hemingway did not fall within the category of Romantics. In any Byron versus Hemingway argument centred on Italy, there can only be one winner.

Here, Byron ruled.

But my presence in Florence threw me off track, and I am not regretful of having arrived here first.

*

To Italians, the espresso coffee should be a break, plain and simple; while you're taking it, there is nothing besides the pause, nothing besides the coffee and the conversation that accompanies it. Coffee is a momentary escape from work, not a companion on the way to, during, or from it.

These words float into my mind as I dip a warm butter croissant into my cappuccino, fearing that too much butter and sugar would send me daydreaming of living here forever. I am at Café Gilli, Florence's landmark café that tops my list of places to drink coffee. This one moved a few times before coming to its current location at Piazza della Repubblica, formerly called Piazza Vittorio Emanuele, at the beginning of 1900. Its history is intriguing, too. Opened by the Gilli family from Switzerland in the year 1733 as a sweet bread boutique in the era of the Medici on Via de' Calzaiuoli, it became an instant favourite among the rich Florentines.

The menu has several interesting varieties of coffee, and while I am partial to my long black, a term used widely in Africa, I intend to drink every kind of coffee on offer here. I'm sure this is not going to be my last visit here.

A young woman wearing a soft pink dress slips into the chair beside me, her eyes doing the talking. I nod in the affirmative. Her long, red hair sits neatly on her bare shoulders. She calls the waiter in a voice so warm and buttery I want to dip it into my coffee along with my croissant. She smiles at me, a warm smile that heightens her resemblance to the Goddess of Love. The waiter arrives with her cappuccino, his eyes dancing in delight. The goddess raises the cup to her nose, breathes in, and smiles.

Once Upon A Time in Florence... I am lost in a daydream.

That is how I will tell my story to anyone who will care to listen someday. In this story, I recall meeting a young goddess who liked cappuccino while I had been looking for the God of Romance, Lord Byron.

I imagine her walking down the streets along River Arno. So charming, so full of life.

My daydream is interrupted by the sound of a chair pulling back. The goddess is gone, and in her place is a man watching me intently. An Italian. I can tell from the way a smile hovers around his lips. He looks like he wants to laugh.

I grab a napkin and dab my lips. When I reach for my coffee, I realize there is none left.

What was in my cappuccino? Where is the goddess? What was in my coffee? Had the goddess really been there?

Unapologetically, the man launches into conversation.

"My dear madam, how are you today?"

"I am doing just great, sir. Thank you for asking. I do feel a little weird, though."

"I say, it is the first time I have seen someone sleep over their coffee. I presume Florence has tired you already. You are a tourist, *sì?*"

Men. They are friendly, hospitable, generous, intelligent, good humoured, and well-dressed, but it takes an Italian gentleman to carry on a conversation with a stranger as if there is nothing to it.

"Madam, may I ask you to join me for a coffee?" He tells me his name. Lorenzo. And he is trying to flirt.

"Well, certainly. Coffee always tastes better in good company." That is me, trying to match his mischief.

Out of thin air, the waiter arrives with two steaming cups of pitch-black coffee. I straighten my back and pick up my cup. Life is slowly returning to me. I hope I am not smiling too much.

"It is good, yes, the coffee?" he asks. "I hope you enjoy it."

"You have such a delightful accent," I blurt out. "You Italians are so... what do you call it... romantic and proper. Charming and delightful."

He warms up to the compliment. A smile lights up his face. I offer my name.

"It is a beautiful name, I think. But may I call you Florentine? It is a name you will go by in Florence, one that will be appreciated by all. A name just as pretty as you are..."

"Sure, Mr Lorenzo, just as long as I don't have to dress the part. Your women are so prim and neat, and my hair, I am afraid, is a dead giveaway. So messy and frayed from the travel."

"Why are you here, in Florence? Is it our love stories that bring you here?

He is very close to the truth. A love story did bring me here: my love story with Lord Byron. I am not going to tell him that just yet.

"Something like that," I say.

It turns out that Lorenzo is a tourist guide, although not for very long. If I am right, he turned himself into a guide for me.

"I always suggest to everyone to take a Vespa tour in Florence, you know," he says. "It is the best way to see the city and connects you with the place."

"You are right. I like the idea very much."

Without saying very much, he has made me his client. Maybe the first and likely the last. Lorenzo has one condition. I am never to photograph him—so that there is nothing to remember him when I grow old.

"When you remember Florence, it must be in your mind and your heart. You feel with your heart. No looking at a picture of Lorenzo. You must see Lorenzo in your mind."

All conditions accepted, I agree to meet Lorenzo the next morning at Café Paszkowski, another Florence's favourite located close to where we are and which, in the early years, hosted the likes of Giovanni Papini, Ardengo Soffici, Gaetano Salvemini, and even Cesare Battisti.

*

Suddenly, I am in the mood for a haircut. I need something to change how I see Lord Byron in one of the most romantic cities in Italy. That done, I embark on a self-guided tour of Florence, feeling, if nothing, a little closer to Lord Byron in spirit and a little more in love.

My tour of the city takes me on the route Lorenzo highlighted for me, starting at Ponte Vecchio. We will come this way again tomorrow, but I want to orient myself with its history.

Ponte Vecchio is a stone arch bridge over the river Arno. This bridge, built by Taddeo Gaddi, was completed in 1345 and is one of the most unique things to see in Florence. From the word go, it was populated, with butchers and tanners setting up shop there. However, in 1593, Duke Ferdinand I decided to allow only goldsmiths and jewellers to operate on Ponte Vecchio because the butchers and tanners produced too much garbage and foul smells. Ever since, the bridge has been filled with art dealers, jewellers, and souvenir sellers.

Interestingly, it isn't the allure of diamonds and jewellery that interests me but the reason Ponte Vecchio made it to history books and lent itself to the concept of bankruptcy. Supposedly, in the past, when a merchant couldn't repay debts, soldiers broke the table on which he sold his goods, and without it, he couldn't sell anything. The word 'bankrupt' traces its origins to *banca rotta,* Italian for 'broken bench.'

Centuries ago, in Italy, money dealers worked from benches or tables. If a money dealer ran out of money, his bench or table was broken in two, and was sent out of business. The word had its French equivalent, *banqueroute,* and eventually traced its way into the English language as a figure of speech and a literal definition of what happened to the affected person.

Ponte Vecchio is evocative and romantic and witnessed great tragedies and a war between the Guelphs and Ghibellines.

The story goes like this: *Buondelmonte de 'Buondelmonti was a handsome and elegant young nobleman in 1216. But on the day of his wedding day, he was ambushed and murdered on the Old Bridge near the statue of God of Mars. The blame for this, of course, was laid on love; this young man had promised to marry the descendant of the honourable Amidei family but later withdrew his intentions. The shame was washed away with blood...*

Centuries later, in 1900, to mark the fourth century of the birth of Benvenuto Cellini, the renowned Florentine sculptor, a bronze bust was commissioned, and it stands in the middle of a fountain on the bridge where very recently lovers have taken to placing a lock on Cellini's monument.

*

Finally, I arrive at the elegant Piazzale degli Uffizi and hear the story of Simonetta Vespucci, an icon of Renaissance beauty. Vespucci was the one desired and loved by nobles, poets, and artists and with whom Giuliano de' Medici fell madly in love.

There are many versions of their sordid love affair, each intriguing and juicer than the other, and I leave feeling as though I have walked through real life.

Head spinning with so many stories, I make my way to the Piazza della Signoria, an amazing open-air museum, to admire the imposing Palazzo Vecchio, the monumental Neptune's Fountain, the perfect copy of Michelangelo's David and the Loggia dei Lanzi with it wonderful statues.

Once again, I am regaled with great love stories of the Medici families, great lords, court intrigues, arranged marriages, and secret romances born in the shadow of the most powerful family of the Florentine Renaissance.

Lord Byron had dismissed Florence as being full of 'gossip-loving English,' but he did express the feeling of being 'drunk with beauty' as he took in the great artworks in the city's galleries in the Uffizi.

He was right in his proclamation.

I penetrate the medieval quarter, where, surrounded by narrow streets and tower houses, I relive the atmosphere of that period, finding myself in the places of Dante Alighieri, who was born here and lived all his life here, and of his wonderful Beatrice, angelic woman, and his muse. His love story, I think, is among the most romantic, and I wish it were Lorenzo narrating the story to me.

*

I finish my coffee in silence and attend to my dressing while the sun is still a warm yellow. Today, we will explore the romantic side of Florence, and it is just as well that I should be dressed accordingly.

The history of Italian fashion is interesting as it is relatively new, taking over from the French after WWII and contributing in many ways to the country's economy. Italian fashion is internationally celebrated as exotic, sophisticated, and romantic. Italians treasure their appearance and *la bella figura*, so if you would like to blend in while visiting Italy, it is a good idea to follow some essential fashion etiquette rules. I want to blend in, or maybe I just want to please Lorenzo. Whatever the reason is, I am thrilled to dress the part. What had he called me? Florentine, yes, that is right. Today, I am going to play the part.

When Audrey Hepburn arrived on the scene in *A Roman Holiday*, it sealed the title of Italy being the glamorous alternative to French haute couture. I won't disrespect Italy's fashion tradition, at least for today.

In Italy, one can never be too overdressed, but one can be easily under-dressed. Despite Italians being casual, the majority of the population is well-dressed. It is possible that Italians express themselves through fashion—though I cannot be the judge of that.

*

I arrive just in time at Café Gilli for my appointment with Lorenzo, flush with the excitement of meeting him. I hope he likes my transformation. Should I have not cut my hair so short? There is no place to put a flower in it now. I like putting flowers in my hair.

But something about the name Florentine goes well with my present haircut.

Lorenzo arrives on a Vespa. In Italy, it is mandatory to ride a Vespa. His punctuality surprises me. I have always maintained that Italians, like Indians, are slow to comprehend the concept of being on time. Lorenzo clearly didn't conform to the Italian standard of time. His Vespa is suspiciously new.

I was right, after all.

"We will do the tour like you have never imagined," he says. "Come, I'll tell you the stories of love and romance in every stone of Florence."

"You are on."

He says nothing about how I look.

I sit on his new Vespa, feeling like a queen taking her throne.

Our first stop is the religious heart of Florence: the place of the Cathedral and the famous Brunelleschi's Dome, the Baptistery with the glittering *Porta del Paradiso,* and the magnificent Giotto's Bell Tower.

"Florence may be famous as the Cradle of the Renaissance, but more than that, it is distinguished by the great artists and the power struggles between powerful families. I will tell you the stories of passion, love, intrigues, and betrayals of common people and lords."

My nod goes unnoticed.

"But I will begin with hot chocolate," he says and leads me to a rather non-descript café facing the Duomo. I follow him without a word.

If a tour of Florence must begin with a cup of hot chocolate, so be it.

Lorenzo puts the cup of the thick hot chocolate and says, "My beautiful Florentine."

I know now how this tour will end. I feel it in my bones.

The hot chocolate is sweet. Like temptation. I am drunk on the sensations the sugar produces. I don't approve of it in the least.

Lorenzo points towards the Duomo and whispers, "Do you see something there? Yes, look... we will begin our story with that."

"What am I supposed to see? The Duomo? Well, that is hard to miss, right? But what I do hear is music. It is coming from everywhere. And yes, I see love. Isn't this the place of love? Painful and everlasting love? You know I, Florentine, have decided to fall in love."

Lorenzo, not in the least expecting a show like this, is staring at me open-mouthed.

I continue with my dramatics.

"You wonder why I am here? I am sure you do. Let me ask you this? Have you been in love? And what is to say you cannot fall in love consciously? There is quite a lot of space in my heart and my mind. I want to write a story of blossoming love right here in this café, in this old neighbourhood, in this very city. Oh, pardon me, sir, but I am drunk on the idea of love. This hot chocolate? This is charming… and this cup…"

I let it sink in. But Lorenzo is about to laugh, not quite following my conversation. I must admit the truth.

"I see you are puzzled. But yes, this is a puzzle. The question is how to make it all fit. Again, I ask you this: why are the greatest love stories of Florence written by men? Why does every story begin with, '*Dantes fell in love at first sight, or Alessandro fell in love at first sight.*' We should change that, shouldn't we, to something more gender neutral like *Florentine fell in love with Lorenzo*… Who is to know the truth? We will create our own truth. So, would you, signor, be the Dante to my Beatrice? Would it be easier if I just called myself Beatrice?"

Mia cara donna!

Who knew hot chocolate could produce that effect on me? Finally, I tell him about Lord Byron, feeling a little like I am turning into him somehow.

Lorenzo laughs. In some crazy way, he sounds like Dante. I have never heard how Dante laughed, but it could have been like this. A full-throated, merry laugh that makes me want to write poetry.

The café is noisy. The coffee machine doesn't stop hissing, and suddenly, a tour group arrives, demanding hot chocolate, croissants, and coffee, and the barista cannot keep up with the requests.

"Romance," Lorenzo says firmly. "Let me tell you a thing or two about Italian romance. And you will forget your Byron."

He dives into the story he knows by heart.

"When Brunelleschi conducted the constructions of the famous Santa Maria del Fiore dome, many artisans and workers were entangled in various love stories. One of them left a permanent mark on the Florence Cathedral. A beautiful seamstress lived in a house at the beginning of Via dei Servi Street; she used to look out the window daily and observe the building works. One of the senior masters noticed her beauty and, when her husband was away at work, contrived to start meeting the woman at her home. After this short story of passion ended, the master decided to 'play a joke'; he carved a bull's head in marble, decorated it with huge horns, and placed it on the wall of the cathedral just in front of the beautiful seamstress's house."

The story is hilarious; we burst out laughing. Because this is Florence, this outburst doesn't attract any attention.

"You are right," says Lorenzo. "Now that I think about it, it is funny, alright. It's quite a funny love story, and thank God, it did not end in deceit or betrayal. The magnificent buildings of Florence have seen its fair share of intriguing betrayals and tricks."

We ride from one place to the other, and Lorenzo has a story for every place we go until I am walking with my head in the past with flashes of medieval events unravelling before my eyes.

*

Florence is built of dozens of bright moments of cleverness, but the single cleverest thing about it is that, while maintaining a careful veneer of breezy symbolism, it refuses to settle for anything easy or unoriginal.

I love my journey into Florence's sordid and steamy past, and I am certain that even this better, more satisfying-than-I-was-expecting ending has opened my eyes to what I really intend to achieve. It trades one cliché for another, albeit, yes, a slightly richer one.

But maybe that's the point. Maybe all conclusions are a form of settling. There will never be enough romantic stories or history to make everything fit, but in that is my completeness.

Florence isn't for everyone. Actually, it is not for most people, despite their claims to the contrary. I may have never liked it as much if I didn't have love in my heart or the kind of obsession that turned Florence into the historical hotbed of steamy romance.

I'm very delighted to be here. The crowded streets, the many tourists—it's all fine with me. My love for fresh pasta, seasonal veggies, fancy restaurants, hot chocolate, coffee, and croissants has only increased. If I'm not actually eating, I'm pretty much thinking of my next meal. Something that maybe I've only recently understood about myself is that I wasn't meant to have a life that was necessarily easy or regular. It's like having an annoying, stubborn child living inside me that craves a good challenge.

*

Finally, we arrive at Casa Guidi in San Felice Square. I have had enough of Florence's love stories, which are getting murkier than versions of Byron's affairs, and I really want it to end, but Lorenzo is turning out to be a good guide. His stock of love stories is endless.

"Robert and Elizabeth Barrett Browning, the eminent English poets, escaped the wrath of Elisabeth's father to find a home in Florence. Here, they lived happily for fifteen years. Their home became the Mecca for the Anglo-Saxon community of Florence. Elisabeth returned to England only after the death of Robert."

I take a deep breath and let it all sink in. It is almost time for us to say goodbye. Then, I suggest coffee. Any reason to prolong the goodbyes will do.

We ride back to where it all started. Café Gilli perhaps will go down in my book of *A Love Affair With Florence* too as the place I delved into the mysteries of Florentine romance and learnt of Medici and Dante.

The coffee appears as if by magic. We sip in silence, enjoying the coffee and each other's company.

"I will miss you, Florentine," he says softly, his eyes coming to rest on my face. "Telling you our love stories is a privilege. The world must know about them."

"And now, the Grand Finale," he announces. "I promise it will move you to tears."

"The most famous Florentine love story is of Francesco I de Medici. In 1563, a wealthy Venetian, Bianca, fell in love with the humble Florentine Pietro Bonaventura, fled to Florence, and got married. But during a reception, she met Francesco de Medici. It was love at first sight for both. Although Francesco already had a wife named Giovanna, this did not prevent him from having a relationship with Bianca.

"Giovanna soon died mysteriously, and the lovers, having nothing to hide, got married. After eight happy years, during their rest in Poggio, a Caiano country villa, one evening they suddenly felt sick and had a temperature. Ten days later, Francesco died, and Bianca passed away on the 11th. People still search for the answer, and the version of poisoning with arsenic is not confirmed yet."

*

This is the ultimate story of love. I am perhaps made of sterner stuff because I am not moved to tears. He smiles sadly. We look at each other, each lost in our own thoughts.

The time has come. We rise.

As he hugs me goodbye, he quotes from Alessandro Manzoni's *The Betrothed*.

The heart tells me that we will meet again soon. Of course, the heart, who listens to him, always has something to say about what will be. But what does the heart know? Just a little bit of what has already happened.

Chapter 8

In Padua, my quest has narrowed down considerably. From here, I will continue to reconnect with Lord Byron, tracking him to Venice and thereon to Rome before concluding my grand tour. In today's context, my travel merits a place in Literary Tourism, although it is a phrase I personally dislike, it fits the sentiment.

The city of Padua was, once upon a time, more venerated than Venice. It is hard to imagine that era, but one must consider history. I suppose a little knowledge of history is always helpful because it allows one to put things in perspective and appreciate a place more. Had I not arrived here pursuing Byron, I'd probably never have known it to be home to one of the oldest universities of Europe, that Galileo was once a tutor there, and that Padua was once considered a centre of scholars and the place where all the big names in Renaissance art converged.

I have two reasons for visiting Padua: first, Café Pedrocchi, an 18th-century café frequented by Lord Byron, Stendhal, and other greats; second, its proximity to Venice.

My visit to Padua is short. I have not factored in a longer stay, hoping to cover as much as possible in a short time and leave for Venice soon after. Little do I know that it is not to be.

*

I make for the 18th-century Café Pedrocchi, seeking directions from a group of young men who walk me to it happily, questioning my presence here and throwing random questions about travel and India. It is a refreshing change to speak with the young and buoyant crowd full of life and vitality. I am happy to answer their questions. We arrive at the café housed in a neo-classical building at one end of the Piazza, a few blocks from the Padua University. That explains the young men's presence. Touched by their keenness to accompany me here, I offer them a beverage at the famed café, but they decline politely. Instead, they invite me to explore their university—the oldest, they say with pride—if I have the time.

"It is a very historical and special university," they say.

I nod in the affirmative.

The café is busy and therefore noisy. Sounds from the street permeate through the walls. The café's occupants are mostly young students and old people, and every one of them appears comfortable and at ease. There are a few empty tables, and I make my way to one by the tall windows.

This unusual café with tall Greek columns and classic décor has a reputation of never closing its doors and serves the best mint and chocolate-flavoured coffee. I baulk at the thought of mint or chocolate in my coffee but accept that times are changing.

However, I make a note to try at least one of the two famed beverages here. It is a hard choice between mint and chocolate, one worse than the other—in my opinion—and I silently curse the creator of this particular drink before ordering my favourite.

I see fit to throw in a little something about coffee drinking in Italy. Believe it or not, there is a huge and mostly unspoken guideline for ordering coffee in this country. And if you care about being judged by the Italians (and they will judge you, even the politest ones) for your poor choices, it is best to pay attention to what I am about to say.

Process this: Starbucks didn't appear in Italy until 2017 in Milan, forty-seven years after it began operations in Seattle. And there is little to be said about its success, too.

To start with the simple act of ordering coffee—I mean the right kind of coffee. To fully understand this culture is to know the time to consume this beverage. Remember, you should not use milk in your coffee after lunch, which means that ordering a cappuccino after a big meal is highly irregular. To keep it simple, avoid milk in your coffee after breakfast. To ask for a syrupy flavour in your coffee is a sin, which is allowed only in Starbucks. The only way around it—if you want something added to the coffee, is to add a dash of brandy and grappa.

Also, it is possible to find a sit-down café in touristy areas, but the local way is to stand around a bar and throw back a gulp of coffee.

I have broken most of these rules in Italy, knowingly and unknowingly, not in the least afraid of being judged, for I love my coffee as much as the next Italian in the street.

We don't agree on the time to drink it, that's all.

This café has witnessed many historical events and served coffee to many famous figures since its inception. It was, at one time, known as a café without doors. I am only too glad that era has passed because the noise level is kept to a minimum thanks to the doors and windows that shut.

The piano comes to life, and suddenly, the noise from the streets dissipates into moments in history where the greats of Europe and Italy put their heads together over coffee and discussed the world.

Historically, this café has been the cultural, political, journalistic, and academic center of Padua, but today, it serves as the centre of cultural activity. It was also a place for students who planned the 1848 riots against the Hapsburg monarchy, igniting the Italian national movement. And here, Lord Byron spent much of his time discussing poetry and politics with friends.

Padua held an important position in Roman history and claimed to have the biggest café in Europe when it opened. Lord Byron and Stendhal have described the café as 'simply the best in the world,' and even if one is not pursuing historical greats, it is a great experience to grab a coffee or a snack here. The rooms are large, historic, and jaw-droppingly beautiful. There is, of course, a high price to pay for this beauty, but to look past this is to enjoy the grandeur of this place.

Before leaving, I reluctantly asked for the special beverage, aided in this adventure by the waiter who pressed me into trying their specialty. The Caffè Pedrocchi: a coffee with mint-flavoured cream and a sprinkle of cocoa powder, made according to a highly guarded secret recipe.

And I did not like it, despite trying hard to.

*

It seems improper to leave the city so soon after consuming its famous beverage and not giving it a closer look, which means I have talked myself into staying the night. Venice is not too far away, so everything is working out fine. This allows me the liberty of running through Padua's highlights and giving the famed Aperol Spritz a go. It was, after all, invented here.

I begin with the University of Padua, Italy's second oldest and the fifth oldest in the world. It was established in 1222 by some professors and scholars from the University of Bologna, Italy's first university, as they yearned for more academic freedom.

The university is well known for another reason—it was the first university in the world to award a PhD to a woman in 1678. The recipient, Elena Lucrezia Corner Piscopia, graduated from this university with her philosophy doctorate.

My first acquaintance with the university is with the Palazzo Bo or The Bo Palace, the main campus.

The main courtyard, with its many magnificent frescoes, is free to visit. However, considering its impressive history, I decide to spend a longer time exploring its grand halls, where numerous scientific discoveries have been made. The campus consists of the world's first permanent anatomic theatre and the desk where Galileo Galilei once taught as a professor in the early 1600s

Padua is filled with marvellous things, but seeing the frescoes of the Scrovegni Chapel is my moment of fulfilment. I'd have missed this rather small and somewhat understated chapel and would have easily passed by it without knowing the wonders that awaited inside.

This 14th-century chapel was built by a banker named Scrovegni, who was trying to guarantee his father a spot in heaven. Its interiors are decorated with detailed frescoes by the artist Giotto; surely, it must have done the trick. Bad luck if it didn't.

The beautiful frescoes depict stories from the Bible, including the life of the Virgin Mary and Jesus Christ. Truly a masterpiece, many art historians believe Giotto's work on the chapel sparked the Italian Renaissance.

Before long, I find myself sipping Aperol, a century-old drink invented in Padua by two brothers, Silvio, and Luigi Barbieri. This aperitif is light, has a unique orange colour, and is slightly bitter, but it has remained a popular drink since it first featured at the 1919 Padua International Fair.

It's just too bad that Lord Byron lived in a different time.

My exploration of Padua ends at the 13th-century Palazzo della Ragione and Sotto il Salone, the incredible covered market beneath the palazzo. The palazzo—with its enormous hall—is covered in astrologically themed frescoes. There is plenty of culinary exploring to do in the palazzo's lower level, where the Sotto il Salone, a market, has been operating for eight hundred years.

I come away feeling that I have had a very close brush with Lord Byron. That feeling of going home to a lover increases as I approach Venice.

*

"The sands are often covered in snow," the Bangladeshi shopkeeper at the Piazzale Roma whispers as I sift through the heaps of souvenirs while waiting for the Vaporetto to take me to Venice.

"But that does not keep the tourists away," he adds. "Venice is always very crowded."

There is a tinge of sadness in his voice, deepened at the sight of his former countryman. His name is Shafi, a Bangladeshi immigrant. I nod absently. Encouraged by this, Shafi produces a rose from under the table, where it rests in a bucket of fresh water, and presents it to me. I accept it in the only way I know. With a smile. I see no reason to refuse it.

The smile returns to his face. A happy smile.

"I am happy to be in Venice," he says, "but sad that I cannot visit my country because my papers are not good. There are many here, like me. But we make a good life; in my country, that is not possible."

I understand what he is trying to say.

He rattles off a story about his arrival to Italy, which I believe is half imagined and half true, but it makes for a lively counter-sales conversation. He gives me a fat discount on a silk scarf made in China.

"Very good silk," he insists. But we both know that it is not good silk, but for the price he is offering, it is a deal. I want to ask him questions—about his life in Venice and his dreams— but it is time to go.

"We will meet again when you come back," he calls out after me.

"Khuda Hafiz," I reply.

It is a goodbye because we both know I am not returning. Shafi raises a hand and waves weakly. I walk past locals lingering over cappuccinos and reach the dock, breathing in the warm, salt water-tinged air.

The Vaporetto ploughs through the stretch of the green Adriatic Sea, widening the distance from the Piazzale Roma. Sunshine sparkles over the waters as I watch with silent admiration. Venice is a dream destination for people around the world. It is mine, too, although my dream varies a lot from the million others.

A one-in-a-million-tourist looking for Romanticism.

The pursuit of that dream includes finding the place that hugely influenced the near-infamous Byron and turned him into one of the beloved Armenian monks.

As the ferry inches into the jetty, the sunlight catches the glint on the golden weathervane of Archangel Gabriel perched on the bell tower, also called St Marks Campanile. To a first-time visitor, Venice appears to rise from the sea like water columns, as described by Lord Byron two hundred years ago. Byron's *City of the Heart*, as he later called Venice, looks unchanged in two centuries.

Nothing could have prepared me for the first sight of Venice. It is so unlike anywhere else I have been. Everything is on the water—buses, taxis, ambulances. Everything floats.

Venice is packed with tourists this morning, like every morning, I presume, and the sea is burdened with cruise ships bearing thousands of tourists. In the parking lot, bobbing gondolas are lined up and secured, waiting to be used. Once upon a time, these gondolas ferried the wealthy, but today, they exist solely to entertain tourists. And the tourists, by the looks of it, are keeping the pizza fires burning in the kitchens of the gondoliers.

I zigzag my way through the milling tourists, not stopping for photographs or souvenirs from the stalls lining the jetty, ignoring the chill and the chance of being photographed feeding pigeons, intent only on getting acquainted with Byron's favourite city.

There is water everywhere, and on each of those narrow waterways are gondolas with excited tourists and a gondolier narrating romantic tales. I walk past many beautiful bridges, but the one I am looking for is the *Bridge of Sighs*. Eventually, I slow down, watching everything and everyone intently, when a colourful gondola disappears under the Ponte dei Sospiri, the bridge connecting the prisons to the interrogation chamber in Doge's Palace. Ponte dei Sospiri *is* the *Bridge of Sighs* because Byron named it so.

I stood in Venice on the Bridge of Sighs
A palace and a prison at each end.

I unravel Byron's thoughts from these two lines. He had invented the name because he thought the condemned would sigh as they walked over the bridge toward their death, seeing Venice and freedom for the last time.

Byron must have felt what I am feeling now—a chill running down my spine.

From the *Bridge of Sighs*, I make my way to the famous St Mark's Square. It is every writer's dream, a lover's desire, and a favourite spot for pigeons. It is as if all the world's beauty

236

converged here. Marvellous architecture, piazzas full of delightful eateries, romance, and memories of Lord Byron.

*

St Mark is lined on three sides with arcades running fashionable shops and cafes. The open side faces the St Mark's Basilica that stands gloriously—a symbol of Italo-Byzantine architecture. On the top of this mind-blowing structure is the statue of Venice's patron apostle, St Mark, flanked by angels and a winged golden lion beneath them. The sheer scale of beauty makes my jaw drop.

On the northern side of the Basilica is a clock tower with an embellished clock face and a massive beam with a bronze statue of an old man and a young man on its sides. The Moors. These young and old moors represent the passing of time. They strike the Bell each hour.

*

Drinking coffee on the move is the most pedestrian of daily tasks elsewhere. But in Venice, coffee drinking is a highly regarded activity—a tradition, if you will—one that signifies a respect for culture and a love for coffee. But taking it a notch above is Caffe Florian, where coffee itself plays second fiddle to the ceremony of serving it. In fact, they are so serious about coffee that they make you wait a while before someone shows up with a menu merely to test your patience in acquiring a cup of coffee.

Once I pass this test, I am in good hands.

Elegantly dressed in white with a head full of wavy black hair and warm brown eyes, the wait-staff leads me to a corner table by the large, beautiful windows with a wonderful view of the porticoes, the church, and the square.

He hands me a menu, gives me a few moments to decide my order, and smiles as he glides away with my order. There is nothing quite so romantic as being surrounded by the glory of St. Mark's Square. I allow myself to fully appreciate my surroundings through the polished glass before turning to the beautiful interiors.

I feel extremely lucky. The café is exquisitely decorated with paintings, golden ceilings, marble tables, and comfortable sofas. It exudes a sense of calm and refinement.

It won't be cheap, but to share the same space with Byron, never mind the two centuries separating us, is priceless. Not to waste any precious time, I take a tour of the café, admiring the exotic figures of the Chinese Room and the Oriental Room and the much more ambitious iconographic project of the Senate Room, where paintings are dedicated to Sciences and Arts. In the Room of Illustrious Men, we are surrounded by portraits of the most relevant characters of Venetian history, such as Marco Polo, Andrea Palladio, Paolo Sarpi, Carlo Goldoni, and Benedetto Marcello.

In Café Florian, the past meets the present. It mirrors the spirit of the intellectuals who visited here. Caffè Florian is almost three hundred years old, established in 1720 under the porticoes in Piazza San Marco, and has been functioning without interruptions these last three centuries, which pretty much means that Caffe Florian has seen it all, glory and bad press, the grandness of La Serenissima or Republic of Venice, and the destructive flooding of Acqua Alta. It keeps on going.

Irrelevant though it might seem to mention it, the fact remains that tourists never stop coming, and the café never stops serving some of the most exquisite and sophisticated fare Venice has to offer.

My coffee is slow in arriving. But when it does, I am shivering with excitement. The monogrammed cup in which my coffee languishes lies on a silver tray. That is when I stop to think of the price I'll have to pay for it.

It is immensely satisfying to wrap myself in its history, surrounded by the ornate and sophisticated Venetian life from the 1700s, while I sip my cappuccino. With that cup of hot, steamy coffee, I travel through history and experience all different emotions and feelings.

Let me not beat around the bush. You do not go to Florian for an espresso… you go there for a strong sensory, cultural, and historical experience, to feel like a Venetian, to become one with the characters of Venetian history. It is a historical place full of beauty.

When the waiter returns, I ask about the Casanova hot chocolate, not for consuming it but for its name. The waiter speaks in perfect English with no trace of Italian. To hear him speak in that knowledgeable way is a delight.

"Casanova was the most famous Venetian, who loved to spend time in this café. I am not sure if he drank hot chocolate, but it's our house specialty and comes with mint-flavoured cream and white chocolate flakes. Would you like to try it?"

"No, thank you, but I'd like to know about Casanova for sure."

He raises his eyebrows questioningly and smiles. "I think you must read about him. I have a book with all the information if you are interested. Even the history of this cafe is in it."

"That is very kind of you—and yes, I'd love to take a look."

Before I have drained my cup, he arrives with a large, dog-eared book, which looks like a wedding album. I thank him before ordering another cup of coffee.

The history of Florian is intriguing, too. It started as a café named *Alla Venezia Trionfante*—or Triumph of Venice—by Floriano Francesconi but was soon renamed to Florian, after the owner. It was a public place, and everyone, including women, could walk in and out, leading to scandals and love affairs, particularly by the famous adventurer Giacomo

Casanova. It was a place where conversations happened, where the first newspaper of local chronicle in the world, the *Gazzetta Veneta*, was sold, and where gambling was quite common.

If I were allowed to go overboard describing it, I'd call it the container of events that contributed to rewriting the city's history. In the years of its existence, it became the meeting place for patriots, poets, philosophers, writers, and journalists, besides serving as a hospital briefly in 1848.

It is unique because, over the past three hundred years, it has been one of the main centres of the cultural life of Venice.

On the fourth page, I come face to face with Venice's original bad boy.

Casanova.

Clearly, he occupies a slightly larger place than Byron in the hearts of Venetians because he even has a drink named after him, which is quite popular, too, going by the number of orders for it.

As I read, my respect for him grows. His infamy overshadows Byron, and Caffe Florian could very well be one of the reasons for it. It was one of the earliest establishments that served women, which worked well for Casanova, allowing him to meet women and form liaisons.

Was it here, at these white-marble tables, that Casanova, and later Lord Byron, drank coffee and dallied with the ladies?

I am beginning to wonder if there is something in coffee houses that encourages scandals. Although I love spending time in coffee houses and sometimes like to linger on, inhale the smell, hear people talk, or simply watch the world go by, I cannot understand how that could cause a scandal.

Just what was Casanova's modus operandi?

*

Giacomo Casanova, born in a family of theatre actors in 1725, showed immense potential since childhood. Growing up, he turned into many things, but his being a scholar, a diplomat, and a spy were among those that brought him fame and infamy. He frequented the high society and seduced women, particularly targeting those who were missing something in their life, like a husband's attention, and providing them just that—attention.

At one point in life, he wanted to be the Pope; at another, he wanted to be a musician, but his main passions were women, gambling, writing, and alchemy. At a young age, he had seen and done it all, including serving jail time in Venice for an affront to religion and common decency in 1755 at the age of thirty. That bit of history is interesting to read and, even more so, the verdict.

The Tribunal, having taken cognizance of the grave faults committed by G. Casanova primarily in public outrages against the holy religion, their Excellencies have caused him to be arrested and imprisoned under the Leads.

After my second cup of coffee, which is duly appreciated by the stern waiter, I set out to find Casanova's birthplace.

Venice is a maze. Walking through the streets is tough with and without navigation. For every dozen steps I take, I walk back half of that. The maze of small streets, bridges, alleys, and canals is endless, and I am beginning to see why this art of getting lost in Venice is marketed as 'The Venice Experience.' As enjoyable as that game of aimless wandering can be, it slows my progress. I do not mind getting lost, but when I have a place to visit on my mind, it is annoying.

The locals help, but it is not their fault there are too many tightly packed lanes. Every time I ask the directions to Calle Malipiero, I am given a smile and a vague direction that sets me off on a completely different track. Never follow Google

Maps in Venice. It is worse than asking a Venetian for directions. Venice does not have proper streets. The gap between buildings is the street.

Despite the constant wrong turns, I am charmed by what I see. It is an atmospheric city, and every house seems to have its own history.

Eventually, I make it to Casanova's family's house on Calle Malipiero, near Palazzo Grassi, slightly off the tourist track, and manage to visit the nearby parish church where he was baptized before winding back to Ponte delle Tette where he romanced topless ladies. By the time I arrive at Calle Vallaresso, once a gambling haven that gave Casanova opportunities to socialize, flirt, and make new connections, I am ready to give up.

Casanova spent the first nine years of his life with his brother and two sisters in Calle Malipiero before being packed off to a boarding school on the mainland in Padua, where he pursued his law studies, finishing at the age of fourteen. Life played a cruel game on the young man after he lost his grandmother, and the dejected young man took up priesthood at the age of eighteen, far away from the women who—by this time—already ruled his passions.

In just three historic stops, I have developed a profound love and connection to Venice through Casanova.

I force myself to end my wanderings and return to Byron.

Byron was passionate about learning Armenian, and here, in Venice, he found what he had been looking for. When he arrived in this city, Venice was the home of the Mekhitarist Congregation, a collection of Armenian monks who had settled there. Impressed by their ethos and the rich language, he decided to invest time in learning the language. His brief interaction with the Armenian community of Venice is celebrated with a preserved room where he worked and the

242

items he used. He was the first Westerner in the modern era to take an interest in the Armenian culture.

Another place in Venice closely linked to the name of Lord Byron is the island of San Lazzaro degli Armeni, where he lived with a small community of monks. He learned Armenian here and participated in the publication of an English-Armenian dictionary.

Tracing him in Venice is easy. Venice is by no means a small city, but landmarks of great men who sought inspiration here are well-documented, which makes it easier to trace, especially Lord Byron, who arrived in Venice in 1816 as a guest of a cloth merchant in Frezzaria after his brief stint in Switzerland. Like Casanova before him, Byron's most scandalous time was spent here, and he eventually made it to the list of Bad Boys of Venice, coming in second after Casanova.

Byron was a sportsman at heart. I know this from my wandering in Istanbul. In Venice, he continued that sportsmanship. One night after merrymaking at Lido, he swam across the Venice lagoon and down the entire length of the Grand Canal in three and three-quarters hours.

In *Don Juan*, Byron talked of his swim across the Hellespont nine years earlier.

Venice gave Byron some of the best works of his life, including *Don Juan*. Many places in Venice are related to him, such as the Palazzo Mocenigo Palace on the Grand Canal, the world's most famous canal, where Byron lived from 1816 to 1819 with fourteen servants, two monkeys, a fox, and two mastiff dogs. It was here he composed the first stanzas of *Don Juan*.

Wedded she some years, and to a man / Of fifty, and such husbands are in plenty; And yet, I think, instead of such a ONE 'Twere better to have TWO of five and twenty...

*

In the evening, I tackle the gondola, Venice's most romantic and recognizable symbol. I hear tourists argue over the price of a gondola ride, a few shaking their heads in disbelief and storming off. I do suppose it is really about the budget and expectations.

My sleek, crescent-shaped gondola is bejewelled with crimson velvet and gold trim and helmed by a gondolier named Giovanni, who sits in the centre of this extravagance, smiling.

It is hard not to like him. We set off, meandering quietly between the grand palazzi, colourful laundry dangling from clotheslines and dancing in the wind, ducking our heads expertly while floating under small footbridges. All the while, Giovanni keeps his smile on. His muscles are shaped by sculling his craft with a single oar in the forcola, a decorative piece of walnut wood carved so that the oar can manoeuvre in different ways. His face is tanned and weathered, and he sports a prison-striped black-and-white shirt, black pants, and a red scarf tied at the neck.

Nothing is more iconic than punting down the Grand Canal in a Gondola. On the Grand Canal stands the Querini Benzon Palace, where Byron met his last love, the young Teresa Gamba Guiccioli, wife of the rich, sixty-year-old Alessandro Guiccioli from Ravenna. Their relationship was described as tumultuous and fraught with tensions. It was the year Byron lost his brother-like friend Shelly and his daughter Allegra.

My gondola takes me along the Grand Canal, under the Rialto Bridge, past Basilica di Santa Maria della Salute, the House of Prada, the Aman Grand Canal Hotel, and out towards the smaller islands. For some reason, I picture Shakespeare's *Merchant of Venice* and the greedy Shylock and his pound of flesh as we sail past the old customs house, which taxed every vessel coming to the city to trade with the merchants of Venice.

I almost imagine Giovanni launching into a rendition of *O Sole Mio* while gliding down the canals, but that is not to be. Instead, in an inspired moment of defiance, he launches into another Venetian song, my favourite.

Nessun dorma! Nessun dorma!

Tu pure, o Principessa

Nella tua fredda stanza

Guardi le stelle che tremano

Then, he breaks into the theme song from *Godfather*.

*

If there is one thing I have learnt thus far, it is to give in to the moment without looking for any justification. We pass under smaller bridges, wave at the passing gondolas, and slowly, I let go of my obsession.

Impulsively, I make up my mind to stay the night in Venice. Fortunately, a room is available at the Rosa Salva Hotel, one of the most historic hotels in Venice, close to St. Mark's Square.

*

I would never know what Ernest Hemingway must have felt when he first arrived in Venice in the fall of 1948, two years short of his fiftieth birthday, with his fourth wife, but I suspect it wouldn't have been far from what Byron had felt. Hemingway promptly fell in love with nineteen-year-old Adriana Ivancich, a beautiful Venetian, and is said to have kept returning owing to this. But that fling helped him revive his writing, and Hemingway soon published one of his last novels, *Across the River and Into the Trees*, a story of love that is kind of crazy, an overwhelming passion that still brings a touch of joy and playfulness.

Hemingway stayed at the Gritti Palace, and like the luminaries before him, he frequented the *Caffe Florian*; he walked around

Venice and often got lost, but every corner threw up a beautiful side of the city for him.

Indeed, the bond between Hemingway and Venice is a love story, but not in a conventional way; it involves falling in love with life with all its shortcomings. Careless in its lightness, mad in its irrationality and immediacy, and all-consuming in its passion.

As a tribute to Hemingway, I head to *Harry's Bar* at the mouth of the Grand Canal.

The bar is an institution in Venice, although I have read accounts of dissatisfied people on TripAdvisor complaining about nearly everything. I try to remain neutral as I plunge boldly into the fully packed bar. Bellini was invented here, and this was where Ernest Hemingway spent many evenings enjoying a few; considering these two historical occurrences, I am ready to brave anything.

Considering the volume of customers, I accept the possibility of delay. I do, however, find a spot at the bar where a group of American tourists are arguing with the bartender about the Prosecco. The irate bartender throws a look at me, and I think he is about ready to have them shown the door.

At thirty euros per Bellini, it does seem a bit much, and I do share the American's dismay when their drink is served in smallish glasses. But that is the price of history and authenticity, and going by the number of tourists queuing up for the beverage, I am not very surprised that it is.

Bemused, I watch the bartender squeeze peach puree from foil packs into glasses while squirting Prosecco from a soda-style tap. There is no blending of peaches. No popping of corks, as I am sure was done in the time of Hemingway.

Nevertheless, it is an experience I cherish.

*

The night in Venice is most beautiful, with all the lights twinkling in the waters. I take in as much glitter in my eyes for memory. Venice is an experience. It fills my heart and soul.

At night, a storm descends on Venice. For the duration it lasts, I feel the presence of Lord Byron. In his letter to his publisher, John Murry, in 1819, he had described the Venetian storm in a somewhat dramatic way, but it is quite likely he had done it perfectly.

We were overtaken by a heavy Squall, and the Gondola put in peril – hats blown away, boat filling, oar lost, tumbling sea, thunder, rain in torrents, night coming and wind increasing.

No oar was lost in my situation, nor were hats blown away, but it seemed like a perfect end. What my gondolier had said earlier in the evening when trying to charm me into accepting his invitation to dinner came true.

"Venice is different at night," he said quite simply. "When all the tourists are gone, and the noise of multiple languages subsides, you hear Venice speak in her tongue. It speaks in poetry and verse. It speaks softly, like the kissing of the angels and poets."

Byron would probably have said something similar.

*

Early morning in Venice is a joyful experience. The streets and canals that were so packed and dirty yesterday look rather pretty. A lone motorboat shoots down the canal on my left, while on my right is a restaurant with upturned chairs resting on top of tables. The window shutters of the flats above the shops are only starting to open. Many houses have peeling plasters, thanks to the cruel moisture rising from the canals. But even in its daily fight against natural decay, Venice is fabulous.

It is interesting how, under the veneer of Venetian history, art, and scandals lies a layer of daily life, a non-stop struggle to adjust to the existence on the water. Venice is a complex city, and many historical events have grown to become legends. Clearly, there is more to this city than just the two famous literary figures I have come to find.

But there is an eeriness to Venice, and I understand at last why many of the more famous novels set in Venice are horror stories.

It is incredibly still as I walk along the narrow alleyways, past the tall, rundown buildings, with nary a human to be seen. I feel as though I am touching the soul of Venice.

As I leave, I hear a small voice in my heart asking me to fall in love with the Venetian magic.

*

Footnotes:

- *Between 1819 and 1821, Lord Byron moved into the apartment of his mistress' husband, Count Alessandro Guiccioli.*
- *Childe Harold's Pilgrimage was published in four cantos between 1812 and 1818. It was loosely based on his own youthful travels around Europe.*
- *Genoa was his final Italian destination in Italy before he moved to Greece in 1823.*
- *Leads refer to the prison of seven cells in the east wing of the Doge's Palace, reserved for prisoners of higher status like political prisoners, defrocked, or libertine priests or monks.*

Chapter 9

Like millions of others, I have been to Rome in the past. Rome is simply one of those places everyone goes. But every time, I have fallen in love with it a little more. And every time I leave, I vow to come back. I usually do, too. I have never known or understood what brings me back, but I do come.

The city's beauty, personality, and chaos envelop me as I get off the metro train at Spagna metro station. Its busy streets enchant me all over again. I cannot say this is especially true for everyone visiting here because I have heard from travellers that no matter what tricks the city pulls, it is just not for them.

But Rome is one of those places that will always be busy with tourists, no matter the time of the year. It is a place one must visit before they kick the bucket. The history, which oozes so much from almost every inch of Rome, can feel intimidating and perhaps overwhelming, and rightly so. Its ancientness is a matter of pride and learning. It was certainly not built in a day.

This time, I am here for a different reason. A vague and imperfect reason laced with so much hope and romance because I know in my heart that having learnt much about Lord Byron, Hemingway, and so many others along the way, I may keep clear of actively pursuing literary greats in the future.

Rome is a great city, and I love it. And I love its art, coffee shops, pizzas, and its association with the past. Its literary offering. Its visual appeal. One of my ever-favourite cities to visit. Like its name, Rome is a truly eternal City, a title first used by the Roman poet Tibullus (c. 54–19 BCE). But more than its glorious history is its Old World charm and pace of life that differs vastly from the rest of the country. It is unhurried and laid back. Here, rest is more important than productivity, and holidays are more valued than workdays.

With its UNESCO World Heritage Sites and prestigious neoclassical buildings, Rome is given the status of an open-air museum, but to me, it is a personal temple where Byron once lived.

*

It is impossible to begin my quest without first visiting Café Grecco on Via Condotti, Rome's most exclusive street just off the Piazza di Spagna or Spanish Steps. This street is lined with designer shops, but that is of little interest to me. I am eager to visit Café Grecco for reasons well-established by now. After its Venetian counterpart, the Caffe Florian, Café Grecco is the second oldest café in the country and a symbol of Italian culture.

And there is no better place to begin or end one's quest.

Caffe Grecco at once catapults me into the past. An elegantly dressed waiter returns my enquiring smile and leads me towards the back of the crowded room, past the walls covered with gilt mirrors, framed oil paintings, and around old wood tables. The red velvet speaks of glorious days of the past. Typical of a period café. And sure enough, it is that, too.

Almost everyone I'd known about or heard of or was partial to has been a guest at this café at one time or the other. It is an institution, a sacred place. Lord Byron, Percy B Shelly, John Keats, Mark Twain, Henry James, Hans Christian Anderson, Charles Dickens, Thomas Mann, Stendhal, and Goethe have all enjoyed a cup or more right here. It is a haven for writers, artists, and politicians and has weathered wars and political instability. Pictures of illustrious patrons adorn the walls. Its furnishings and artworks are protected property. It is more of a museum than a café.

The café is nearly full, mostly with tourists taking a break from the walking, and a few of them genuinely appear impressed with the café's history. The waiters shuffle quickly between tables, taking care to avoid tripping over extended legs and camera bags placed carelessly on the floor.

Naturally, the coffee is not cheap, but it is a small price to pay as I get to create an imagined moment of romance with Lord Byron. And anyway, I never deny myself a coffee, whatever the cost.

I am drawn to the similarities of its former patrons—Byron, Shelly, and Keats. They were the rulers of romanticism. I suppose if there is a thing as a *Romantic Trinity*, it must have been them. The 19th century's best poetic trio were the cream of British literature, each unique in their loves, life, and rivalry. *And all of them died young. Shelley died at 29, Byron at 36, Keats at 25.*

Close to *Café Grecco* is the house of John Keats. My interest is suddenly aroused. Curiosity leads me to see for myself the life of one of the greatest poets of the 19th century, who was enamoured with Lord Byron and wrote a poem to that effect when he was just nineteen. Interestingly, without even meeting him. This feeling later changed.

Keats's short poem, not one of his best as the critics claimed, includes the lyrical imagery for which he later became known.

Byron! how sweetly sad thy melody!

Attuning still the soul to tenderness,

As if soft Pity, with unusual stress,

Had touch'd her plaintive lute, and thou, being by,

Hadst caught the tones, nor suffer'd them to die.

I do not actively seek to learn the life of John Keats, but I am driven by curiosity. I want to know why Keats didn't like Byron very much and vice versa.

John Keats thought Byron a snob with privileges he did not work to gain. On the other hand, Keats was a poor and struggling middle-class poet whose work was often harshly judged by the critics of the time, so naturally, there was an element of jealousy of Byron's success. Neither liked the other's work, and both were very bitter about it.

This unexpected detour in the search for Keats has me enthused. A brisk walk brings me to the Spanish Steps, where scores of people are posing against the historical steps. The Spanish Steps, built between 1721 and 25, leads up from the Piazza di Spagna to the Egyptian obelisk and the 16th-century Church of Trinita dei Monti on the Pincio where the 16th-century Villa Medici sits amid formal gardens.

My eyes wander to the nondescript and faded building at the foot of the Spanish Steps—the Keats-Shelley Memorial House. I shiver with excitement as I enter, only to notice that the entrance and stairway look like hundreds of others in similar buildings throughout Rome. I pass through this public entryway, take the stairs to the main floor, and enter through a small vestibule into the rooms where Keats and Severn lived. It is another world altogether. I am blown away by the sheer collection of books. Like Café Grecco, this is a museum.

As if stepping back in time, aside from the drawings and manuscripts displayed on the long table occupying the center of the first room, known as the Salon, everything appears just as I imagine it would have when Keats lived here. Small paintings and drawings line the walls. The rooms are beautifully decorated—tall shelves filled with books and so many paraphernalia associated with the lives and works of Romantic poets, Keats included. There are over eight thousand volumes displayed. The house contains a fine collection of Romantic literature, besides manuscripts, paintings, sculptures, and memorabilia.

While I tour the museum, a group of young students arrive for a poetry recital session. I ask to be allowed to sit in with them to establish a connection with Keats.

Soon, I find myself in Keats's bedroom. It appears intact—the way it would have been. But then I realize I am looking at a reconstruction. A replica of his narrow, spartan bed lies against the opposite wall facing the doorway. A chair sits against the wall, and beside the door, there is a cabinet with a few artifacts. When Keats died, the Vatican had ordered everything in this room to be burnt for fear of spreading tuberculosis, the disease that eventually killed him. The room appears close to the original. Above the bed is a drawing by his friend Joseph Severn.

From the window, the view is that of the piazza, the fountain, and the Spanish Steps. Back then, the area of the Spanish Steps was known as the English Ghetto, but today, it is expectedly crowded and, I bet, noisy. But in Keats's bedroom, the noise doesn't bother me. I have had my moment.

I turn my attention to Pietro Bernini's Barcaccia fountain. The fountain looks like a marble boat sunk into the pavement at the base of the steps; it must have refreshed passersby for generations. Perhaps Keats refreshed himself in its clear, cool waters and enjoyed the sounds of the fountain on cold, lonely nights.

He'd passed away in this room at 26 Piazza di Spagna, aged twenty-five, critiqued, loveless, and mourning his lady love, Fanny Brawne, whom he had left behind in England.

Prior to his death, John Keats wrote a letter to his brother George in September 1819, where he addressed the differences between himself and Byron. *You speak of Lord Byron and me —*

There is this great difference between us. He describes what he sees – I describe what I imagine – Mine is the hardest task.

The rivalry, it appeared, was more acutely felt by Keats. Keats's death did not seem to change how Byron felt or put an end to this prolonged rivalry; in fact, after Byron learnt of Keats passing away and the reason for his death—stress at receiving negative reviews—Byron found it hilarious, and in poor taste, even made fun of Keats, posthumously, in his famous poem *Don Juan*:

"John Keats, who was killed off by one critique, just as he really promised something great,

If not intelligible, —without Greek, contrived to talk about the Gods of late,

Much as they might have been supposed to speak. Poor fellow! His was an untoward fate: —

'Tis strange the mind, that very fiery particle, should let itself be snuffed out by an Article."

*

From here, I come to the final destination of my literary journey—the statue of Lord Byron in Via della Pineta, within the Villa Borghese.

Byron is everywhere.

The beautiful marble statue, a replica of the original sculpted by Danish sculptor Thorvaldsen, portrays the elegantly dressed poet seated on Roman ruins. With a cloak on his shoulders, he holds a pen with his right hand, waiting for inspiration, while with his left hand, he holds a fragment of a book.

The inscriptions on the marble pedestal on which the statue rests are verses of the poet taken from *Childe Harold's Pilgrimage* part IV, CXXXVII:

But I have lived and have not lived in vain:

My mind may lose its force, my blood its fire,
And my frame perish even in conquering pain,
But there is that within me which shall tire
Torture and Time, and breathe when I expire.

*

It is curious how Byron's personal life often overshadows his works. It did so during his lifetime, and the problem only worsened after he died in 1824. For the last two hundred years, most studies of Byron have been buried beneath the confused mess of his life or unduly influenced by it. The scandals have a life of their own. No poem—not even the great satire of Don Juan—can rise above them.

I suppose it is all his fault, although I seriously believe he wouldn't have cared. Byron would have probably preferred to be the subject of gossip rather than a footnote in a book.

He arrived on the literary scene in the early 1800s and still adorns the scene. It seems as if a new biography is published every other year. He simply won't go away. Truth be told, no one wants him to go, for even if you dislike poetry, you can always read about his life. Often, it seems that most people prefer it that way.

Byron was no ideal poet. Even to me. Much as I love the man himself, I do not revere him. But he was a great poet. His work is timeless. It has stood the test of time. His poetry speaks to me; it fascinates me. He was far from perfect, but he did write perfectly.

*

It was in Greece that Lord Byron died a national hero, but my quest ends in Rome. I decide to put my obsessions to rest. Greece will remain off my Byron map because I want to think of Lord Byron as the eternal traveller and poet, looking for solace and new pastures. Byron, the hunted, and hunter of new experiences. Byron, the living, breathing human I have come to love.

I'll never forget my days in Italy. I arrived here in pursuance of romance and found it everywhere. Some permanent, some fleeting. Some just. Through my literary adventure, I have broadened my spiritual horizons, too, and gained sufficient knowledge of history through the characters of their books. It has made me think.

"… But words are things, and a small drop of ink,
Falling like dew, upon a thought, produces
That which makes thousands, perhaps millions, think…"

George Gordon – Lord Byron (Don Juan)

I have one last thing left to do before I leave the country. I push my way past the crowds towards the Trevi Fountain. For those with wishes to fulfil, this fountain is called the Wishing Fountain, and I hope that it will, after all, keep to its reputation as the Wishing Fountain.

There is a huge crowd near the fountain—mostly young tourists looking for that perfect photograph. Trevi Fountain is a classic example of Roman craftsmanship. Besides its beauty, it is a historic landmark and Rome's oldest water source.

As the legend goes, General Agrippa, a close ally of Emperor Augustus, was looking for water with his troops. Suddenly, a virgin appeared and pointed to the ground, and upon digging there, the soldiers found water.

There is a happy, wishful vibe here, like people looking for something more than pictures of a fountain. People are digging into their pockets and purses for coins to throw in. Some of them are restricted by this act—a punishment for going cashless! I see joy, disappointment, and hope on people's faces.

Luckily, I have a few coins in my pocket. I fish one out and make a wish, hoping no one is watching me. I toss the coin. It falls with a small splash five feet from me. That sound works like a balm for my soul.

My wish is for Byron to come back to life.

But the Wishing Fountain is not granting wishes today.

So, I will continue to think of Lord Byron in the manner of essayist William Hazlitt.

In slovenliness, abruptness, and eccentricity… Lord Byron surpasses all his contemporaries.

And that is the way he will always remain in my mind.

About the Author

Anjaly Thomas

Anjaly Thomas is a lawyer turned writer/traveler and author of *Plentiful Springs*, *Almost Intrepid*, *There Are No Gods in North Korea*, *Lonely Planet Dubai* and *UAE Country Guide*. Her solo travels around the world are a result of a conscious decision to sketch a world map based on her travels. From a novice backpacker who fled a mundane job at a newspaper to having visited North Korea pretending to be a schoolteacher, she has pretty much seen and done it all. She strongly believes that traveling solo sets the foundation for a better and more fruitful life because it teaches you everything that textbooks don't.

www.anjalythomas.com
www.travelwithanjaly.com